The Service of Clouds

The Service of Clouds

Susan Hill

Chatto & Windus
LONDON

First published 1998

2 4 6 8 10 9 7 5 3

This edition published in Great Britain in 1998 by
Chatto & Windus
Random House, 20 Vauxhall Bridge Road
London SW1V 2SA

Random House Australia (Pty) Limited
20 Alfred Street, Milsons Point, Sydney
New South Wales 2061, Australia

Random House New Zealand Limited
18 Poland Road, Glenfield
Auckland 10, New Zealand

Random House South Africa (Pty) Limited
Endulini, 5A Jubilee Road, Parktown 2193, South Africa

Random House UK Limited Reg. No. 954009

A CIP catalogue record for this book
is available from the British Library

ISBN 1 85619 279 2

Papers used by Random House UK Limited are natural,
recyclable products made from wood grown in sustainable forests.
The manufacturing processes conform to the environmental
regulations of the country of origin.

Typeset by Deltatype Ltd, Birkenhead, Merseyside

Printed and bound in Great Britain by
Biddles Ltd, Guildford and King's Lynn

For
Jessica and Simon
The brave ones.

Out of perfect light and motionless air, we find ourselves on a sudden brought under sombre skies, and into drifting wind; and with fickle sunbeams flashing on our face, or utterly drenched with sweep of rain, we are reduced to track the changes of the shadows on the grass, or watch the rents of twilight through angry cloud ... The aspects of sunset and sunrise, with all their attendant phenomena of cloud and mist, are watchfully delineated; and in ordinary daylight landscape, the sky is considered of so much importance, that a principal mass of foliage, or a whole foreground, is unhesitatingly thrown into shade merely to bring out the form of a white cloud. So that, if a general and characteristic name were needed for modern landscape art, none better could be invented than 'the service of clouds'.

John Ruskin, *Modern Painters*

PART ONE

One

'Where am I?'

'Well, you're in your bed.'

'Not my bed.'

'Are you not comfortable, dear?'

'Not your dear.'

A thread of spittle worked its way down a seam in the flesh beside her crumpled mouth.

'Where am I?'

'In the hospital. Let me just wipe your chin now.'

'Who am I?'

'Well, you're Mrs Annie Hare.'

Silence then. The young nurse with red hair wiped the mouth of the old woman, Annie Hare, and looked at the clock, which made no sound either, and twitched the top sheet and the hand that rested there, yellow as a chicken's claw, twitched with it.

'Who am I?'

'You're Annie Hare.' She hated to sit with the dying.

Rain beaded the windows, and slipped down them, making no sound.

'Who was I?'

The girl panicked then and rang the bell and ran for Sister.

(Later, at home, the story would expand, puffed out by her own little hysteria. She would say that the old woman had known,

3

hadn't she, had surely been given some vision or other premonition of her own impending death. *Who was I?* she said, not *Who am I?* 'which you could easily understand, oh, that happens almost every day with people who are delirious, in some bit of fever or other, you don't have to be dying to lose yourself temporarily'. No, it was, *Who was I?* She knew then. They do.)

'Who was I?'

They had telephoned him, even at half past one in the morning.
She was his patient; it was not that they needed him.

'He'll come,' the Sister had said, snapping the curtains sharply around the bed rail.

The old woman did not start; she had slipped way down beyond sudden noises now.

'There won't be anything he can do, will there? Why ever would he bother coming?'

'He likes death,' she said, and turned her back on the girl and walked away down the long room.

(Which would make more to tell, in the confident, off-hand tone of one who knew about all such things, the tone of voice that impressed the girl's father and made her mother proud and her brothers sneer. 'He likes death, that doctor. Well, some do, it's well known.' Though she herself could not fathom it, not in any way.)

The ward was half empty. Flat, un-pillowed beds were lined against the window, with great spaces in shadow. The girl moved closer into the sheltering circle of light around the desk. She was nineteen. She hated the night duties when one of them was dying.

*

Molloy got out of his car and stood for a long time in the dark quadrangle. The air smelled sweet and mild; there was rain in it and smoke on it. But not the sea here. He lifted his face, to feel the slight movement of the damp air, looked at the steps that led up

4

to the swing doors, and the lights showing through the yellowing curtains. Thought: There is this night; there will be a few dozen more. After that, I shall not belong here. I will never come to this place again, and in a while the place itself will not be here.

(It was to be demolished, the old buildings were done with now.)

He turned his head quickly, as if it would help him turn his mind from it too. It was unimaginable to him, and painful beyond bearing, though he could have expressed none of it. He looked vaguely into the darkness towards the bushes beside the drive, but saw nothing except old images, revolving and shifting behind his eyes.

When he opened the doors into the hospital, the smell of it drowned him, the smell he had known as the background to his life, every day, every day – scrubbed sluices and antiseptic floors, sheets and sick bowls and the rank stems of flowers, and sweet, faecal decay.

He heard his own footsteps, coughs, the wind sighing suddenly at the door, saw the shaded light at the end of the ward, and felt a great surge of joy and rightness and satisfaction at where he was, and at his own place here, before the bleak misery seeped into the edges of it, souring it, blotting it out.

He put his hand up to the door of the ward and held it there, staring at the shape of his outspread fingers against the wood, and thought suddenly that at the moment of his own dying he might see something so ordinary as this, in the last flaring of the light. Then went on, into the quiet, waiting place.

They had pulled the curtains right round the bed so that, within the narrow cubicle, he was alone with the old woman. They knew better than to come near, or in any other way to disturb him.

It was as though the air was slowly leaking out of her body as she breathed little, shallow breaths, so that she seemed flat beneath the sheet. Her hands were clutched to the cover, as a baby will clutch close to its own face, her skin smooth and almost transparent to the bones below, the flesh already receded.

But she was not dead. The pulse still leapt at the side of her

5

neck and, now and again, swallowing moved the knotted gristle under the skin of her throat. She was Annie Hare. He knew nothing about her. By the time she had come here, there had been little for him to do, which was so often the way. Only the old came to this place now. It made no difference to him. When his patients were dying, he came to them, sat beside them, watched and waited for death with them, and could not have kept away.

If he was too late, away somewhere, or it happened too suddenly, he felt a frayed, hollow sense of having uncompleted business that would now have to be carried within him forever. Whether they were aware of him or not did not signify, nor what others said or felt. He was called a saint, and a conscientious caring doctor – or else he was thought odd, and his consorting with death disturbed and puzzled them. None of it mattered. No one spoke to him about it. They were not close to him, nor party to his thoughts.

He loved the sense of concentration, like the beam of light from a torch, focused on this spot, the stillness and expectancy, the feeling that everything that had ever been in this one human life was packed now into the smallest space, as he sat quietly on the hard chair, hunched close to the bed. It was unchanging, though the people changed, and where he wanted to be, where he felt rooted and belonging, even if they themselves meant little to him. Every so often, he reached for the claw on the sheet and held it, slipped his thumb over the parchment skin, feeling the thin blade of bone beneath.

He did not enquire about family. If they came, they came. He would not see them, the Sister had to do with all of that. It was none of his concern. This was his concern – the woman in the bed, and her dying, and his own nearness to it. He felt death sidle into the cubicle and settle down to wait a little with him, before moving in.

From the first time, he had felt its absolute importance to him, to sit in silence like this, watching for the tide to turn, and been overwhelmed by the certainty that this small, uninteresting space contained everything of significance. Within it, time shrank to a pinpoint, steadied and was still, the focus of the past, present and future, at the centre of the turning world. (So that when he left afterwards, he was dazed and bewildered by the ordinariness of life in the streets outside, the unregarding movement sweeping by. He could not get his bearings straight away, but had to go somewhere to be alone, adjusting gradually, like a revenant waking, a traveller returning from long away. As a student, he had walked the night streets in every weather, cycled far out into the hills overlooking the water, or simply stayed on his own bed, staring at the wall, or into the neutral darkness.)

It was not true that death always came quietly, and met with no resistance. But this, tonight, would be quiet, and so he would simply sit by, watch, wait.

The wind caught at the casement suddenly and shook it by the throat to gain entrance, and, once it was there, prowled about the old, half-empty building, pushing at doors, lifting floorboards a little, restlessly, and like the wind, the old woman, Annie Hare, moaned and shifted on the pillow. Her nose was hooked like the beak of a bird, the flesh seemed to be dissolving as he watched. The skin was taut across her forehead.

And the wind raced across the roof and keened in cracks and probed with thin fingers beneath slates, and out in the ward, some slight movement, a voice, a demand attended to. Silence again. The Sister sat at the desk within the circle of light.

The girl had been sent down to the store, two flights of stone stairs, past closed doors, which unnerved her, but in a different way from the presence of the dying. She could endure being spooked, like a child would be, by mere shadows and hollows and empty corridors.

The wind dropped, gathered itself again. But the next gust came to nothing, and the building fell quiet.

Molloy shifted heavily on his chair. He was watching intently, sensing some slight change, seeing the old woman's breathing subside. He touched her hand. 'Annie Hare,' he said softly, for reassurance, encouragement. There was a response, the faintest stir within her like an electrical charge, just perceptible to him.

'Annie Hare.'

What he was doing for her, in what way he was assisting her,

7

he could not have said, but that it was so he never doubted. She was not left alone, he had made sure of it, for her, as for all the others, that was the point and purpose of his work – his existence, even.

His mother had been alone, and all these deaths since could never make reparation for it. But his own intense satisfaction in death's presence, his craving for it, was something quite other, quite separate, and of no concern to those he sat beside for company.

Somewhere, beyond the cubicle, beyond the ward, someone dropped a metal dish, and the sound went on, like a coin running round and round and down a tube, reverberating until everything else gave way to it for those moments. And after that sound, the wind blew again, as if at a signal.

He looked intently at the yellow, beaky face, the downy hair sprouting in tufts from the old skull, the claw upon the sheet beside him. The sound had not reached her. He put out his hand, covered hers with it, and felt the stream flow out and away, leaving the stream-bed empty. Dry. Then time stopped and was held suspended in pure and stunning silence, and with it, Molloy held his own breath, before the wind, snaking under the far door, puffed out the curtain surrounding the death bed. He folded her hands with care on top of each other, left them empty, and went away.

Two

His mother's christened name had been Florence Hennessy, and she had become Flora Molloy.

She had hated the first name from childhood, though, until she was ten, she had suffered it, not knowing any other way, and, from her family, continued to suffer it until she left them.

'That was the name we gave you. That was the name your father chose,' her mother had said, as if the business had nothing at all to do with the girl. 'You are Florence.'

But when she reached the secondary school, she had announced herself from the first day as Flora. And, as the school was in a town twelve miles away to the north, and not the one to which everyone else from their village and its surrounding district went, she was able to begin this part of her life on a new page, with perfect success.

She felt herself to be two people, and that was her salvation.

Only when school reports and occasional correspondence to her home wrote of her as 'Flora' did the two lives, the two girls, come into conflict.

'You are *Florence* Hennessy. I will not have this. It is not up to you to change your own name. Why do you insist on telling such a lie?'

'It is not a lie.'

'It is not the truth. Flora is not your name.'

9

'I like it best.'

'Why? Why?'

Her mother had written to the school. 'She is to be called by her proper, christened name of Florence. We do not approve of the name she has given herself. She is not of an age to make such a decision.'

She had torn the letter into small, even fragments on the bus and during the course of the day dropped them, one or two at a time, into different waste paper baskets around the school.

The Hennessys had once been quite significant farmers. Her grandfather had owned more than seven hundred acres, all the land up towards Doyne and Ballymunty. They were 'gentleman farmers', May Hennessy said, people of note in the whole district, they had horses and pony traps, they had hunted, they had even been able to travel abroad and stay at hotels, they kept accounts, not merely at local shops but in the smart department stores of the city.

It was not any mismanagement or financial trouble which brought them gradually low, simply ill-health. From grandfather to father to son, the men were not robust. Heart trouble, kidney trouble, tuberculosis led to weaknesses and disability, and the need for a succession of treatments. It was none of it their fault, and so they believed that, in spite of having lost land and property bit by bit, relinquished it reluctantly by selling here and there to neighbours, Hennessys had nevertheless somehow retained their status, and the respect of the community. They no longer farmed seven hundred acres, no longer employed dozens of men, no longer lived in the biggest house for miles around and had tenants in half a dozen cottages, too, and yet, somehow, they suspended disbelief in their new, reduced situation; in their own eyes, they were gentlemen farmers, landlords, squires, people of some importance.

By the time Florence was born, the loss of most of the land and property was two generations away. Her father, John Joseph Hennessy, was the grandson and third male in a line to suffer deteriorating health, so that his daughter never knew him other

10

than as an invalid. As a small child, she had spent time with him, sitting on the floor beside the chair, which was pulled up close to the hearth, and in which he spent most of his day, wrapped in a plaid rug. But although fond of her, he found the restless company and chatter of a small child irritating and tiring and, learning that quickly, she retreated, not to her mother, but into herself, where she patiently began to build an iron will and reserves of determination and strength of character, but in secret, aware of the potential value to her of such a carefully harboured resource.

She was a self-sufficient, quick, observant and contented child. She understood her father's situation, and felt sorry for him, in a detached though affectionate way. But she was not privy to his thoughts nor he to hers, and both were happy that this should be so.

There was some land left, mainly for sheep grazing, but they lived away from the farm, in a severe, dull house, surrounded by an acre of uninteresting garden, just off the road to the village. She could remember her father going out in boots and a cap to the fields with one of the black and white dogs, and driving with him in the trap to market. But that had been almost four years before. Now, he sat in the chair, beside the fire in winter, near the window in summer, a thin, sallow man with a small moustache and pale, grey-blue eyes and receding hair, and with always a handkerchief in his hand, ready for when he coughed, and sometimes a faint blueness about the mouth.

She went to the school in the village, and disregarded her mother's lesson about their being in some way apart from, and superior to, the ordinary children, quite able from an early age to see through pretensions and fantasies to the plain truth. She played with whatever companions of the moment favoured her, always amicable, never close, and at home spent her time by herself. She was a solemn, rather beautiful child, very tall for her age and curiously unlike either parent, though with a certain Hennessy fragility about the skin beneath her eyes. Her inner life was rich, complex and satisfying to her, her outer life reserved, calm and uneventful. She took little notice of the dramas and emotional atmospheres that eddied from time to time about her parents and their concerns. What she thought about the future, even as a small girl, was that it would mean not only adulthood but freedom and independence, for she had always had an innate sense of not properly belonging to this place, these people. It had nothing to do with unhappiness, nor with love or its lack, it was a simple fact, this sense of otherness and detachment, just as she was a child who played willingly with others and yet, when she turned her back, forgot and did not think of them at all.

But her own state was not something she considered very deeply; she was as she was. Otherwise, her life was even and unremarkable, and she would not, until the distant attainment of adulthood, have expected it to change, as children do not.

Within a month of her eighth birthday, her father had died and, two weeks afterwards, her mother had given birth to another child, a shrivelled, sallow-skinned premature daughter, whom she named Olga, because May Hennessy had an inclination towards the romantic, the exotic and the foreign-seeming, as an antidote to the reality of her own life and diminished horizons.

Flora had not been told about the coming child and, afterwards, had wondered at what point her mother would have brought herself to speak of it – for surely she had never meant the whole, momentous business to have been unprepared for, surely there must have been some plan for a careful disclosure. (Though she found the thought of any such talk between them unimaginable, and later came to realise that in any case none had been planned. May Hennessy had been too shocked herself, and thrown into emotional disarray, to know how to tell anyone at all of her pregnancy. She had only prayed that Florence would not notice it and question her, for the girl was perceptive enough, with an intelligence her mother was afraid of.)

But Flora had noticed nothing.

And then, before the time of birth, the death had come.

Three

Saturdays were for longing. That was their point.

They took the bus to the town shops, not to buy from them, but to gaze into their windows, at fur stoles and mahogany furniture, shiny black gramophones and underwear fancy with lace and appliqué, china candelabra and fruits in syrup, packed into elaborate jars. It was tacitly understood between them, though never openly stated, that they were here to admire, to compare and to covet only, as though these objects, resplendent upon their stands and counters, were crown jewels or rare artefacts in a museum and quite unattainable.

They walked slowly down one side of Lord's Parade and up the other, looking, and, having looked, felt quite satisfied, and then went into Maud's for tea and lemonade, cakes and an ice.

It was understood, too, that acquaintances would barely be acknowledged. These outings were private occasions, separate from the rest of life and undertaken to appease some desire of May Hennessy's for ritual. Flora thought that, though they shared nothing else, her mother would still have preferred not to be with her, but to enjoy the outings entirely alone. They scarcely spoke unless, once they were installed at a window table in Maud's, a memory of something just seen and admired might float before May Hennessy's eyes and so be singled out, set, as if on a pedestal and turned this way and that between them, and commented upon.

13

The child had always felt cool and detached, never restless with the desire to take home and own anything they saw, partly because nothing in the shop windows ever seemed to have much to do with her; she could have had no possible relation to black velour coats or crystal vases. But she had inherited a certain dispassionateness, and was able to hold herself aloof and see the slow walk down Lord's Parade in the same light as a visit to a series of dull tableaux. Only at Christmas did a spark of something like excitement or happiness leap up in her at the sight of the glowing coloured caverns hollowed out behind the glass.

At Maud's, Flora liked the atmosphere, the bustle of waitresses and the chink of china on trays, long spoons in tall glasses, the pastel ices with cochineal syrup running like rivulets of lava down the sides. Then she sat and held her spoon poised above the glass, looking around at the women in hats, and longed to reach out and hold this bright, chattering place, carry it about within her. It satisfied very easily any craving for change or interest in her otherwise grey, plain days.

She had not learned peevishness or dissatisfaction. Her life was as it was, and she accepted it, as children will, and if she recognised that the Saturdays had a different or disturbing effect upon her mother, she did not question that either. What May Hennessy thought, felt or wanted was her own affair.

It was February, cold and bitter and black as a burned-out coal. They had made their way more quickly than usual down Lord's Parade, seeing no one they knew, and eaten tea-cakes, not ices, in Maud's, which shrivelled the usual pleasure of the day a little. The place had been quiet – there was influenza about. Flurries of hail blew like pips on to the windows. May Hennessy's face was drawn, with puffiness around the eyes.

'Well, perhaps it would have been better not to have come,' she said.

Flora did not reply. But she was conscious of the difference in things, of a disappointment, and, afterwards, would remember, and mark the day out as the beginning of the change in their lives, and the end of everything familiar.

After supper was eaten and cleared, the maid Eileen went out, walking two miles to the village to stay one night with her own family.

It was the only night of the week they were left alone, and, occasionally, they would play cards at the table in the back parlour next to the kitchen. They had a fire there, as well as in the front room where John Joseph Hennessy sat, and because it was the weekend the oil cloth was taken off and they played directly on to the polished wood, which was another thing that helped to set the day apart.

It was difficult to know afterwards how much she had really sensed of the change in things. But, after the card game, her mother had simply sat in her chair, looking down at the table, seeming tired, and Flora had sat too, and, then, something happened to time which slowed and stopped, and hung there, like a heavy, still object, a weight suspended on a chain. She felt it pressing in upon her. The house was quiet. The wind and rain had died down, the coals in the hearth did not shift or stir, so that after a time she became a little frightened by the silence, and fidgeted, wanting to bring everything back to life, nudge the clock to make it go again. But her mother sat and did not notice, went on with her thinking, and then the girl slipped off her chair and out of the room, and was quiet in closing the door.

In the hall, the silence was greater, like a thick cloud, a substance through which she could move forward only slowly.

She put her hand on the knob of the sitting room door. Her father's room. But for a moment she did not go in, only stayed frozen there, as if fearing that, once she had opened the door, she might find herself in some strange other place, where she would not know herself, and the arrangement of things would be quite unfamiliar.

For the rest of her life, she remembered everything about the room and her next few moments in it, alone with her father, though for years she did not speak of it but kept the memory stored away, untouched and perfectly preserved. She was able to close her eyes and smell again the smell in the parlour, to hear the pressure of the silence there, and to recreate her own feelings as she sensed its different and disturbing quality. It was not until she was no longer Florence Hennessy but Flora Molloy, and her own son was five years old that, for no apparent reason, she began to tell him of it, as she might tell a story, and after that he would ask to hear it sometimes, as if it were indeed *Rumpelstiltskin*, *The Pied Piper* or *The Little Matchgirl*, all of which she told him in the same way and the same voice. (For her favourite stories became his, they liked exactly the same ones for the same reasons. Their delight in this, as in so much else, was mutual and perfectly matched.)

She had gone on slippered feet that made no sound into the soundless room.

The fire had burned low, though the coals still glowed at their heart. The lamp had burned down too, the light was tallow and flickering.

She stopped. She had been about to say his name, but then did not, only stifled the life out of the words as they rose into her mouth. She looked at him, waiting, and then after a few seconds made her way not directly to him but by edging round the room, holding on to pieces of the furniture, afraid to let them go and be somehow stranded, without support.

'I knew,' she said, all those years later. 'I knew when I opened the door, only without knowing that I knew.'

She had reached him at last, but then could not bring herself to look, had stared at the hearth and the pattern of the green tiles around it, and the shape of the lilies that were printed on the tiles. There had been no smoke rising from the nuggets of coal, only the strange, dim, staring redness.

She saw his hand first, the handkerchief held in the palm and trailing down between his fingers that hung loose over the chair arm, and the hand was like a wax candle. She knew at once and quite certainly that there was no life in it.

Then, inch by inch, she had let her gaze travel up his arm, up the grey woollen sleeve, to his shoulder, to the shirt collar, then

16

above that to his thin neck. His head was back, resting on the small cushion. She followed the line from neck to jaw, as she had felt her way around the edge of the room. She stared at the bristle of hair, thin, colourless, at his temple and wisping back behind his ear, examined the coil of the ear, intricately.

The silence in the room tensed itself, tight as a coil about to spring; an absolute silence, such as she had never known before, but which penetrated her now and wove itself into the innermost recesses of her being, and settled there, bound itself in and around like a mesh, knotted, inextricable.

She was holding her breath, her throat and chest hurt, wanting to explode, she heard her heartbeat, as though she were trapped with it inside the skin of a drum.

She looked suddenly, quickly, right into his face, before she had decided that she would do it, or was able to prevent herself.

His eyes were not closed, they were open, and they were eyes she knew, yet they were not, they were different, a stranger's eyes, staring, staring back at her but not seeing, nor able to let any light or life out. They were dead eyes, cold, glazed, opaque.

The silence gathered itself and rushed towards her, she was engulfed in it, and then from far away, as at the end of a black tunnel, she heard herself begin to scream.

Four

The year that followed was the worst of her life save only for one, that came after. Of that she remained certain.

The time before her father's death, right up to the moment of walking into the front parlour and feeling the terrible different silence, became not merely the past but a complete, finished piece of the past, which was not joined on to the present or the future at any point, save by the thread of her memory. It was an island, forever inaccessible, inhabited by people she had once known but knew no longer, and to which the causeway had been sealed off. It floated there on its own, separate sea.

At first, her insecurity was total. She was unsure of her own surroundings, and people behaved oddly towards her. Children who had never seemed to like her, or to want her company, sidled up and hung about her, as if she were an object of fascination. Those she had regarded as enemies offered her sweets, yet friends remained aloof and stared at her across the classroom, as if she had become another person. At these times she would go into the cloakroom and look at her face in the pockmarked bit of mirror behind the door, half expecting it to be unfamiliar. But, apart from a wariness in her eyes, which she recognised as an accurate reflection of her inner feelings, it was her own face that confronted her.

What she remembered always and most clearly, afterwards, were not merely individual days and events – the day of his funeral, or of the birth of her sister, though these were seared on her memory. It was the disarray and displacement she felt, the way days were ordered quite differently now, so that even sounds were changed, everything felt temporary and time was a mire to be waded through on weighted feet. The rooms looked odd. The front parlour belonged to no one and was without a purpose, they did not go into it, but huddled together beside a poor fire at the back of the house. Strangers called at odd times, relatives, whose existence she had scarcely known of came, and sat awkwardly about the house, uncertain how to talk to her.

Her feelings about her father were the most confusing of all. She had enough to do, all day and far into the nights, to make her way to the heart of them, to sort them one from another and range them to her satisfaction.

When she had realised that he was dead, she had felt cold and afraid, urgently hysterically afraid, but that had lasted only a short time, until people came and took her away. Then, she was lost and bewildered, not knowing what her role should be. She felt anxious about the future, and at odd times was filled with desire simply to run away, to separate herself altogether from her mother, the house and what had happened. But she felt no real sadness. She had loved her father, yet that love had been a dutiful, subdued thing, not vital or rewarding. She had not known him or felt close to him, for all his vague kindness and affection towards her. He had been too distracted by illness, too wrapped up in the simple, daily struggle with his body and its malfunctions and weaknesses to spare energy for emotion or any relationship that might have been a further drain upon him. He had had nothing left over from the business of keeping himself alive.

It was wrong, she thought, not to feel pain and grief or the need to cry passionate tears. She felt unnatural and guilty at her own coldness and detachment, at the same time understanding that this was her greatest source of strength.

19

But the worst of it, after all, was not the death but the birth, not the absence but the new presence. The change begun by her father's dying was made absolute the day her sister was born.

They had taken her away. She had been driven in the trap, very early in the morning, wrapped in a thick rug against the cold and sleet that blew off the hill all day, to the house of a girl she hardly knew, Leila McKinnon, and her questions had been unanswered, except by a curt: 'Your mother is not well.'

The day was one that scarcely seemed to come light; even at noon, the lamps were lit and the sky lowered down on them, blotting out the view. The McKinnons lived in a house with a gravel drive that swept up to the door. She never understood why she had to be here, rather than at the home of some friend she could have chosen for herself. But her mother had always felt the equal of the McKinnons. Flora understood that perfectly, recognising May Hennessy's pride as a formidable force.

No one had told her anything. The rooms were large, high-ceilinged, formal. She had walked in and out of them, touching things gently, running her fingers along the cold marble of a fireplace, standing at the tall windows of the library looking out at a cedar tree, perfectly set in place upon a bare lawn. Leila McKinnon had followed her in silence, told to be kind, told to allow Flora to do as she pleased, and mildly resentful of it. They had trailed about the house for an hour, scarcely speaking, unable to find a common interest. Lunch had been eaten at either end of a dark refectory table. A maid had served them, and a dog had been lying sprawled beside the hearth, a wolf-hound, like some creature out of a fairy-tale.

'When am I to go home?'

'Your mother is unwell. It's better that you are here. You will go back just as soon as it is time.'

'When will it be time?'

'She needs a rest, you see, Flora. There is the doll's house in the attic now. Why not go up to see that?'

They had climbed the stairs, as they were bid, to take the chairs and beds and sideboards out of the doll's house and re-arrange them desultorily, never looking at one another. Beyond the attic windows, the sky gathered in to rain.

The maid brought up tea and scones and soda bread with jam, and iced biscuits. Flora felt oddly light-headed, as if she were in a dream, or else catapulted into some foreign country where they spoke a language that was like her own and yet incomprehensible to her. She could not get her bearings, did not know what she ought to feel, all her points of reference seemed to have been jumbled together and set back wrongly, like signposts you could no longer trust to show you the way.

It was night when she was returned home. She had felt anxious, pierced all over with unhappiness and profoundly alone. Perhaps it had shown, for on the doorstep, Leila McKinnon had come forward and embraced her awkwardly, and thanked her for coming, as if there had been a party, and Flora had held on to her for comfort, smelling the starched smell of her collar, and then she had understood that she was an object of pity, someone to be treated carefully, and that the death of her father had set her apart.

She held herself stiffly, as if on a set of strings that kept her together not merely bodily but in support of all her feelings and thoughts too. She tried not to let herself be jolted about, and clenched her hands together tightly under the rug. Only a small part of her was allowed free, and that part needed protection from the unfamiliar present, the unknown future.

The lamp shone in an upstairs window, and she went towards it, as to the source of all strength and reassurance. She was afraid, climbing the stairs. Her father was dead. Might not her mother be, too? The memory of the thick silence in the front parlour, and of her father's hand, as cold as wax, bobbed about within her.

And then the door of the bedroom was opened to her, and, standing on the threshold, outside the circle of light and warmth and quite set apart from it, she looked in upon them, her mother upright against high pillows, her hair disarranged and

21

damp-looking, a stranger to her. And the little shrivelled baby, on the cover beside her.

Five

In the new life – for that was what she felt it to be – she could have loved her sister, and indeed, began by doing so willingly and easily, and in spite of the shock of her presence. But it was clear that her love was neither wanted nor returned, because Olga had no need of it, claiming as she did all love, all attentive devotion, from their mother.

She was an ugly baby, with thin, scrawny limbs and peeling skin, and discontented and unsettled too, ceaselessly crying, a grizzling, mewling little cry. But as she grew she became pretty, in a complacent, doll-like way, and then she commanded devotion and was petulant when not receiving it. Flora felt neither jealousy nor resentment. The effect of her sister's presence upon her was far more penetrating and painful. She felt herself to be in some way guilty, because inadequate. Even her own physical being seemed wrong and distressing to her, her hands and feet were elephantine and clumsy, her height and paleness and plainness were like blemishes, outer symptoms of her unsatisfactoriness. But, more than anything, she felt a pit open up within her which nothing could fill. When she woke, it was like the ache of hunger. Sadness accompanied it, a pure core of sadness that she learned to accept as an inevitable part of her present life, though she did not attribute the sadness to any one cause, not her father's death, the birth of her sister, or the child's dislike of her.

23

Her salvation was her own inner detachment, a clear-eyed resolution and strength of character and a steeliness which was not harsh or cold, merely utterly reliable.

She watched May Hennessy and Olga, saw their mutual adoration and interdependence, and recognised that she had no part in it, and looked on her sister's porcelain beauty and outward charm without envy. She knew that she no longer belonged here – perhaps, indeed, had never done so, and was merely marking time until she could leave, though the business of growing up seemed infinitely slow, infinitely tedious.

As she grew, what crystallised within her was not only the desire to be away and make her life elsewhere, but also an intense pride, inherited from her mother, a sense of her own status which was related to May Hennessy's passionate defence of their position in society. Flora did not care for that, yet nevertheless she felt, in some way she could not yet define, superior to and set apart from others. It was as though she were marked out. It did not cause her to behave badly, to sneer or to be in any other way disagreeable – she was outwardly unchanged. Others liked her well enough and were happy to have her company, while sensing a permanent reserve, almost amounting to an aloofness, which was not unattractive. They respected it.

Eighteen months after her father's death, Flora could barely remember him. It was as though he had never been wholly with them, never been physically strong enough nor sufficiently dominant in character to make a lasting impression, and so he had faded, as a photograph exposed to the light, his features became hard to recall. There was only a lingering atmosphere in the front parlour, which Flora sensed acutely, something about its coldness and silence that reminded her of the evening of his death and his thin, empty body propped in the chair, so that she went there as rarely as she could and never lingered.

May Hennessy did not speak of him. What he had thought of the coming child – even if he had known of it at all – how much interest or concern he might have felt, were also never mentioned, and, although intelligent and perceptive about their situation in general, and aware of all the nuances of her mother's nature,

Flora did not choose to unsettle the fragile equilibrium between them by asking questions. That this was a relief to May Hennessy she was certain. They were amicable together, living parallel rather than intermeshed daily lives. Flora became more than ever an intensely private person, needing no close confidante nor any outlet for her innermost thoughts and feelings. She read a great deal, choosing her books with much care and going through them slowly and methodically, seeming to exert control over them, as over everything else in her life, and never allowing herself to be taken by surprise, or to be out of control.

The child Olga kept away from her, until she was old enough to be inquisitive, when she would pry into Flora's things, question and tease, before running back to her mother's protection. But Flora dealt with her mildly enough and was never roused to ill temper. She looked into her sister's pretty, spoilt face and staring blue eyes, and felt mild affection and a certain scorn, because of Olga's total dependence upon others for admiration and approval. Olga could not be alone for even a few moments and, when in company, could not be silent or concentrate on anything except her own chatter and the reaction it provoked. Observing that, Flora was only grateful for her own inner resources. Life had dealt its blows. She thought that she had defences and to spare now, against those that would come.

Six

Molloy did not go home yet. To leave would mean one more bead told, of the last few.

He turned, out of the cubicle in which he had left the body of the dead woman, Annie Hare, out of the ward.

The girl, running back up the dark stone steps from the stores below, saw his back and stopped to watch him go away.

'Why would he go down into the old part, Sister? Why would anyone have business there, that's all shut up and empty? What interest is there left in it?' She would not have gone, not for anyone, and besides, could see no reason. The building was dying, wasn't it, and almost dead? It would be bulldozers and then rubble, within the year, and good riddance.

She quickened her own step, going past the abandoned blocks and doors leading to wings that had been cleared, hollow stair-wells.

'He's like a spirit. He'll haunt the place. He can't leave it, can he?'

'He cannot.'

'Funny that. Doesn't it seem funny to you? Don't you think?'

'It is not my business or yours to think anything about it at all.' The Sister pinched her lips and would not say anything more, out of some slight sense of loyalty to the doctor, the natural respect

26

she had been trained up to, as well as wanting to put the younger woman down.

Molloy walked. Away from the occupied wards and from the pools of quiet light, away from people to whom he could not have spoken about any of it.

Molloy walked.

It was as if a tide had turned and run out, leaving what bit of life remained in the old buildings washed up in one corner, and the people huddled together in the last of the light and warmth. They talked, and went about their vestiges of business; occasionally there was crying or laughter and the smell of meat stewing. Beyond, emptiness and darkness. Long high wards, curtainless windows. Echoes. Cold, dead air, stirred by no one in their breathing of it, any more.

Only tonight, the wind blew in through the cracks and shifted it about, and, when the clouds parted, moonlight shone down the abandoned rooms and through the dirty window glass at the end of the tiled corridor, lighting his way (though he did not need it, knowing every step).

No one followed him. He had walked through the empty buildings often enough in the last months, recording everything, touching his hand to the flaking walls, running it along the cold tiles, standing to stare ahead into the empty spaces, as if he wanted to imprint his own presence here, while it existed at all. Remembering.

Since childhood, he had been haunted by places. He dreamed not of people but of rooms, of hallways, porches, attics, of the curve of a pillar, the moulding of a ceiling, the grain of a wooden beam. Of banisters, steps, window-frames. By day, some part of a building he had known would be thrown upon the inner screen of his mind, and he would gaze at it. Time and again he would find himself walking, in his imagination, up some particular staircase and through a once-familiar door. He carried imprinted within him a plan of every house in which he had lived or worked, and of others too. There had been a convent, set up a

27

dark path behind trees, not far from his secondary school. He had hung about there, looking through the bars of the gates. Now, he could recall every detail, of the chimneys and the roofs, the pattern of the bricks, the lie of the tiles. He never wanted to go inside, but preferred to guess how it was, to walk about the rooms in his imagination only.

When he was six, from the bus windows he had seen a small castle beyond a dry moat and, later, a black hovel in a field with smoke coming from a hole in the roof. The cottage of a witch, his mother had said. 'Look. Go on. Look.' And he had looked. For it had come from her, this fascination with mysterious buildings. She had told him about the empty school, one night before he went to sleep, sitting beside him in the dark, and he had taken it into himself, and dreamed of it straight away, and afterwards asked her again and again, 'Tell me about the school. Tell me about the school.'

It was when she had been a governess in Kilmoyne. There were so many smart houses on the road that led to the sea, new houses, and brash, not the real, grand places of the old families, like Carbery, where she worked. She had enjoyed looking, she said, watching people drive out between the stone pillars, proud in their shining motors. Everything there had been new.

(Though now, he thought, those are the old houses, and that is the solid, old-fashioned part of the town, which is so changed, so grown. Now those houses have old, old people struggling on in too many big rooms, behind overgrown, unmanageable gardens. There is nothing brash and new there any more, only decay, and sadness for that bright past.)

She told him how she had walked up a grassy track, thinking that it was a short cut to the coast road, but instead, behind some rough fence and barbed wire, she had seen the soft grey buildings, the courtyard and broken steps and entrance of what had been a school. 'St. Teresa's Convent School for Girls.' The board, with flaking gold letters, was still there, but pasted across with strips of tape. 'Private. Keep out. Trespassers will be prosecuted.'

It had been spring. The hedgerow was a tangle of guelder rose and quickthorn, the old cracked paving stones sprouted daisies and groundsel. The grass was high as her waist. She had found a gap in the wire and climbed through, and, after that day, she had gone back several times, found a way inside through a door that had blown open and was left swinging.

In his dreams, he went where she had gone, into the classrooms of the empty school. Into the hall. Up the stairs to the dormitories, where swallows had got in and were nesting, and mice ran about over the broken floorboards. It had been frightening, and dangerous, perhaps, and, at any rate, forbidden. He had heard the old excitement still in her voice as she told him about it. 'I can't forget it,' she had said. 'It's there. I go round it in my mind. I shall never forget.'

It had come to him, as everything that had value or meaning in his life had come to him, from her, so that now, walking the empty hospital corridors, it was of her that he thought. But although he could trace every inch of every building in the past, his mother's face he could never see at all. He had not been able to do so, since the day he had heard of her death. He had only her voice, very occasionally, like a scrap of music played in the distance, before being broken off abruptly. He would hear something she had once said to him, a fragment of a sentence spoken without warning in his ear. The photographs he had of her did not help him. There were four, and she gazed out of them, but not at him. She would not come to life for him.

What he had of her was not a memory, not a face recalled. It was his past, and it was rootedness, and a place to which he went in order to feel safe. A sanctuary. But it was also an anguish. Desolation. Unhappiness, and the purest pain.

But the places, the buildings and her feelings for them, he knew as well as he knew his own places. She had given them to him.

He went on, through every corridor, into every room. Walking. ('Like a spirit,' the girl had said.)

But after an hour, his spirit came to rest, as it so often did, in the one place to which he was always drawn. He took the back stairs,

29

and then went outside, across the yard. A single, blue-white light above the door lit his way, and then he felt his restlessness ease, and strain and all anxiety leave him. He was quieted. In the deserted corridors there had been silence, but a silence that was uneasy. He had felt oppressed by it, and made melancholy. He went there but wished that he had not.

Here, the silence was of a different kind, and a balm to him. He pushed open the inner door.

Seven

The mortuary was lit only at the far end, where the attendant sat beside the trolley. They had brought her down already. She lay like the skeleton of a bird, scarcely heaped up, lightly and softly beneath the sheet. Annie Hare.

The man glanced up. Nodded to him. He was used to Molloy coming here, to sit for minutes, or for an hour, recognised that the place seemed to serve as church or chapel to him. Sometimes they spoke a word or two.

Molloy went to stand beside her but did not lift the sheet to look beneath, did not disturb her. Then he turned, pulling out a stool to sit on.

'Quiet,' he said.

'Just this one, and two from yesterday.'

The man went on writing in the file of Annie Hare, and the desk lamp shone on to his hands, huge and thick, with tufts of black hair over the backs, like the pelts of a small animal. He was younger than Molloy, but he would be leaving at the same time. He was not going to the new hospital. He was moving away, north to where his sons were. 'Time for a bit of new life.' He did the job because it was a job, and thought little of it, a cheerful man, easy with the living, untroubled by the dead.

' "The Gateway," ' someone had said to Molloy, the first time he had gone there, as a student. 'We call it "The Gateway".' Though

31

the mortuary was called other things too; they had to make light of it to be able to deal with it, as with the horrors they saw. They had to get used to things quickly, and never brood. Molloy brooded. It would be his failing, his tutors said, it would break him. A doctor could not brood. A brooding temperament would not see him through.

They were right to believe it, but not right about Molloy. Only by taking things deep down into himself and brooding upon them there in silence, until he somehow transmuted them and was able to feel easy, could he do his work, and retain a sense of balance and sanity. He could not make crude jokes, as his fellows did, and never ducked nor swerved away from the worst there was to know. And the worst was not death. For him, death was often the best of it, a right and fitting conclusion. Death led here, to this cool, white place, into this quietness and stillness and solitude. 'The Gateway'.

He did not believe any of the customary creeds that he had recited at school. She had not. 'No one knows,' she had said. 'They'll pretend to you. They will all claim the truth. None of them knows it, and we do not either, and you will not. Only never close your mind. That's all. Never.'

She had always spoken to him, as to an adult, in this way. There had never been baby talk between them. In the conversations he remembered still, word for word, so that he could hear them over in his head, there had never been any sense that he was too young to hear about this or that, not ready to understand. What she had wanted him to know, she had told him, what she had wondered about and needed to discuss openly, she had talked to him about.

As, death.

'We do not know. No one does. Nor ever has.'

He would not have doubted her, in this as in anything else. No one knew. Yet she was all-knowing to him, he was certain of it, as well as all-powerful and all-providing. He needed no one else.

'The Gateway.' He thought the word now, looking towards the outline beneath the heavy sheet. In all the years since his mother's

32

own dying, he had come to it time after time. This far. If there was a farther, he could not follow. It was the best he could ever do. It had to satisfy.

The first time he had entered a mortuary, in the teaching hospital, he had been sick with dread. They had had to give him leave, for two days after. He had been sweating and grey in his terror. He would have to leave then, he had been sure. Blood was nothing to him, incised flesh or protruding bone, the stench in the open gut, pus in a wound. But his imagination had shied away from the place where silence and finality would confront him with the things that were in him. That he could not bear. He had begun to strip his bed and to empty his things out of the drawers, for he would be asked to leave, there would be no other way. He had shown his weakness, a fatal flaw.

Instead, they had frog-marched him back there, propelled him through the doors, saying nothing, the pressure brutal, of a knuckle between his shoulder blades. He had smelled the cold and the formaldehyde. The silence had rushed into his ears like a wave, to drown him. The world had dissolved like water beneath his feet.

They had ordered him to open his eyes. After a moment, he had done so, and found himself alone with the attendant, who sat on a stool beside the waxen body of a man. He had looked at Molloy, with understanding and absolute kindness. 'It's nothing,' he had said. 'Do you see? Nothing at all.'

But it had been everything. The realisation had crept towards him and overtaken him, like the dawn of understanding. In this functional place of death, and later, at bedside after bedside, Molloy had reached the only destination of any importance to him.

He had borne their amusement, knowing that he made them uneasy. 'Mortuary Molloy' they had shouted after him then. It had not troubled him. Something had cleared in his mind, some log-jam of dread and uncertainty and confusion, as he had realised his own calm and strength, in the face of the dead, and his sense of rightness when he witnessed the moment of dying. It had been utterly sure, at once, and had never left him, and his life as a doctor had been transformed by it.

Nothing touched him, nothing threatened his certainty, ever again. He did not speak of it, nor answer questions about it, except with a shrug. There was nothing he could have said, no words with which he could have conveyed his feelings to the others, so that, after a time, they withdrew. They did not isolate or ostracise him, and he shared his days with them amicably enough. But he did not need them.

Beside those who were dying, and with them after death, his loss of her, the desolation of it and his absolute sense of abandonment, were eased. Nowhere else. For the rest of time, he suffered her absence unrelievedly, and the accompanying absence of the feeling of all love and all sweetness.

Now, sitting quietly in this basement room, within this place of safety, he suddenly felt a sense of his mother's person, so entire and vivid that it was giddying. He smelled her smell. Her body was as close to him as his own breath. He saw her face and almost cried out, with the reality and then, at once, the searing unreality of it, so that he swayed on the stool and caught his breath. The other man glanced up.

But it was over, as it had come. It had taken a second, and pressed him down in that second with the weight of forty years, and then was nothing. The man looked away again, and so, after a time, Molloy got up, and went to stand briefly beside the hidden body, to put his hand up to it, touching the dry cotton of the covering sheet, as if it were sacred cloth.

Eight

Flora built her plans calmly, and in an orderly way, as others might accumulate savings little by little. At school, she worked methodically, never trying to impress, never asking too many bright questions in the class, and so the others neither scorned nor resented her. She maintained her cool, pleasant manner with them, walking round the school grounds after lunch, or playing tennis.

Towards her teachers, she was polite, neat, pleasant. None of them could find fault with her. None of them knew her. She was not secretive nor furtive, merely quite separate. Her real life went on somewhere within herself.

She liked to walk in the lanes and fields near her home, and as she grew older, through the streets of the town too, and, in her walking, discovered for herself the things that were of value – the castle, churches, gates leading to small, elegant houses tucked away. She grew to distinguish the façades of buildings, to see what was beautiful and elegantly proportioned, what cheaply built, cluttered and ugly. Her own taste was austere. She liked clean, straight lines, spare detail, plain handsome shapes, was irritated by over-elaboration.

In summer she went into the public parks and gardens, but although she found them pleasant enough, and shady on the hot afternoons at the end of the school day, they did not move or excite her as the buildings did. She thought of them as unsatisfactory, being neither town nor open country.

Then she went into the largest of them, Maclayne Park, one Saturday in December. She had taken the bus to town with her mother and Olga, and later would meet them in Maud's, after they had walked, as she and May Hennessy had once used to walk, solemnly down Lord's Parade, looking into the shops. Shops, and their window displays, were not interesting to her now, but Olga made up for her, in over-excited acquisitiveness.

It had been cold, with a pale, bright sky, and the sun had been setting in a damson-coloured band, at the same time as a wire of bright moon emerged slowly, like an outline impregnated on some magic paper. Flora had wandered in through the park gates half absently. But, as she looked up, she saw the lake in the hollow ahead as the sun was striking the surface, flaring and copper-coloured before it sank. Then, the lake had gone black. Behind it were the trees, bare and austere, some skeletal, with an intricate mesh of smaller branches, others dense, solid and erect. Everything had been tidied, everything was cleared of the softening mass of foliage and flowers. She had walked slowly around the darkening paths and seen shapes revealed, the open spaces between setting them apart from one another. There had been a cold, bitter smell of bare damp earth and holly berries. And she had stood, taut with the excitement of this place, and her own intense pleasure in it. In that moment, the point of the gardens was revealed to her.

If she did no more academic work than was usual for an intelligent and diligent girl, she read a very great deal, and her reading, like everything else, became disciplined and steady. She read as soon as she woke and for an hour or more before sleeping. On the light mornings of spring and summer, she would come downstairs long before her mother and Olga, and read sitting on the back doorstep and, in her reading, she allowed herself to be led from one book, one subject to another, gradually enlarging her taste. The public library educated her, she would say afterwards. She went there several times a week, enjoying the smell of the place and the soft sound of turning pages, the muffled coughs, the oblong reflections from the windows on to the polished floor. She liked its calm and orderliness, and the sense of concentration that was pressed into it, like the sense of reverence in a church, and the way both places seemed to exist outside of ordinary time.

Until she was seventeen, the library, certain handsome streets, and the parks and gardens in winter, fed and enriched her, supplementing the plain fare of her school lessons. Otherwise, she had a little companionship, much solitude and, for the rest, the everyday routine of her life with her mother and sister.

She did not spend time in analysing her own feelings, though on her plans and ambitions for the future she dwelt a good deal. She would have said that she was contented, and, for the time being, had what she wanted, secure in the knowledge that the rest would come. May Hennessy did not understand her. There were no quarrels between them, because they had few points of contact, and she knew nothing of Flora's plans. She herself never looked ahead. The strain of surviving in the present was all-absorbing to her, though of this Flora was for some time quite unaware.

She had had little interest in the drawing and painting classes at school which were dull, and seemed to have no connection with her own growing visual awareness. Bowls of fruit, vases of tulips, arrangements of uninteresting objects, were set on small tables and trays for them to sketch, and the periods, although quiet and rather soothing, were tedious.

Revelation came at the Rotunda Museum. They were to draw what they chose, and Flora wandered off by herself through room after dusty room full of fossils and stones and bones, helmets and coins, shards and broken pots and dark old furniture, searching for something of interest. No one missed her. She climbed an iron staircase that spiralled to the domed roof, and went slowly around the balconies, into rooms that led off a gallery. Up here, where the light came in clear and bright through beautiful windows, were pictures, portraits of pompous men and bland-

37

faced women, artificially posed dogs and horses, religious scenes and brown varnished landscapes full of mountains and cataracts and ravines in which Flora thought no one would surely ever wish to walk.

The rooms led out of one another like a series of Chinese boxes, and they were quite empty. It gave her a quiet pleasure to go through them alone, in silence. And then she turned, into a long, white gallery, filled with north light. The walls of the other rooms had been crammed with pictures. Here were only a few, and at once she was drawn to one at the far end of the room, and stood in astonishment before it.

A young woman reclined on a couch beside an open window. She was dressed in soft folds of cream and white and ivory and pale grey, and her arm hung over the edge of the couch. A hat dangled loosely between her fingers. Her face was turned away. Beyond the windows ran a thin, glittering line of sea. Otherwise, clouds trailed across the sky, and the clouds seemed to billow in through the spaces in the room in which the young woman sat and to be part of her dress, and of the very air. There was no colour, save for a ribbon in her hat, which was red, the red of flames, geraniums, poppies.

On the other walls, other pictures, in which skies and clouds both reflected and gave back an inner light, as well as the light within the room. And here and there was the same small patch of red, or else a single dense block of vivid blue. The rest was light and air and scudding movement.

But it was the girl at the window who compelled her, and, then, as she emerged from her concentration upon the picture, the vision of the whole room in which she stood. She felt the shock of discovery like an electric charge.

38

Nine

Hazel catkins came out overnight. The bare cherry boughs were hazed with pink. Hawthorn hedges pricked green. An early spring burst, in warmth and birdsong. And each day, because of the pale pictures in the Rotunda, Flora opened her eyes on a new world and felt changed by it. But the change was not merely in outward things and in ways of looking. In the part of herself deep below the surface, she considered new questions, and answers occurred to her which were sometimes shocking in their strangeness.

Her plans became clearer. She took book after book on art from the public library and when she had exhausted their supply asked for the loan of more from other, distant libraries, and was flushed with gratification and a sense of power at the ease with which they were all obtained for her. Many were rare and she was not allowed to take them out. She spent more and more hours at a table in the reading room, before returning again and again to the pictures themselves on the gallery walls. But although she never tired of looking at the young woman in her pale clothes seated before the window, and at the landscapes of clouds, she became frustrated that they were all she had and greedy for other, quite different pictures.

The new idea came to her like a bubble rising to the surface, one afternoon as she sat at her classroom desk, and the wallflowers were thick and heady and pungent in the flowerbeds beneath the open windows.

She would go to a college, in London, or even in Italy – Florence or Rome. She would study there and live among pictures. She felt quite calm, in her immediate certainty that it would be, and so did not trouble to consider details. The strength of her ambition, and a hard fixity of purpose, would be all-powerful. She had no doubts, saw no obstacles. There were colleges, and teachers, and places in which young women might live. She had read of them. She would go. She had only to concentrate on getting a place, through her intelligence and application. Flora knew herself.

And now that her plans were formed, in the summer of that year, she began to feel a terrible sense of restriction and restlessness, and walked through the streets and in the fields, as if trying to walk out her frustration at the present, and the irritating slowness of passing time. The days were rich and heavy and slow with scents, the grass high and thickly green. The house, in which she spent as little time as possible, seemed to shrink. The rooms were dim and brown and stale, the windows let in too little, too dingy a light. Outside streams dried, soil baked and cracked. The birds fell silent. Flora's skin seemed to teem just below the surface, as though something within her needed to burst the bounds of it and leap away. She walked and read and thought, and lay awake through the sticky, airless nights. But each morning, she was surprised again by the promise of the year ahead of her, a last, short, steep hill which she must climb.

Olga went to parties, dressed in frilled dresses and satin shoes, hair be-ribboned, ringlets bouncing about her bland forehead. Olga considered herself silently in mirrors and pirouetted for approval. Olga was popular and fluttered about the house, never able to settle to anything, never happy to be alone. Olga was a bright, pretty thing to have about the sour dark place, and her mother was mesmerised by her, as if amazed by the child's very presence in her world.

They will be perfectly happy together, Flora thought, at least for a few more years. They will be attentive to one another, dance round one another in admiring little circles, before Olga outgrows it all, and flounces away, leaving a terrible silence behind.

By then, she herself would be long gone, and she knew that her own slipping away would scarcely be noticed, her absence leave no gap. She was happy, relieved that it would be so, and behaved indulgently towards her sister, out of gratitude. They had nothing in common at all, no meeting ground. But she was oddly fond of the vain, attractive, ephemeral little creature, because she saw her vulnerability, and that she was fragile and insubstantial, and her power of commanding attention and admiration would not last. And when it failed, Olga would disappear and be nothing.

Summer shrivelled and burned and was tossed away by the first gales of autumn. Flora revealed her plans to the headmistress. Colleges in London, and also in Edinburgh, were discussed – Italy, it was thought, would come later. There must be an order in these matters, Miss Pinkney said. (Though the girl's self-possession and coolness unnerved her. She could not get the picture from her mind, as she sat in her spinster lodgings that night, of Flora's grave and meticulous control.)

'It is to be hoped that the future will meet your expectations,' she had said, wanting – what? To warn? To chasten?

The girl's eyes had been steady on hers, her face shadowed by the faintest of frowns.

'Why should it not?'

Miss Pinkney had been unable to answer.

'Why should it not?'

The crab apples were eggs of gold and blood red, the branches bowed under the weight of them. The front path was lined with blowsy, rinsed-out hollyhocks. At night, hedgehogs snuffled and snorted for grubs, in grassy corners.

Why should it not?

*

Olga had been prinked and petted to bed, her ringlets screwed up in papers. She had stared at her own self in the glass, and been reassured.

And, then, the house was quiet. No wind blew tonight. The trees were still. Nothing went by along the road.

They sat in the old balloon-backed chairs, on either side of the kitchen hearth. Flora read. In a little while, she would speak the sentences she had prepared, in their exact order.

But suddenly, disconcertingly, she remembered her father, in a few seconds of absolute clarity, saw his crumpled body inside the clothes that were too large, the ill-fitting grey cardigan, the stiff collar that gaped away from his neck, and with the recollection of him came a piercing realisation of what she had never until now understood – that he had been unhappy and lonely, in some profound way, and quite unreachable in his sadness. She was bewildered by the uprush of grief and dreadful longing that came to her then. It was as though she were crying hot, urgent tears. But no tears fell.

'Why should it not?'

She turned her mind away from the recollection and, in doing so, looked up, and across the space between them at her mother. As so often now, May Hennessy was doing nothing, not reading, nor even fidgeting with something of Olga's that the child wanted to be altered or embellished. Her hands were still, folded in her lap, and she was leaning forwards slightly, staring, staring into the coals. Her face was old, furrowed and bleak and infinitely disappointed. Looking at her, Flora felt a shaft of pure, detached sorrow. Thought: Her life is over. And what has it been? There was my father, always unwell. Then dead. There is Olga, and Olga has been everything to her, her treasure, her delight, her investment in the future. But Olga will go. There is no future for her in Olga.

And she herself was about to tell of another separation, though she did not think that it was one May Hennessy would care about, for there was only incomprehension between them now. She might be envied, but Flora knew that she would not be missed.

42

Several times, the words were in her mouth, waiting to be spoken, and yet she held them back, feeling this stillness and silence lying between them to be important.

She would not break it.

And as she had been struck by a truth about her father, now she understood her mother's profound disappointment in life also. May Hennessy had been happy in childhood. Flora had always heard her speak with joy and respect and longing of it, though she was clear-eyed enough to see that her mother's memories were selective, and that any unhappiness or tedium had been forgotten, and all pleasures highlighted, gilded and smoothed.

Marriage had appeared as an opportunity, not so much for personal happiness as for self-establishment and social advantage. The Hennessys had standing, money, land and prospects. Reality had been cruel. At times, Flora had caught her mother looking, in distaste and bewilderment, around this small back room, as if unable to understand how she came, on the brink of old age, to find herself here. She seemed to have become smaller in her disappointment, as he had in illness, to have no colour, no brightness of eye or lightness of step. Her pride had been chastened. The things that counted to her in life she had either lost early, or never attained.

What is there? What has she? What future can there be for her, Flora thought now.

Her mother's hands were working together, thumb rubbing against thumb. Her life had no compensation, so far as the girl could see, no interest or expectation. Her own determination quickened in her. For she had a future. This life, here, would not be hers.

But the words she spoke then startled her. She had not known they were in her head. They were not the words she had prepared.

'Why did you marry my father?'

She heard her own voice speaking confidently into the silent room.

May Hennessy turned her head slowly and stared, her face

43

open and unmasked, before distress and some bewilderment clouded and darkened it.

Flora could not have predicted her mother's reply, but now, in this new and very different silence, she realised that she expected honesty, and that the honesty would prompt words like, 'Security.' 'Money.' 'Esteem.' 'Position.' Those were what May Hennessy cared about; for those she had felt it worth risking her happy childhood. 'Betterment.' 'Advancement.' And Flora would have understood, for to a large extent, though in quite another way, those were her own ambitions. Hers were private and intellectual, her mother's had been social. That was all. Marriage would not be Flora's means of achievement, but she recognised that her mother had no other option.

'Why did you marry my father?'

The question was suspended between them, each word still somehow heard, hearable. May Hennessy's hands, which had been twisting together, her mouth, which had been working, were still, and the stillness was adamantine and dreadful. Flora shrank away from it, back into her chair. But she could not drop her gaze, could not avoid her mother's eyes upon her. She was afraid of bitter anger and reproach, of having her question, and the presumption of it, repulsed, afraid of what she would hear. But her mother's words, when they came, were spoken very quietly, and with infinite tenderness, and the truth was in them unmistakable, complete.

'I loved him. I loved him as well as a person can love. Did you never know that? There was no avoiding it – such love.'

Flora wanted to shy away from the words. They were too much for her. She could not cope with their meaning.

But hearing them spoken, nakedly, without pretence, she knew, in some shadowy way she also could not fully comprehend, that they marked a rite of passage. On hearing them, she had taken a step forward and broken altogether from her own childhood.

Ten

The old moon, shadowed, held the new moon in her arms, a woman dying at childbirth.

Molloy walked quickly to the car. He did not look back. He wanted to be away from here; the urgency of it made his heart pound. But as he turned out of the grounds on to the main road, he told off the visit automatically, slipping it like a rosary bead through his fingers.

So he supposed that he might feel as a condemned man, counting the last days to execution. It was not a death, but to him it felt like one, and he could not make out the life beyond. It was there, a fact, yet unimaginable.

He drove on through the shuttered town and then took the coast road which curved around the bay for four miles, bungalows straggling beside. His headlights caught a blue painted gate, a run of white fence, a slinking cat, amber-eyed. Then the cliffs began, the road running between them and the sea.

He had emptied his mind of the day. What happened happened, and for the time he immersed himself in it, then walked away. He would not think of Annie Hare again. As a young man, he had woken and slept with his head full of the images of pale faces and still, cold limbs, the absolute contrast between the living and the dead dominating him. But he had taught himself to step back from his preoccupation, set it aside.

He would not go home yet.

Just before the point, the road divided. To the left, it led inland, towards his own village, but the main road went on, following the bay. Molloy stopped. He would walk. His limbs felt huge, cramped and restless inside the confines of the car. All the frustrations and dissatisfactions, mute and undefined, seemed suddenly to have transferred themselves to his body.

When he stepped on to the grass, he was aware first of the stillness of the night. The wind had dropped and the clouds moved away in a mass, leaving the stars and the two moons. The tide was far out. He took the overgrown track that led through the marram grass down to the shingle and then on, until he reached the hard, wet sand at the rim of the water, where the tiny waves rolled over and back upon themselves with a soft, lapping sound. He had been holding on to his breath, clenching it within his chest so that his lungs and muscles ached. Now, in releasing it all, something else was released too, leaving him oddly exhilarated.

The bay was small. It was not far to the point, awkward to reach and quickly filled by the tide. Few came here, summer or winter. He began to follow the line of the water and then for a moment or two, as if opening a door and peering through the narrowest crack, he allowed himself to think glancingly of the future. But it was impenetrable to him, and bewildering. It was the utter change that would change him so that he would no longer know himself. His life had been defined by his work in that place, and his own place in it, and, before it, by the other hospitals, other patients' lives and deaths. He had had no other reason or being since the day that the news of his mother's death had come to him.

He had been married. His wife lay at home now, in the bed at the other side of the room from his own empty bed. He had made a careful decision to marry her, needing a solid background to his life. He had liked her and she had loved him and so would be entirely content with what he was able to offer – a situation, a home, a measure of company. Fairness. Openness over money. And nothing whatsoever of himself. He remained inner, private and inviolate, and never within the reach of another person. For the woman asleep, quietly alone, it had not been a bad bargain, though perhaps now she felt the colder winds of age she would have welcomed the warmth and protection of a greater closeness. But nothing was said, nor would it be. There was simply an understanding.

He liked to feel the firmness of the sand, yet with the slight yielding when he lifted his foot. As he walked towards the point in the silken darkness, his body fell into a rhythm, and then his anxieties quieted and dropped away. And into the stillness and silence that were left to him came other thoughts, which flowed through him like a slow-moving river through caves. They came not formed into words, but as images only. He saw the permanence of rocks and the earth's strata, and sensed sudden, huge molten upheavals that happened without warning, and faults and cracks. Then there was the sky and the shiftingness of clouds, and the sea, turning, turning, endlessly renewing itself. The pebbles dragged back, mumbling at the seething water's edge. The whole world seemed to be within his head and he viewed it there. He thought of flesh and blood and bone, atoms forming and re-forming, saw human bodies, the same from birth to death, and yet not the same in any way, changed utterly as the atoms reassembled.

When it was like this, he seemed to be on the brink of some simple, vivid comprehension of things, as in a dream when all is explained, all made clear, only to dissolve into paleness and confusion with the return of consciousness. Such times contented him. The fact that there were no answers to his questions, no resolutions to the workings of his thoughts, had long ceased to trouble him. Rocks. Sea. Stones. Atoms. Flesh. The flicker of brightness that was intelligent life. Raw, relentless misery. The stone-like state of death, that permanence that became in itself the final dissolution. He turned to them, as others would to invisible holy things, for sustenance and strength, reassurance and a kind of comfort.

He reached the point and rounded it, and then, the darkness of the whole wide shore beyond was huge as a mouth, to consume him if he stepped into it. He did not. He turned and began to walk calmly back, contained within the circle of cliff, and the moon rode, beautiful above him.

Eleven

The smell in the cold hall was the smell of a childless house, and the silence was the same and oppressed him. Dust never settled. When anything was put down on the polished chest, it remained exactly so.

The air was deathly still, and his own feet made no sound on the thick pile of the carpet. It was a woman's house. They were a woman's rooms. He felt too large, too clumsy in them.

In the kitchen, lit by a white strip of light, the surfaces were clear, a dish covered. The table wore a cloth. The calendar was set straight, lined precisely below the clock. He went into the living room, and stood, among coffee tables and cushions and lamps and china baskets, and the odd sensation returned, of being a giant with swollen limbs, a huge, ungainly thing.

Home.

It was hers, and he had never once begrudged it to her, having other things. Now he could not breathe here. The fawn-coloured curtains and tapestry sofa, the rugs like the matted backs of sheep, seemed to be stuffed into his lungs, choking him. He tasted cloth and wadding and dryness.

In the future, he would be here at times he had never known the house. At noon, and two o'clock and five. He would carry trays of small china cups and embroidered cloths into the scone-smelling kitchen. He would have nowhere else to go.

The blood roared like the tide through his ears, seething to be released.

He let the water run from the kitchen tap until it ran free of any staleness, and drank a glass of it, and the coldness on the back of his throat soothed him. He had thought of taking a little whisky, but after all had no need.

In the bedroom, there was a sweetness of powder and scented things. He did not switch on the light, considerate towards her. But she slept silently through his return, as always, after years of practice in it. At breakfast, she might remark, ask a quiet question. He would say just enough. He had never talked of things, his concerns, the other life. Those like Annie Hare. That was well understood.

It had not been unhappy. It was a solution, a way of everyday living that suited him – and suited her, or so it had always seemed. He had never regretted it. It took up so little of him. Now, he lay in his bed in the cottony darkness and it seemed that he was strapped to some toboggan or train that was hurtling downhill towards an unavoidable tunnel in which it would stop, never to move thereafter, and that would be his future and the end of things.

He slept little, five hours at most. That had been so since the first years as a doctor. It had served him well. He could be out half the night, and still be awake and alert at dawn, and until now had thought nothing of it.

But now, he thought. The light fell on to his face. He lay hearing birds break the silence into fine fragments, like cracks running over the glaze of china. Today would be as days had long been. Today, he would leave at seven-thirty, to walk up the steps of the hospital before eight. Today. Tomorrow. The day after. But after that, the beads would slip further through his fingers, and could not be caught and held; he could feel how far ahead the last was placed, and it was not far.

Then, he would lie, as the light filled out the satined and quilted bedroom, catching the bevels on the glass of powder bowl

50

and decorated mirror, and she stirred, and still it would be early, still there would be a day as long as a lifetime ahead.

Annie Hare, he thought, hearing the young blackbirds. Did Annie Hare, whose ears were stopped against the song, and eyes against the light, have the best of it now? He did not know. He had never before been so uncertain of himself, and his own ordering of the future.

The cleanness of the kitchen was like that of the mortuary, or the operating theatre, the air as cold. But the sun fell, lemon-coloured on to the sill, and he looked out to the old stone wall and the pear tree at the edge of the garden, with sudden pleasure and a spurt of hope.

'I'll go,' he said in the hall, as he always said, the moment before he left the house.

'I'll go,' not knowing whether she heard him.

He had taken the kettle off the hob and left it with the water warm, the tea tray laid ready, fed crumbs to the birds and put away the board. His own cup and cutlery were washed and put away. The kitchen, flooded with sunlight, settled again after his brief presence, and there was no disturbance there, no mark.

If he had ever longed for warmth and grease and the clutter of old things discarded in corners, or for some animal, yeasty smell, he did not acknowledge it. He was conditioned to order and the cleanliness of things; silt and disarray troubled him. Yet in some cell of the honeycomb memory was a different way of living, richly, densely coloured, heaped up, a cave for him to return to, huddled together with the Florence Hennessy who had become his mother, Flora Molloy, and that was home.

Twelve

The coals shifted and slipped, sending up a little puff of ash. Time passed. May Hennessy had not spoken again, and had not moved, only sat forward still, staring into the core of the fire.

She is seeing the past there, Flora thought. And then, I will not love.

For where had it led? The sad, grey man who had been her father had withered the love and the passion away. It had failed as his own health had failed – could never have been sustained. She had been born. He had died. (Olga did not come into it, Olga, born afterwards, and being the child she was, did not belong to the old life in any way at all.)

I will not love.

Flora looked round the room. The walls felt darker and pressed in upon her, the air was thick, with age and neglect. There seemed to be no energy here; the effort of living used it up and there was none to spare.

Her mother's confession had discomforted her, hinting as it did of experiences from which she was excluded. She had not existed then, and the idea of her own non-existence was terrifying, for she needed all the confidence and sense of purpose, the full assurance, that her own self-awareness could give her. She had come to know, very early on, that she would have no one and nothing else to rely on. Now, seeing her mother bent forwards over the fire, she thought she saw the reason not to indulge in the weakness of love, for it had led May Hennessy here, to this state of defeated unhappiness. And what guarantee would there ever be that it would not let her down too, in some similar way? She could not have borne that, and the thought made her sit up suddenly, as if to shake off any possibility of it. As she moved, the picture came to her mind, of the young woman before the open window, the cool paleness of her clothing, the airiness of clouds, and it steadied her, and excited her too, symbolising and containing as it did her own visions of the future.

What she had to say was said then. The words had been arranged ready for so long, it was easy, and soon done. She told of her plans and the cities she might go to, the colleges and where she might live, repeating Miss Pinkney's words exactly. The speech lay as if unrolled between them for her mother to examine.

The fire needed coal. It was dark and shrivelling into itself, and the cold crept in towards them from the edges of the room. Flora had not imagined anything beyond her own words, her confident statement of her intentions. There had seemed no need. She presumed that the arrangements would simply be discussed, and the details picked over; things would dispose themselves, if not now, then before very long.

Otherwise, for the moment, the milk pan would be filled and the worn green tin of cocoa taken from the shelf. The maid Eileen had seen to the dishes, as she would see to the hearth early the next morning, before any of them woke. The maid was an invisible part of life, and unregarded. (But Olga loved her. With Olga, the girl shared laughter and furtive giggling conversations. Only Olga had been to the cottage in which her large family lived, close and foetid as a litter of puppies.)

Flora would offer to make the drinks, and then, they would sit companionably. The fire would be pulled together and stirred into life again. There would be talk of London, Paris, Rome. She would tell May Hennessy what she had found out, the nearness of her absolute freedom warming her to openness and generosity.

53

But her mother sat like stone, and, after a long time, Flora felt herself begin to turn to stone also.

The words of her little speech were fading from the room, as the warmth of the fire faded, and in the coldness could no longer be imagined. A panic flared up briefly within her, but she would not acknowledge it, for fear. Then, there was nothing. The world outside seemed a dead and silent place, secret within itself, impenetrable. It seemed to Flora that they were people in some fairy-tale, frozen in sleep for a thousand years and caught in mid-thought as they sat, and that, until they were touched again from without, nothing could progress or change, and they were powerless. But, also, it seemed to her that the helplessness was not the worst of it. The worst was the consciousness.

'You are seventeen years old.'

The words, dropping into the silent room, did not startle her, but merely seemed infinitely strange, as if heard from far away. Flora's limbs were numb, heavy things, her tongue thick as felt.

'You are seventeen years old.'

May Hennessy had not looked at her, but only dumbly into the dying fire. Now, she turned her head slightly, and Flora saw that she was staring, as she had stared at the question about her marriage, and on her face was only bewilderment. I do not know you, her face said. I have never known you, and never understood. Where did you come from? How? Whose child are you? What kind of child? You are a stranger. I do not know how I am to speak to you.

But in the past few moments, before the speaking did begin, after all, Flora felt a sudden understanding, and the possibility of closeness between them, just because they were strangers, without the obligations, the muddiness, of any ties of blood, or long familiarity. In the silent look, there seemed infinite possibilities. She might have said anything of her own feelings. Confidences could have been proffered, without embarrassment, as between those who meet in the interlude of some journey, and then move apart, the truth having been absolute between them. Her childhood, her mother's own pride and scorn, might not exist.

And then, the truth-telling began, and it was harsh, raw truth, coarse and grainy as rough bread, not refined so as to be made palatable, but truth, complete, matter of fact and, to Flora, terrible.

The truth was this. That she had been indulged, and it must end. School, education, the heady days of personal freedom, of walking about the town alone, of the gardens and the gallery, all these had been allowed to her as a privilege. Others did not remain carefree and irresponsible for so long. Others, when they were the unlucky working girls, left school at fourteen, and came to be maids, like Eileen. Those from their own class might stay one more year, and after that they would be at home, and gradually, in local society, until their own marriages. (And if not marriage, then the living death of being bound to parents as they grew older.)

Other girls.

Flora had been allowed to drift on a little longer in the pleasantness of girlhood, because it was what her father had wished for her. She was to have longer as a child, longer without anxieties. But that had not been easy for the rest of them. For her mother, it had been hard because of her loneliness and her widowhood. But most, because of money. There was no money. No money to educate Olga in the way she deserved. No money for the keeping up of appearances (and it was inconceivable that they should not be kept up). No money for the best cuts of meat, or clothes, or outings, for coffee and ices at Maud's. For years there had not been the money May Hennessy felt was their right, because of her husband's illness. Instead, there had been scrimping and concealing, worry and shabby sacrifice and a meanness about everything, borrowing and debt.

No money.

'You should know it. You have to know it. Why not? You are old enough. I have borne it alone, because he wanted you spared. But you are seventeen years old, and I can tell you that there is no question of it – colleges and learning for years to come. None, and there is an end of it. Can you not see that?'

She saw. She understood at once, and her future plummeted to earth like a stone until it struck the ground below and was

55

obliterated. She did not bother to look down after it, for where would be the use?

'You should have known.'

'Yes.'

'Plans. Dreams. Going away. How was that ever to come about? Whoever gave you the idea that it might?'

'No one. It was my own idea.'

'You are to leave in July.'

'Yes.'

'Seventeen! I was taught at home. We were. We had no opportunities.'

'No.'

'I married.'

'Yes.'

'It was not his fault. Never think it.' Her voice was suddenly loud, angry.

Flora pressed herself back in her chair, not wanting any talk of her father, any intimacies or emotion. Mention of him now could not be allowed. She wanted him to be ringed by an impenetrable fence, and private to her.

'You could not even go to Portmayes. There is not even money enough for that.'

Portmayes House, off the Doyne Road, where the Misses Clanfy taught needlework and simple cookery. She despised Portmayes more than she could have said.

'No.'

And then her mother stood up, and took a step towards her, half-raised her arms in a curiously pathetic, vulnerable gesture, offering or asking for – forgiveness? Understanding? Love? Flora looked up at her in dread. Her mother's hair was grey, thin and dry, her face crumpled in disappointment, and a terrible, colourless exhaustion which Flora could not bear to see, but she simply turned away from any feelings, knowing that, once expressed and admitted, they would rise up and overwhelm her.

Her mother went heavily, stiffly to the door. Nothing else was said. The drinks were not made, and the fire was left untouched, the ashes to go cold, anyhow in the grate.

*

Flora sat absolutely still until after she had heard May Hennessy's last tread on the stairs and the closing of her door. Then she got up carefully and went to bed, keeping her mind quite blank as she did so, locked against all thought or feeling, and, there, lay on her back, hands clenched to her sides, quite sleepless, until the first light of morning, when she dressed and left the house and did not pause until she was far out of sight of it. Then, off the path, she began to run, ran and ran stumbling across fields, making for the open country, and there let loose her anger and hopelessness and the pain of devastation, bellowing like a calf taken from the cow to slaughter.

Thirteen

She raged about the fields and woods for the whole of that day, which was beautiful, mellow and soft, with a purple mist on the far hills, and slanting light lying over the corn. She saw no one, kept away from the village and the farms. She did not eat, only once or twice dipped her hands into a stream and after drinking let the water run over them, silky, cold, but not in the least comforting. She would not be comforted. She had only this day in which to give vent to her feelings, and they must be allowed to spill over violently and run their course, before she clamped them down, buried them and made them impotent forever. Only, for now, there should be nothing to soothe her, nothing to smooth the jagged edge of bitter disappointment.

She scrambled down ditches, and sat in the rough spiky grass, crying and never troubling to wipe the tears from her face. She saw the future she would have had, the streets she would have walked through in her new life, felt the weight of the books she would have carried on her arm, went quietly into the galleries and libraries of her mind and felt the grave and serious stillness of the air within them, crammed with words and colours and thoughts. People did not enter here. She supposed that friends would have come in time, when she had needed them.

She would not go over the real life as it was to be now, in the house with her mother and Olga. It would be. She would deal with everything. This day was not for any of that, this day was for wild grief over what she had lost, for mourning, and self-pity, and hate.

She went to sleep in the warmth of the early afternoon, lying on dry leaves and bracken in some woodland, and, when she woke from the dark turbulence of her dreams, lay looking up at the sun that pricked here and there through the dense tent of leaves above her, and gradually reined in each feeling, one by one, and took it under her control again. The place seethed with the secret life of birds and insects, tiny unnamed creatures, furtive within the undergrowth and the boles of trees. Flora felt strength and decisiveness and calm seeping back into her as if through the pores of her skin, from the air around, and the earth on which she lay. Her head, which had felt hot and painful, cooled and cleared.

It occurred to her that if she were simply to remain here, she might not be found, and that she would eventually, perhaps painfully, die. But she had no false sense of romanticism. She was realistic, without any wish to make useless gestures. She would take charge. Get what satisfaction she might. Yield nothing.

After a time, as the sun slipped round and the wood darkened, she got up and brushed her skirt carefully, wetted her hands in the pool and smoothed them over her hair to neaten it.

She had thought earlier that she would simply never return to school, not even to collect her things, for those things were of no use or interest to her now. But she saw that such a response was petulant and resentful and so, childish, and she had done with childhood.

The following morning, she went on the bus and into class as usual, read from the usual books, made the familiar, reserved responses and gave away nothing, as she had given nothing to her mother and Olga on her return from the fields. They should not know anything of what she thought or had felt. She had those things locked jealously within her. They were her strength, and altogether private.

59

Fourteen

It had been May when the truth had been told her. Now, it was the end of August. But between that day and this, a thousand years might have passed.

Her mother would have said that she could not possibly arrive at the house, which was called Carbery, on foot, for what impression would that give of her? But she had not asked her mother. Her mother knew nothing about it. When it was settled – for it would be, Flora had a grave and absolute certainty of it – then would be the time not to ask, but simply to tell.

She left the bus a mile before the stop she had been given, because she wanted to approach the house gradually, to get the measure of it for herself. She trusted to her own instinct completely. But she had taken some trouble over what she wore. She had not many clothes and was untroubled by it. Money for those went to Olga, to whom such things mattered greatly. But some impressions counted, she understood that perfectly well, and so she had tied her hair back in a careful knot, which made her look older, and carried a straw hat, to put on before she arrived at the house.

The sun shone, and the air was thick, dusty and grain-smelling, until she reached the top of the long lane that was cut between high banks, dense with undergrowth, and came suddenly out into the open, and there was the glitter of sea a little way off, and the air was fresh and smelled of it.

There were wrought-iron gates to the house, which was stern-faced, of bare, plain stone. The symmetry of the windows pleased her. There was nothing dark or concealed. She stopped. Looked. Would come here, she thought.

A cedar tree, and a great Wellingtonia. A peach house set against the west wall. The blinds were half drawn down. There was no movement. But anyone might have been looking at her. And so, she began to walk there, holding her hat against the dark blue skirt, and felt herself to be tall, an adult, and equal to this house.

It was cool and immaculate, pale and light, in the way all the other houses she knew were not. Sunlight filtered into the long hall. Beyond the windows of the ground floor, she saw the shadows of the trees, dark upon the grass. There were no flowerbeds, no colours nor distractions. Only, in the distance, the thin steel line of sea.

For the rest of her life, which was to promise her more than it ever paid, and in this, hatefully to resemble her own mother's, Florence Hennessy, who became the woman Flora Molloy, remembered every detail of this day.

The house called Carbery in the dusty afternoon sun of late summer became an inner vision, important, as the picture of the woman in drapes and cloudiness was important. It was never to blur or fade nor become confused with anything that came later to muddy and clutter the simple outlines of her life, so that when she talked to her son of it, it was vivid to him too from the beginning, and he understood at once the absolute importance of it to her. It marked the transition between the home of her childhood, and those more mundane and unremarkable houses of the rest of her adult life, between her hopeful youth and the later, patchy compromises, accidents and shrinking horizons. For all of this it was important. But also in itself, for its seriousness and plainness and air of absolute and settled calm. Carbery mattered to her, together with the picture, and the lake in the park, in some

61

permanent and symbolic way, filling and feeding her mind, and her imagination and memory, until the day of her death.

She had set about finding the situation alone, and with caution, rejecting other possibilities in favour of this one, and replying to an advertisement placed in the daily newspaper, and which she consulted in the library – for no papers came to the house.

'You are very young.'
  'I am seventeen.'
  'That is very young!'
  'I shall be eighteen at the turn of the year.'
  'We had thought of a mature person.'
  But he looked at her sharply, as if considering her afresh.
  'My wife is resting,' he said. 'She will be here presently.'
  Beyond the tall windows, the lawn, the shadows flat on the grass. Stillness.
  He was a pale man with fair, flat hair and small features. But his voice was pleasing. Tiny, transparent specks of dust jazzed inside a beam of sunlight. The house was silent.
  'You have been to a good school. You have an excellent report.'

'Flora is a conscientious girl, though she is not altogether easy to know. We had hoped for her to go on to some form of higher education, but family circumstances have not permitted this. Her father died recently. She will make a good and thoughtful tutor.'
  Miss Pinkney had sat alone at her desk, hesitating with her pen, struggling to find the words that would convey the essence of Flora Hennessy. 'Reserve.' 'Self-possession.' 'Determination.' No. When the girl had come to tell her of the cancellation of any plans for college, she had looked out of defiant blue eyes and Miss Pinkney, faced with the look, had been unable to offer help or sympathy. Do not pity me, the eyes had said. Do not dare to question, to suggest any word of affection or warmth, or any regret for me.
  The girl's pride was absolute and, seeing that, Miss Pinkney

had said nothing at all, merely inclined her head and made a note upon her pad.

She had supposed that Flora would simply sit at home with her mother, be a companion in the house and hope for a husband to provide for her future. When the letter had come from the MacManuses of Carbery, asking for a reference for the girl as a tutor to their son, she had been surprised, but also admiring. She had wanted to be of some help, though she thought that she would not see the girl again, that she was part of a past that had somehow failed her.

'She presents herself well, is sensible and mature. I am confident that she would take her place properly within the household.'

Flora sat quite still on the straight-backed chair, hands crossed together in her lap. She would come to this house. It seemed to her to have been arranged a long time ago. The interview was superfluous. She saw herself moving about in these high, light rooms. Flora Hennessy. (For Florence was quite dead. Florence might never have been. Florence belonged to her home, and to the years with her father and mother and Olga, years which she had already consigned to the past.)

She continued to look out of the windows, at the cedar tree and the Wellingtonia, and the silver haze which was the sea. Then, after a moment, she heard the footsteps of a child. But she took a little time before she turned her head slowly, and then stood, to face her future at the moment it began.

Fifteen

'Are you a woman?'

'I am not a man!'

'I don't mean that.'

'You should say what you mean.'

His face paled, with the effort of concentrating. She would not help him.

'Or a girl. Are you just a girl?'

'No one is "just" anything.'

He looked at her in despair.

'I am neither then,' she said. 'Not old enough for the one, but past the other. Neither.'

'Like a unicorn,' he said quickly. And then, as she burst into laughter at him, laughed too, in relief.

His name was Hugh. He was six, and his graveness and oldness sorted with hers. They kept an invisible, formal barrier between them which suited them both, teacher and pupil, girl and child. They respected one another. There was liking and, gradually, complete understanding. Yet he too had a reserve, a privacy, to match hers. She looked at him and did not have any idea what was going on in his head, what places he inhabited. They shared a love of stories of a rare kind, fairy-tales and grim dark fables, curious legends. Their lessons revolved around mythical creatures, crones who lived in caves, impenetrable forests and magic plants, stones by which the future could be told. The emotions and deeds that filled their talk were strong as black tea. Thirst after revenge, passion for power, tyrannical rage, the jealousy and plotting of evil stepmothers, crusts to eat and rags for clothes and beasts that spoke and consoled, and trees with spying eyes.

She planned their timetable of lessons with the help of books, and followed it exactly. Spelling. Mathematics. French. Scripture. Natural History. Art. Conversation. But within the lessons, they roved about as free as wild, parentless, naked children in the mythical wastelands, plucking nuts and fruit from trees and berries from bushes, and drinking asses' milk. They read the books in the long library, and made the stories fit the timetabled subjects, as they chose, learned poetry and turned stories into plays and painted the plays into pictures, and went down the garden, on to the cliffs and out to the rocks on the beach, to gather whatever was there in season – seedpods and grasses, limpets and crabs and shells, cones, skeletal leaves, wild poppies and chalk-blue scabious and the chrysalises that clung to stalks. In the schoolroom they labelled everything, and decorated the labels elaborately, like the letters of illuminated manuscripts. Scripture was stories. Moses in the Bulrushes. Daniel in the Lion's Den. David and Goliath. The Parable of the Seed and the Sower or the Labourers in the Vineyard. And then there was their mutual discovery of other, stranger gods, and more exotic legends. But there was no catechism and no morals were drawn or preached, and when these were doled out to them on Sundays, in the musty church, like so many portions of cold gruel, both of them, quite instinctively, set them aside untouched.

They spent a large part of every day together, in the house full of airy space and light in which their voices and footsteps echoed, or else sitting out on the grass under the great trees. She had nothing to do with the business of his eating and sleeping and dressing, there was a nursery nurse for that, and so their time together was not spoiled with domestic irritations or conflicts. She was surprised how much the company of the boy pleased and interested her, and what satisfaction she achieved in teaching him. He was alert and quick and their interests and dislikes coincided. In teaching him, she continued to learn.

Any other life had ceased to exist. She scarcely thought of her home at all and had closed the doors of her mind on the farther future. She neither dreamed nor yearned nor allowed herself to regret, but for the first time since very young childhood lived wholly in the present, and in those imaginary places which she and the boy inhabited.

Carbery itself gave her great satisfaction. The parents were often away and the other servants kept to their own quarters. She always ate her evening meal alone, after the boy had gone to bed, and later, sat in the library, or a small upstairs sitting room which had a view of the sea from its windows. Sometimes, when it was still warm in September, she went out, to walk in the garden or the fields beyond the house, and on to the cliff path beyond. She was given one day off, and very often part of Saturday and Sunday, when visitors came or they took the boy out, and at first she went out too, almost dutifully, walked or took the bus into the town, and went again to the gallery, and walked through the streets of familiar houses, and sat beside the lake in the park.

Once, she met Miss Pinkney, and went at her invitation to have tea in Maud's. The place seemed strange, as if she was seeing it from the other side of a looking-glass. She drank tea, which she had never done here, and ate an ice, which was the same and served in the same tall glass, with a long spoon, and yet which tasted quite new, and unfamiliar.

But it was at this meeting, sitting straight-backed and composed at the table in Maud's, that she felt her composure weaken, too, and her iron self-restraint fail her, so that she was suddenly giddy and uncertain. One moment, she was sipping her tea, intrigued at the idea of things being as they had always been, and, the next, she felt a peculiar frightening sense of unreality, as if she had forgotten who she was, and why she was in this place. For after all, who was she? She was Flora Hennessy, who would never again be Florence. She was tutor to Hugh MacManus, of Carbery. At the turn of the year, she would be eighteen. But her limbs felt strangely elongated, her fingers tingled and would not grip the cup, and when she glanced around, the walls shifted as if they were clouds which might at any moment dissolve.

'Are you quite well?'

Who was this woman, with the brown mole on the side of her mouth and hair like wire? Where did she belong? Her own back ached with the effort of keeping taut and stiff, the muscles of her stomach were sore, because she was constantly tightening them, as if, in relaxing, she might collapse to a soft, confused heap upon the ground.

'Would you like some more tea? I will ask them to make it stronger.'

The voice came and receded, ballooned out and grew horribly, like some aural fungus. Who was the woman?

'Florence?'

'No.'

'Flora.'

'Yes.'

'Would you like some more tea?'

'Thank you.'

Who am I? Where am I? Who is she? What has happened to me?

The tea came.

'Use both hands. It will be steadier.'

She obeyed like a child. No. She struggled then. Not a child.

'Do you eat properly? Are you given enough time to yourself? The company of a young child can be exhausting. Are you able to meet your own friends?'

Gradually, the ordinary questions calmed her and she was able to reply. The room settled, solidified and became Maud's again, and comforting.

'Teaching is tiring. When one is conscientious. You will need to replenish your own stores of energy.'

Hearing the assured words, the sense, the anxious tone, she felt touched by something she had not realised that she lacked, affection, concern, the caring of another person, and in the light of

67

Miss Pinkney's kindness, she felt herself open, there and then, and grow, in an instinctive and immediate maturity.

Sixteen

Nobody tended the gardens now. Dandelion and ragwort came up through the broken paving stones and were left to blow to seed in a sudden wind, and the great horse chestnut split up the side, making a heavy branch unstable. But nobody sat there now. (Though they sent a man two or three times that summer to mow the grass, and, because he liked to make the best of the job, he planted wallflowers in the earth beneath the windows of the wards. It was hot, and the smell of them, coming faintly to their nostrils, sent the old men and the old women in their narrow bedsteads sailing back to childhood past, and cast them up on its beach, to lie there.)

And the emptiness crept up and up, like a slow tide, to where they were left huddled together. Vans came, to be filled with the contents of wards and offices, and then the doors of the rooms were closed and padlocked, and the high ceilings seethed with the dust, as it settled back in the sun. (For winter went out one night and spring came in the next day, and, it seemed, summer the next, the blossom flared briefly and was over.)

The whispering began, broken sentences drifting by like smoke or clouds, shredding away, half-heard, and those words that were heard troubled them, the talk of closing, leaving, going away. Where? Where? They dropped suddenly down a black hole of sleep, and dreamed of abandonment, forgotten in the high ward alone, after the doors were closed and locked and the last van had

69

driven away. Where? The blackness lightened to grey, and, in the cloudiness, they wandered again about the rooms of childhood homes and married homes, finding odd brown pots carefully filled with pennies, and a calendar ringed in red, a geranium bright on the window-sill, and the insurance book tucked behind the clock. Familiar beds and chairs and shoes, and handles that fitted familiarly into the hand.

But the wheels of a trolley that no one would bother to oil screeched at the corridor corner. A bell rang. Those who remained raised their voices, and, waking, the old people were startled by the sunlight through squares of high windows, by brightness and the green bed rails, and the smell of warm meat and vegetable water blotted out the scent of the wallflowers. They grasped in a panic at the sheets, trying to grasp this present, this place in which they found themselves (for they could not hold the wallflower-filled past from which they had woken). They reached out hands, to clutch at the hand of the nurse. The last blossom fell on to the grass like stars.

Another death, and then another, on the same day, disturbing them. Would there be no one left? Was this the way they would all go?

Molloy came and sat with them in the white mortuary, and walked the deserted corridors and in among the beds, huddled together at the end of the long rooms, saw bleeding gums, and eczema that scaled feet and between fingers, and sores where sticks of bone pressed up to the skin. Their eyes were filmy, sight veiled, ears muffled, there was a blurring and felting and silting over of each sense. Yet, within, flames flickered and leaped up behind their eyes, quick, bright, darting movements of perception, understanding, fear, before they retreated back, into the safe carapace of memory.

The hands of the clock scarcely moved. An hour was a dreadful shuffle of nothingness and tedium. (Yet Molloy's days raced crazily away from him, and he careered downhill with them, powerless.)

70

The leaves of the chestnut tree spread, and fanned out like fingers. The candles had never been so many, or so bright.

(They would fell the tree. The trunk was a danger, and in any case, it was old. An obstruction.)

The doors were open, on to the broken paving of the terrace. One or two of them sat outside, in basket chairs. An old man shuffled on to the grass and stood, feeling the dryness of it, against the dryness of bare feet.

Swifts screamed about the clock tower, and dived and sped like skaters around the blue rink of the sky. And after a last morning of babel and hurtling, reckless flying, left, and the silence after them was absolute and terrible.

Seventeen

The back of the house got all the sun, afternoon and evening, and the living room had doors on to the garden. (In May, the pear tree was clotted with blossom, like paper snow along the branches. The leaves were thick, and darker now, the little hard fruits already showing.) In sunlight, the house gleamed in its cleanness. The rows of books were tight, edge exactly to edge along the shelf. The clock ticked with a very precise tick into the ordered kitchen.

Sometimes, during these days, his mind would be full of it. It was as though he had suddenly walked in through the door and stood there, huge, bringing in dust from the road and the smell of antiseptic, something alien. He felt that he was set down in his own house without use or purpose, and blundered from room to small room among the ornaments and objects, in a panic, like some cornered animal.

He never saw her. Whichever rooms entered his mind, she was always in the next, and he did not disturb or intrude upon her. The way of the house, and her life when he was away from it, were mysteries to him. He knew at what times the woman came in to assist her and when she left, and, sometimes, if there had been a visitor. Nothing else. He did not know how she spent her days. When he returned in the evening, the house seemed untouched, as empty of life or even the after-echo of life, as when he had left that morning.

72

Soon, he would not leave.

On fine days, she sat at the open window, looking at the birds on the bird table and flitting in the branches of the pear tree. But she did not go out there. She felt the cold too easily now. Or the heat.

Walking the corridors, pushing open the swing doors, listening to the odd, disconnected cries and mumblings of the old men and the old women, he felt his heart lurch as he remembered, as if he were waking from oblivious sleep to the dreadful reminder of some tragedy. He turned his mind away. He would not face the future. He preferred to go into it blindly, and unprepared.

He did not speak to her about it, nor know her feelings, whether she dreaded the thought of him filling up her solitary days and the neat silent spaces, pressing the smoothness out of cushions, dirtying crockery at the wrong times, breaking the tight clean pattern of her routine, and fraying it. When they spoke, it was of the insignificant, the time of this, the news in the village of that. Radio. Weather. Household necessities. They did not talk of her physical state. It never changed, and so there was nothing to say, and of course, he was not her doctor.

(Though he saw that she moved less now, and was slower, shuffling on the sticks from chair to table. She went to bed an hour before him and the routine was stumbling, awkward, painful.)

She smiled. Her smile was a fixed thing on her soft, powdery mouth. She had determined some years before on her role, which was to be sweet acceptance, meekness, patience. A refusal to refer to her condition, or ever to complain.

Smile.

The sun moved around the house from front to back, lightening the opposite wall. In the kitchen, the clock ticked.

No one entered the silence. No one broke into her days, once the woman who helped her had left. Only the birds hopped on brittle legs about the terrace.

In the bathroom, mirrors and white enamel surfaces flashed, as

73

the sun struck them through a chink in the frosted glass. The bedroom was dim and peachy, blinds half-drawn. A china ballerina held the lamp up in her arms.

The afternoon slipped imperceptibly down. The light hazed and reddened. The dead grate held fir-cones, piled together in a little, dry, careful pyramid.

No one came.

There was ham and tomato and potato salad, cold plum tart, ready under the plates. The milk was covered by a weighted muslin cloth.

It seemed that there would be another death. Molloy would not leave the ward yet.

From high in the pear tree, a blackbird sang and sang to her, for some sort of company.

Eighteen

That time of Flora's life was like a clear bubble, in which she was perfectly happy and perfectly suspended, quite separate and detached from the rest. She would sometimes look back on herself there, in surprise and curiosity, as though upon a young woman in a picture, another person, in another life, unconnected to her own later self except by the thin thread of memory.

In the three years at Carbery, she learned the moods of the sea, and those moods defined her days and nights. The house was like a ship, sailing by itself high above the bay. She knew when she awoke to a strange dullness of the air that the sea fog rubbed its back against the windows. The gauzy mornings of early spring, and the black nights out of which the wind gathered itself, to come marauding over the garden, delighted her. She spent hours sitting on the window ledge of the empty attic rooms, looking towards the sea.

They were excellent companions, she and the boy. He had a sharp, inquisitive mind, flashing a sudden question like a blade that cut to the heart of a thing. His face was always pale, the skin delicate and transparent as petals beneath his eyes, and, on his stalk-like neck, the bones infinitely slender.

He had sudden silence, periods when he withdrew into himself as she withdrew, so that there was a complete understanding between them. At other times, he did not belong to her at all but

75

went away, across some invisible line, and then he was theirs, and withdrew wholly into their world, excluding her.

He had his seventh birthday. He wore a sailor suit. He became formal to her, his eyes guarding private thoughts.

She went home dutifully once a month, for a day and a night, and dreaded the time, and could bear the visits back to the old world only in the knowledge that she would leave again and return to Carbery. She would not talk of her life there and in any case her mother was not interested. She looked inward, or back to the life she now saw as entirely happy, satisfied, fulfilled, when John Joseph Hennessy had been alive. Her only other concern, in a possessive, cloying, anxious way, was for Olga. She lived her own life through the child, busying herself with her activities, her friendships, and so Flora could feel detached, freed from her mother's interest and curiosity by her younger sister.

She would not yet think of her own future. She would stay at Carbery until the boy went away to school, when he was eleven. She spent no money, but saved her salary in the Post Office bank, and at times, seeing the steadily increasing figures entered in the columns of the account book, felt a flare of excitement, and in the light and brightness of it, saw the promise of the life she had once planned, briefly illuminated again and possible.

In the library at Carbery she read widely, as she chose, and looked at books of paintings, learned to love areas of literature and the work of certain artists with an instinctive and acute response. Others were puzzling and impenetrable to her. She learned not to struggle for long, but to drop them like a mouthful of some unappealing food, discarded on to her plate.

The year turned. She was twenty. But, still, she watched the sea, and the bubble held, and the rest of her life was far away.

Nineteen

It was May. It was a perfect day, as warm as high summer, the air still, the sea brilliant, stuck over with little white boats.

They had gone out, the boy with his father and mother in the large car, visiting on the other side of the county.

She was reading about lost cities – Troy, Atlantis, Lyonnesse, and from time to time looked up and out to sea, from her high point on the grassy cliff, and imagined them there; if she half-closed her eyes, they rose up and glittered again in all their beauty before her.

She thought of the hedgerows of bridal hawthorn, wreathing the fields around her home, saw the buttercups and dandelions, gold everywhere upon the grass.

At four, she walked slowly, contentedly up the sloping lawn towards the cedar tree and the tea that would be set there.

Except that the tea was not set, and she saw the maid come running out of the house, a scrap of white hurtled as if by a sudden wind towards her, arms outstretched wildly, eyes black and huge in her stricken face.

The boy was dead.

The words came over and over again as she ran, incoherent, garbled, from the mouth that was so mis-shaped in shock and grief.

Flora had watched them leave, from her window. He had been sitting with boot-button eyes in his pale face in the high, open back of the Lagonda car, stiff, serious, expectant.

There had been an accident then, and he was dead.

She stood, very calm and absolutely still, after the girl had shuddered into silence and the sea and the sky had hardened and glazed over, and become dead, for all that the sun shone down on them. They were frozen things in a picture. But she looked on it from the outside now, as if already she had no place here.

She had turned her back on the sea and followed the maid into the house, and inside the air had smelled different and unfamiliar, as though the rooms were already a part of the past.

It was the first grief of her adult life, and she had no idea how to bear it. For there was only a short time of numbness, and the odd sensation of distance, and then the pain of it began. She felt it in her body, and crumpled up, bending and holding her arms tightly around herself. She could tell no one of it. When they returned, and she saw them, she could not speak.

The silence of the house and the dimness of the room behind the drawn blinds was no longer a peaceful welcome and altogether soothing to her, it was the airless, choking silence of death, in which she was taut and alone. Frightened.

'It was the worst of all,' she said to her own son (who had been named Hugh), 'nothing else was ever so.'

She had not explained, nor said more.

Later, he had stared into the mirror at his own face, trying to match it to what she had told him of the other boy. The worst. Nothing was ever so. (Though there had been the one other thing, but of that she never spoke to him at all.)

He had not dared to ask if anything might ever be worse; if his own death would affect her, in some mightier, more important way. But that night, looking up at her as she sat on his bed, he saw the absoluteness and strength of her love for him, and for no

78

other one, and the dead boy withered back into that remote past of hers which did not concern or trouble him.

May had never been so hot. Things came crowding out together, lilac and laburnum and the great smoky plumes of the wistaria hanging from the wall.

But on the day of the funeral, the fog came up from the sea, stuffing itself into the rooms, like soft, damp pillows, greying the garden. The house was muted. She could not believe that anyone would be alive there again. They were stiff, waxen things. She was invisible. For them, she had simply ceased to exist.

They had brought him home the day before. The coffin stood beneath the tall blind windows of the long room, on a pedestal. It was taken for granted that she would go in, at the time set for all of the servants, and so, unable to refuse, she did so, but kept to the last and, when she came up to him, closed her eyes, so that she never saw him again, in any way. (And for the rest of her life regretted it, and never ceased to be haunted in her dreams by a hollowness, as of something unfinished, unknown. There was no resolution, and so in the dreams, she continued to search; she followed after and almost glimpsed the boy. But never caught him, never did see. Rooms were empty, blinds snapped abruptly up, and then, in the sudden flooding in of summer light, were bare and echoing. She ran down lanes and over the grass to the cliff edge, and even, sometimes, flew off it and fell, into waking consciousness before she could discover him. It was years before she spoke to her own son of it, though after she did so there was an easing and blurring of the dreams, which then came rarely until, in the last few days of her life, they returned, vivid, as if freshly painted, before her.)

She had followed the black funeral figures, out of the house to the waiting cars, but, just at the door, turned back, and retreated unnoticed by any of them.

Her steps had terrified her, sounding through the empty house.

An hour later she had walked away, alone, down the long drive between the trees, in clinging fog which had nuzzled her, like

79

some dead, vaporous creature, and crept in through the sides of her mouth, tasting peculiar and metallic there.

She had not looked back, nor seen the house, Carbery, or any of those belonging to it, again.

But to return home was unthinkable. She had gone to Miss Pinkney and asked, white-faced, pinch-mouthed, for a room, and one had been given to her, a room and infinite, quiet, tactful kindness. There had not been prying questions, nothing was expected of her beyond the formal, bleak words of explanation she had given.

She had lain in a high bed among dark furniture and lace curtains, lace coverings, and worked, as at a difficult but finally not impossible exercise, at turning her thoughts and imaginings away from the place she had left, and from what had happened there. She felt old, in some exhausted way, enervated by shock, and the knowledge of grief. It was as though her childhood, indeed, her whole youth, had not ended, but been taken from her, like limbs in some dreadful amputation.

It occurred to her that she had loved the boy purely and unconditionally, in a way she had loved no one else save her father – and how much of that love had come later, with hindsight and his absence, and her vague sense of guilt at the loneliness of his death? As she thought of the man and his life and his illness, so her love had blossomed. But he was not there to receive it and so, inevitably, it had shrivelled too. But her love for the boy Hugh had been a fresh, alive, springing thing, called up by the keenness of the understanding between them, by his nature, his perceptiveness and quick intelligence, and by the simple liking they had had for one another's company.

She spent a week, bruised and exhausted by grief, and by the shock of the abrupt ending to a part of her life, sheltered unquestioningly by Miss Pinkney, eating and drinking little, but sleeping, in great, deep draughts of sleep, from which she woke suddenly, aching and unrefreshed. Then, the thoughts and memories and visions of the past were like flares lit and burning

80

in her brain. She wanted to climb out of herself, or close some door in her own head to escape from them, and could not; she was imprisoned with them in a sealed room, and they were insistent, unrelenting. She went out sometimes, to walk about the streets in a frenzy of restlessness that was like an eczema on her skin which was intolerable when she stayed still, and indoors, but was scarcely eased by walking – except that there were distractions then, the sight of trees, the calm, unchanged façades of the old buildings.

After a week, she roused herself, as if at the end of some feverish illness.

She made her plans.

'You should see your mother,' Miss Pinkney said.

But she would not. She was too proud, and too afraid, also, of being sucked back into the dark, claustrophobic, stale little house. Her mother's drawn face, sunken in its folds of disappointment and bitterness, would make her falter, out of guilt. She would lose her nerve, and it was frail enough already, she was aware of that.

She went to London without seeing them.

Twenty

No one was there on Fridays. She exulted in the silence.

Only the sun came, clean as a knife on to her pillow, and then fanned out across the wall, milky white. There was no one she had to smile for, though sometimes she caught herself smiling, out of habit.

'I'll go then.'

She never replied, always pretended to be asleep, and undisturbed by his morning movements.

'I'll go then.'

After the door closed, and the car went away, the house settled back upon itself, and then she heard the birds, vociferous in the bushes in spring, the robin and blackbird through the winter. She hated the dead, silent garden of high summer.

He had set the tray of tea beside the bed, with boiling water in a flask. It scalded her mouth, but then seemed to burn down into her joints, and, in burning, to ease and loosen them.

She would read then, the same books her mother had read, genteel old-fashioned novels which resembled one another, and from time to time took up *Pride and Prejudice* again, or *Jane Eyre* and *Anna of the Five Towns*. From childhood she had had the knack of immersing herself so deeply in a book that her lungs seemed to fill with it. But surfacing into the pale, cushioned bedroom was the greatest pleasure of all.

On Mondays, she was taken for physiotherapy – like laundry,

she thought, collected and delivered back to the door. On other days Mrs Hoyle came. But on Fridays, she was alone.

She dared not look into the future.

They were not unhappy, or ill-suited. They did as well as many, she thought. But the house, its emptiness and silence, were hers, she was greedy to be alone in it, restless and nervous when she was away. As a child, journeys had terrified her, and she never liked to be in any strange town. The idea of foreign countries was unimaginable.

The sun slipped down the wall and splashed on to the white stool.

It took an hour to get up, to dress. It was worse in the cold of winter, when her joints set hard as posts in concrete. But when it was over, she could sit at the window, and feel the house around her, for reassurance.

Her name had been Elizabeth Connor, and her father had kept the pharmacy, which was where Molloy had seen her, the first week of his work in the town practice. He had been twenty-eight, but a qualified doctor and so had seemed even older, and on the same level as her father. Set apart. He had come in to introduce himself – though word had gone round, they had known all about his coming, his history. He had wanted a special prescription made up, for Miss Gogarty of Chapel Finn, and even began to go into the exact detail, before she had blushed, hurrying to stop him.

'Oh, that is not for me. My father will see to it. I'll call him down.'

She could not even handle the medicines. The tablets and powders and jewel-coloured liquids had fascinated her, since she had been lifted up on to the counter as a small child. But she was only allowed to sell hairbrushes and shaving brushes, toothbrushes and pastes and vanishing cream in opaque white pots. She had never thought of doing any other job. Her life was securely bounded by their home, which was the adjoining house, and by the shop.

83

*

The next afternoon, he had come back. They were only five minutes off closing for the day.

'Oh, I'll just fetch Father.'

But she was the one he wanted, he had said.

The blackbird hopped suddenly from nowhere, on to the terrace, and froze, sensing change, the open door, her figure in the chair. She exulted in the thought of the day ahead, divided into its small, individual portions of pleasure.

The clock struck.

Twenty-One

When the door closed behind the woman, whose name was Miss Marchesa, and her footsteps had gone away down the bare-boarded stairs, there was absolute silence, for all that this was a house in London, and then Flora felt such acute and sudden loneliness that she caught her breath, as though she had been slapped stingingly across the face, and wrapped her arms about herself, for comfort and for protection. But it was not only a momentary feeling she must bear. This was the fact. She was alone in London and of no interest or concern to anyone.

The room was small and narrow, partitioned out of the corner of another larger room, so that the window was only half a window, and oddly placed to one side. It was early afternoon. Eventually, she became used to the deadness of the house at this time, when those who did not go out slept, as she would also begin to know the small creakings and stirrings of five o'clock, and then the early evening noises of women returned from work, when doors banged and water flushed and drained away down basins.

There was a border of Greek keys around the top of the walls, and then dirty white space up to a high ceiling, and a radiator with rust marks, squat and serpentine.

When at last she crossed to the window, she saw that she was above the tops of the plane trees, as well as the roofs of the houses opposite, and that the weather vane on the spire of a church glittered, white-gold, against the insubstantial summer sky.

Miss Marchesa was known to a friend of Miss Pinkney's. Together, they had tried to do the best for her. The house, in Kensington, was perfectly respectable. Unmarried women who worked as confidential secretaries lived there, and widows with older daughters, thin, quavering, blameless women, with a little money that would never be quite enough.

Flora was too young, Miss Marchesa had written in reply to the enquiry, she had never had a girl alone in the house at such a young age; she could not be responsible. But Miss Pinkney's friend had replied that supervision would not be expected, and only an inexpensive room, with breakfast and supper, were required.

It was the first week of September. The streets were dusty, the grass in the parks worn brown and threadbare. But the air shimmered with warmth that lasted from dawn until dusk, as London hung suspended, between high summer and a gilded, roseate autumn that ran on and on into everyone's memories.

Flora left her things still packed and the grainy towel untouched beside the washbasin, and went out of the silent, soup-smelling house into the hazy streets.

For the rest of her life, she was to feed off the glory of the next few weeks, when London lay at her feet, open and friendly towards her, and she walked it, as over some richly patterned, vibrantly coloured carpet, exploring every pathway of the intricate design. For this time only there was no loneliness, but simply the state of being alone, and this was entirely satisfying. She would not have been able to absorb and respond to everything so fully; the impact of the buildings, pictures, open spaces, and of the golden autumn days and soft nights, would have lessened, if she had had private company to distract her.

Public company she had, and it delighted her. She sat on city steps and park benches and seats beside the river, looking, questioning, so that, in sleep, her mind still seethed with images, like some crowded picture by Hogarth or Brueghel.

She went to classes, in art history, Italian and French, both language and literature, at the Institute at which Miss Pinkney had obtained a place for her (and to the fees of which she contributed more than half – though Flora was not to discover it until years after). Apart from these, and the hours she spent in galleries or simply walking about London, she worked as a tutor to two fat, bland Belgian girls living with their father in Wimpole Street, who were uninterested in anything but staying dully at home, between trips to Ghent and Bruges. The hours Flora spent with them were a form of torment, because they passed so slowly, and were so infinitely tedious, and unrelieved by any lightness, any humour or liveliness or affection. Money was earned from them, that was all. Within their heavy, gloomy house, and inside Miss Marchesa's in Kensington, Flora felt suffocated, as if her chest were stuffed with dry woollen cloth. The lack of light in the rooms oppressed her, so that only when she was outside or else in the great airy galleries and marble spaces of the museums could she breathe freely and feel a lightness of body and liberation of her thoughts and imaginings. She became two separate people who did not relate to one another, but the one who returned, like the shorthand typing women and the widows, to Miss Marchesa's lodgings, and who went dutifully, four times a week, to Wimpole Street, was not the real, the living Flora Hennessy.

She came to love London intimately, and allowed it to absorb her, using it to block out all thought of her years at home, and of the house Carbery overlooking the sea. The boy, Hugh. She would never think of that. It was like an open sore which she must not touch or disturb in any way. But somewhere, at the back of her mind, floating and pale, he sat, as she had last seen him, very upright, button-eyed in the back of the open Lagonda car, hours before his death.

Home, her mother and Olga, lay somewhere else, unregarded, and without interest.

The classes at the Institute were enjoyable, and she was well taught. To the staff, she was an enigma but, because she seemed entirely self-contained, self-reliant, after a time they simply accepted that it was so. She impressed them with her application and the doggedness she showed, which she never allowed to become muddied or diverted by other concerns. She had a good eye and a talent for detail, she remembered things conscientiously, she was too detached, too serious for her age. Yet it seemed that she did not fully belong, did not allow herself to become wholly absorbed or committed, and never for a moment lost or forgot herself. To the other students, she offered friendliness but never friendship. They did not know her. To them, this was at first a tease, a challenge, but later, as they failed with her, it became merely an irritant, so that after a few weeks of probing, and attempts at discovery, they simply left her alone. Most of them, in any case, were young women in the charge of chaperones, aunts and older married sisters, marking time, and only mildly interested in the lectures and classes and outings. Flora, for whom life in London in these early weeks was miraculous, a gift and her salvation, could not understand or sympathise with them. She felt infinitely older, in experience and in understanding. Life mattered. She had been given this chance, and seized it, drank from it greedily, as from a beaker of intoxicating liquid.

London began to fill again. There were grand cars in the streets, and the evening pavements were bright with men and women in dinner dress. Flora watched, listened, enjoyed, but never envied, in the same way as she noted, and pitied, the bundled old women asleep on churchyard slabs and the wild-eyed beggars with bare, broken feet – pitied, but did not weep. To her, they were a warning. Otherwise, they did not touch her own life.

That was not true of the other women in Miss Marchesa's lodgings. She was afraid of them, because they tried to intrude upon her, to know her. But, in allowing them any intimacy at all, she felt that she might somehow grow to be like them, and she recognised the women as failures, sexless, genteel, faded creatures in retreat from life, whose rooms she pictured as sterile places, with a staring doll set on the counterpane and little china animals dotted along the shelf.

On her first evening, mistaking the time by fifteen minutes,

Flora had come late into the dining room, and opened the door on to a roomful of women eating soup. They had frozen, spoons half way to their mouths, silent, staring. She had not known where to sit. Her face burned. Miss Marchesa had come self-importantly out of the swing doors that led to the kitchen, and scolded her, and put her at a table with others, a Mrs Vigo and her daughter, with a secretary, Miss Braise-Compton, just beside. Flora had tightened her elbows into her sides, for fear of touching any of them, and barely replied to their questions, but set a ring of aloof silence round herself, while the vegetable broth congealed on her plate. There had been neck of lamb and then plums and custard, and her throat had seemed to constrict, and an impenetrable barrier to form there, so that she could not swallow.

The next day she sought out Miss Marchesa before breakfast, in the brown cubby-hole she spoke of as her office, and asked to be given a table to herself. Something about her coolness and self-possession, her confidence in speaking out, made the woman (who had been quite willing to patronise) feel in some way criticised and set at a disadvantage, so that from that morning she did not conceal her indifference to Flora's welfare, and a measure of straightforward dislike.

But the single table was made available, wedged across a corner by the door into the kitchen, so that she had to ease awkwardly in and out, and could not easily see her food in the dimness.

Mrs and Miss Vigo, and the secretary, affected not to notice, and, beyond the faintest of smiles, ignored her. Flora drew her own isolation about herself like a curtain. Behind it, the air was cold as ice. But she preferred that to any encroaches upon her. She took a book into meals, and felt suddenly older, in a dry, austere way that was not altogether comfortless.

Twenty-Two

The hot September blended into an autumn of translucent early mists over the river, out of which the sun rose. The days drifted down imperceptibly, and Flora felt herself caught up in them effortlessly, lightly, untouched by reality. And if she made no close friends, out of choice, she did at this time acquire a companion. Leila Watson came to an afternoon class in the history of classical civilisation. It was a passion – she was training to be a school teacher in Surrey, and travelled into London by train. She was twenty-five, and a widow. Her husband had been killed a week after their marriage. She had told Flora the bare fact, and stared out of slightly prominent, green-flecked eyes, defying questions. Flora asked none. They spent an hour together and then, before Leila caught her train, ate poached eggs or cheese on toast in a tea room, and looked at antiquities in the British Museum.

The cool, pale statues and grave ancient images impressed her. She felt respectful of them, and in some awe. But they did not move her, as pictures did. She saw Turners, and the painting of the light, the speed, airiness of the sun bursts and the blown spray and cloudscapes, lifted her heart. The dim, tranquil interiors of the Dutch satisfied something different in her. The wise, still expression of men in velvet robes, and the pale women with high foreheads, as well as the scenes within scenes, landscapes beyond landscapes, of the Renaissance, were altogether delightful.

90

'What will you do? Do you plan to teach the history of art?'

They sat on the steps of the Albert Memorial. It was five o'clock. Flora looked at the beautiful curve of the prince's stone back.

'What will you do?'

Children were playing with a little dog, chasing around and around, and a small boy held the hand of a man, a kite in the other.

'What will you do?'

But she did not know. She had not thought of a future, only of this present, in which she exulted in knowledge and pictures and the life of London. Her bank book showed a sum of money that was becoming smaller, drop by steady drop. (She ate the poached eggs with a single cup of tea, but no sweet, and walked everywhere.)

'What will you do?'

But there was no future, and the past was not allowed to exist. (Though she had begun to invent a different past for herself, and to tell it, as a small child will create another life, in fantasy. And while doing so, it occurred to her that, as she might become anyone, so, in some terrifying sense, she was nobody.)

Now, she sat watching Leila Watson walk away from her across the Kensington grass, for the bus which would take her to Victoria station, and her real and unknown life.

'What will you do?'

(You. Who?)

I am Flora Hennessy.

But the words were peculiar, a pattern of sounds only, making no sense.

The park was emptying, children and dogs and nurses going away down the long paths and out of sight. Leaves were spilling down. Over the rooftops of the Palace, the sky was lilac and rose-red. The beauty of London, and of the last, late days of this summer, might save her. Or perhaps they would not. Perhaps, like all the pictures in the galleries, they were not themselves enough, were apart from her, and impenetrable, as self-contained in their way as she was in hers. Yet she had nothing else, nothing at all. The thought was like a chip of ice, lodged in her heart.

Twenty-Three

Night after night they sent for him. He was scarcely at home. Three deaths came together, as well as the slow death of the place itself, like that of a tree severed at roots deep below ground, so that it stood and yet was withering, branch by branch, the life blood draining away. Leaves fell. But the real leaves on the chestnut and beech trees held on, the days were still warm, the sun lingered into October. The doors were opened for most of each afternoon.

Molloy sat with them, listened to whimpers and mumblings and confusion, little starts and cries of fear.

At the beginning there had been visits from officials, meetings had taken place all around them, strangers came and went in the old building, making it their own. But as the summer trailed on and the old ones died, the people left and the place was quiet again. They had the last of its life to themselves. It was not worth anyone's while to resettle them now. They had only a little time to wait, and the job would be done. After the swifts had flown, the swallows and housemartins seethed about the eaves and ledges in a panic of feeding and final fledging, but went at last (and the next year, would return to nothingness, to empty air, and desolation).

Meals were brought in now from kitchens miles away in heated metal containers that were never hot enough. Gravy and sauces and sweet custard congealed on the plates.

For Molloy, whose life was shrinking and shrivelling with them, and with the buildings, the last days were rich, and he savoured them. None of his past work seemed to him to count for anything. The injuries and sicknesses dealt with, children delivered, limbs set, wounds dressed and blood staunched, all rolled away, dropped out of sight into a black pit and were forgotten, of no consequence. He clung to those who were here, listening, touching but little else.

They liked him to sit with them. The nurses kept out of his way. He was more than just the doctor, now.

'Is there a secret?'

The old man gripped his hand. They had called him, thinking that here was to be another death, grown accustomed to them. But when Molloy had walked down the ward full of rolled, chrysalis-like bodies to the lighted tent at the far end, he had known better. They left him, just the same. He had helped the old man to sit up against the pillows.

'Is there a secret?'

'What is it troubles you?'

'You'd tell me the secret.'

'I surely would.'

'If you knew it.'

'If I knew it.'

'Am I to die?'

'Not yet.'

'We're all to die.'

'As to that, yes.'

'I've no one. They're gone.'

'It happens.'

'Is there a soul?'

'I believe it.'

'You don't know it.'

'I've never doubted it.'

'You'll be with me when I die?'

'I cannot promise that. How would I?'

The room was silent. No one coughed, no one stirred or cried out for a few moments. The man beside him had been a tall man, and strong, his hand was still huge on the sheet.

'They're leaving us to die.'

'But there is some summer left. The days are warm in the sunshine. Think of that.'

'We're not given enough to eat.'

'Rubbish, man.'

'They're starving us to death.'

'I said, rubbish.'

'There's words tumbling about in my head like stones in water.'

'Words?'

He had a strong, a good, sound voice. It rang out of the curtained cubicle and down the ward.

'They that go down to the sea in ships,
'That do business in great waters.'

The response came to Molloy's lips before he knew it.

'These see the works of the Lord,
'And his wonders in the deep.'

'Were you ever an altar boy?'

'I was Protestant.'

'The heavens declare the glory of God,
'And the firmament sheweth his handiwork.'

Then they sat in silence, and presently the old man slept, tranquilly, his head resting back upon the high pillows. The pulse beat, vigorous and steady in his neck.

Sister Mcgale brought tea.

'You'll be weary of it, doctor. Night after night. But he was shouting after you. I thought it best.'

'I'd rather.' The tea was weak, but hot, rousing him. 'You can be sure of that.'

'There's not many like that,' she said to the night nurse, hearing the sigh of the door as he left the ward. 'Not many.'

And she did not, like some of them, think it peculiar, the way he was so ready to attend upon a death.

At the end of the ward, the old man slipped sideways off his pillows, snoring. They settled him deftly.

Out on the empty night road, the rain came suddenly, lashing off the sea into Molloy's windscreen, startling him, and the rain marked the end of summer. The words set going like a ticking clock by the old man, went around his head, phrase after phrase.

'What is man, that Thou art mindful of him?'

He had them by heart.

Autumn raced in with gales and great, bulbous clouds over the countryside. The roof leaked.

They locked the doors of the terrace and bolted them, for the last time.

Twenty-Four

The Bible was on the kitchen table. She found it after he had gone, with a marker slipped into the Psalms.

Save me, O God.
For the waters are come into my soul.
I sink into deep mire, where there is no standing.
I am come into deep waters, where the floods overflow me.

At one time, he had read the Old Testament aloud to her, in his soft voice. His love of the words, and any understanding he had of their poetry and wisdom, came from his mother, he had said. (Though he rarely spoke of that.)

She wondered now, throwing crumbs out of the window to the birds, how it could be that she could have lived with him and yet not with him, known him and yet never known him.

He would not go to church. When she had asked to be taken, at Christmas or on Easter Day, he had always driven her up to the door, and helped her into the pew, before leaving to wait in the car, or at home, until the service was over and he collected her. For years, the Bible had gathered dust on the shelf, between the black leather dictionary and her father's old *Pharmaceutical*.

Hath the rain a father?
Or who hath begotten the drops of dew?

One corner of the page was creased down. She did not read on, but turned her mind to him, nevertheless, as the rain came in sharp bursts on to the window, concern and the desire to know quickening again in her.

Twenty-Five

It was the last day of summer. Everyone knew that afterwards. But Flora knew it at the time, from the very intensity of things, the way people enjoyed themselves with such passion, throwing themselves into each moment (and no moments were wasted). There was an odd brightness about the light, a sheen on things, hard as varnish.

On an impulse, she took a steamer down the river, stepping up the plank from the Embankment behind a family all wearing hats, with a picnic basket and a little brown dog, wanting to be part of them, though on the boat she moved away and sat separately, looking up the river, and did not speak or try to intrude. She had learned that any eagerness to attach herself to others sent out a signal of loneliness, or some other inadequacy. People gave off loneliness like a smell. She would never acknowledge any need of them, and on this day, in any case, knew none. She was content to have paid out a little of her precious money on this pleasure, and, now, to sit among the families, the couples and children, and the cheerful elderly, watching the steam puff up rhythmically out of the funnel and the water rise, fold over and fall away. The sun shone. It was the second week of October. The river smelled of fish and tar.

That morning, there had been two letters beside her plate in the dining room at Miss Marchesa's. Few of the other women were down, because it was the weekend. They would sleep on, or else

99

had left already, on outings to relatives or to the shops of the West End.

Miss Pinkney had little items of news, and some brisk encouragement and affectionate concern, a newspaper cutting about an exhibition of art, due to arrive in London from Berlin. Flora had never been oppressed by her attention. They maintained a polite, adult distance from one another, a certain respect and reserve that she appreciated, and tried to imitate carefully in her replies.

The letter from her mother was entirely of complaint, the pages steeped in whining discontent. Olga had been unwell, had been seen by a specialist, which had cost a good deal of money, had an infection in her kidneys, or her blood. Her mother could not help her mind dwelling on all the illness on their father's side. The roof tiles had slipped in a storm, and would leak through the coming winter, because there was no money for repairs. The great elm had been struck by lightning and fallen, toppling part of the walls. Neighbours did not call. Old friends had moved away. There were mice in the house. Did Flora plan to remain in London indulging herself forever? Had she work? Should she not think of returning home, to find a position? Olga's illness had prevented her from going to a private party at the Hall, where she would have met many of the County children. The doctor's bills were worrying. She had had to let Eileen go. (Which in any case was for the best. A young man had come calling, hanging about the yard for her, and even been discovered trying to talk to Olga.) Her own back had ached for the whole of that summer.

Flora had skimmed the words, and did not alight on any of them, so that minutes later they had left no trace on her mind. Yet the mood of the letter affected her own, dulling and greying the brightness of the day. But the wide river and the great trees that lined its banks as it ran out of London, and the laughter of the others on the steamer, filled her heart.

When they moored, everyone spilled down the gangplank at once, and on to the grass, spread out rugs and opened baskets and drank beer and lemonade from the bottle with their heads tipped back. She looked, and saw them as a picture (and so it was to remain, frozen as a bright canvas forever in her memory).

The boat moored beside the river bank for an hour. It was the early afternoon, still cloudless, still warm, the shadows soft upon the grass. She sat looking at the water, and the willows that dipped into it. The leaves were yellow, scattering down. A horse chestnut tree was half bare, its lower branches still full, like dropped petticoats falling about its feet. Flora, held within the day, knew suddenly, piercingly, that this was all, and the last of summer, and looked and looked, at the picture of the people on the grass, wanting in some way to make this scene, this bright, late day that was before her, into something more than a memory.

The steamer hooted, and there was a stirring, laughter and packing up and the crying of children. The picture broke into fragments. But, looking back at the empty bank, as they turned and moved slowly away, she saw everything in that green and golden empty space as it had been until a few moments ago, fixed indelibly, out of time, in some other, immortal dimension.

She turned from the rail. A breeze blew chill off the water, and the sun was setting, not as it had set day after day for these past weeks in a blaze of scarlet and violet and gold, but hazily, sinking into sullen, leaden cloud. The banks dropped dully away. The trees were gaunt.

It is over, she said.

A tune was being played on an accordion, and people began to sing. A woman made room for her on the slatted bench, sharing her own rug. A bottle of beer came round. When she drank, it was bitter-sweet and curious in her mouth. The woman's child fell asleep and, in sleeping, slumped against Flora, and she moved a little, to make it comfortable. She had had nothing to eat since breakfast, and now the beer came round again and she drank more and the accordion and the singing blurred and swayed together inside her head. The dusk crept in from the banks on either side, as the fog began to rise off the river.

And then, out of nowhere, she saw the face of the boy, Hugh, his sloe eyes looking at her out of his pale face, and, feeling the other child heavy against her, she began, shielded by the darkness and the singing and the sound of the steamer's engines, to weep the tears she had never wept, but, seeing them, nevertheless, the

101

woman reached for Flora's hand and held it under the warmth of the rug, and then they simply sat in silence and the gathering dusk and the air was raw and chill and smelled suddenly of winter.

Twenty-Six

The summer was paid for at once. There were no clear, cold, bright mornings, with early frost crisping the grass. The days never came fully light. An acrid fog clung about the buildings of London, yellowed the streets.

She woke to the gurgle of the basins above, and the sheets of her bed felt damp, the windows were smeared with fog. The faces of the women at Miss Marchesa's were pinched and sullen at breakfast. Everywhere, people coughed. But in the Institute the rooms were overheated by coke boilers and their stuffiness felted her lungs. She retreated again into the cold galleries. But pictures had inexplicably become dead things, and she found no comfort there. She read John Ruskin, on the painters of Italy, Florence and Venice and Rome, and longed for them, and for the warmth and the sunlight.

November dragged into December. She supposed that she must go home for Christmas. She was worried about money, and no longer ate in the café with Leila Watson, but bought a bruised apple or a few plums from the street barrow, at the end of the afternoon when they were cheap, and ate them for lunch the following day. Her shoes needed repairing, she had walked so much through London. But the fat sisters went back to Belgium for good and there was no other demand for her teaching. No money. She read more and more, lying for hours on her bed, or else simply sat at her window looking into the fog. She felt neither happy nor unhappy, but detached from all feeling, as from all other people. It occurred to her sometimes that this ought not to be so, that her solitary life was abnormal in a young woman and would make her strange.

'What will you do?'

But there was nothing.

It was colder. A bitter wind blew exhaustingly all day, and at night roared into her dreams and banged doors about there. She felt deranged by it.

Turner's wild stormscapes billowed by her head.

She ate too little. Miss Marchesa remarked several times in the kitchen on her scarcely touched plates.

The term ended at the Institute. She had taken her preliminary examination, shivering in the hall in spite of being at a desk close to a radiator. From time to time she pressed her hand on to it, trying to get the heat to penetrate through to her bones. But it would not. The questions were not difficult, she had everything ready to set down and yet the words would not come, or else they appeared, jumbled together. When she looked at them, they were little black spiky insects crawling about the paper. That night, her sheets turned to water, and she drowned in them. In the morning, the walls of her room collapsed softly in upon her, when she tried to get out of bed.

Twenty-Seven

The world woke to winter, day after day. A new ice age, people said. A comet had been seen in the sky, or so the talk went.

The earth hardened, nights were black with frost. A tongue of ice inched up the river.

Miss Pinkney left everything – a letter, half-written, the ink-bottle all uncapped – and came at once when the news reached her, travelling to London through hours of the bitterest cold.

Braziers burned holes here and there in the freezing fog.

Never such a winter, never such cold, they said.

(But so people always do, so they will fifty years later, when temperatures drop down hard again, and cold creeps along the corridors of the hospital, which is empty now. Icicles pierce down through holes in the roof and cracks in the ceilings.)

Never such cold, as they blunder clumsily about, wrapped and muffled through the freezing streets.

Out in the countryside, the fields are ghost white.

May Hennessy does not eat for a week, from anxiety, she says, but then eats and eats too much, sitting about, hollow-eyed. But Olga has recovered and is bright and becoming insolent, makes unsuitable friends. Of course, she is too young to be left. May

Hennessy cannot come to London. Besides, her back has ached all winter.

Never such cold. Cats freeze to death, along with small rabbits in hutches, and little frail birds everywhere.

Miss Pinkney sits beside a shrouded lamp all day, all night. It does not matter that the mother has not come – for Flora is too ill to recognise anybody.

Twenty-Eight

There is a camp bed which Miss Marchesa has put up, grudgingly, in the room. None of this is convenient. She does not like to have illness in the house. But Flora cannot be moved, and must not be left. Miss Pinkney is quite adamant.

Ferns of ice thicken on the inside of the window panes each morning.

They are skating on the river, lit by flares. It is tremendous pleasure.

But the old die alone, or else merely suffer swollen, stiffened joints and cracking skin and sores; every day brings some new misery. Bundles of rag and paper lie heaped in doorways, and are turned over, and found to be tramps, or old women, frozen to the step.

Miss Pinkney reads, which has always been her salvation, Swift and Sterne and Smollett, Dryden and Pope, for she is still in love with the calm, cool eighteenth century, after all these years. But it is hard to concentrate.

She wipes Flora's face and hands with a damp flannel, smoothes her hair, and, needing a little more warmth and rich, teeming, comforting life, turns to Trollope and Dickens, and some historical romances found on the landing here.

And then, in a night, without warning, the fog evaporates, and the sky is pricked all over with stars, fever bright. The moon hangs, a great lantern above the silver river. At dawn, the sun blazes up out of a hard, pale, brilliant sky.

Never such a winter, people say. Look, how extraordinary! How beautiful.

Miss Pinkney embroiders a table runner, badly. She has asked for her food to be brought up to the bedroom but, after the first day, this is not convenient. She must go to sit in the brown dining room with the secretaries, the mothers and daughters, and when she does so, looking round, cries out silently for Flora, stiff and proud and young, alone in the midst of them.

Upstairs, later, she stands, looking out of the window at the transparent sky and the branches of the bare trees outlined with ice, that cracks sharply under the little warmth of the sun. But it will harden and freeze again, there is no easing of this cold. The washbasin is plugged with ice.

*

[The sinks and basins in the old hospital are empty and the water drained, the sewerage pipes disconnected and hanging bare from the walls. But still, here and there, a tap drips, and the drips are seized and held by the cold roof. Slates slip and cracks run across the tiles of the mortuary.

The rooms are completely empty. There is not a scrap of paper or cloth left in any corner, everything was swept away. The bolts and padlocks freeze to the doors.

But Molloy still walks the empty corridors in his mind, sleeping or waking, hears the moaning and stirring and sudden little cries of the old men and the old women (dead now) and the rush of wind up the basement stairs, the hushing sound of the ward door as it closes.

But this is more than fifty years away.]

*

In the late afternoon, the sun glows, and the light stains the frozen

108

snow and the fronts of the houses rose red, and splashes on to the white wall opposite Flora's bed. Children race home, arms whirling, still gleeful in the snow.

Never such a winter.

But Flora knows nothing of it, neither the darkness nor this new, bright, glittering beauty, she is lost down labyrinthine corridors and passageways, where mists blind and confuse her, and bats cling to the walls of her head. Her skin is raw and her eyes burn in harsh, dry sockets. Or else there is cold water running between her sheets, and she shivers, her body is cold as the ice in the frozen water trough. She stumbles and falls down into a deep pit, and the pit hollows out to a cave in which sudden lights flare, and there are booming, terrifying echoes, and then, blank, thick dark. She breathes through a mesh of rusting wire that grates, making her cough, and her mouth is full of nails, foul, sour, metallic.

An old doctor came once. But now, there is a different, much younger one, sent and paid for by Miss Pinkney.

He touches Flora's forehead very tenderly, with the back of his hand, fearing for her.

Twenty-Nine

The house emptied. The basins in the rooms above were silent. Even these women had people to welcome them for Christmas, friends, aunts, and married cousins. Miss Marchesa's family, a sister and a widowed brother in Putney, would be together, though she would return to the lodging house each night, preferring her own bed, she said (and sometimes they found each other's company a strain).

Miss Pinkney was given the use of the house and kitchen (and it was helpful to have someone there, in the event of emergency, Miss Marchesa had decided. Though she would have liked the whole thing over, and the girl well enough to travel. She regretted having accommodated her at all. 'Kindness never pays,' her mother had so regularly said).

For almost the first time in her life, Miss Pinkney felt of use and needed by one other person – not merely in general by a whole school. She was content to have had no family. Her life and interests satisfied her. But, now, her devotion to Flora Hennessy, who might die, was absolute.

Spending Christmas here alone did not trouble her. She had her books, and ate plainly. But hearing the bells at midnight ring out through the freezing air, she felt a moment of bleakness and disorientation – and of anger, too, that the girl's mother had only

110

written in greeting (and in complaint), sent a plaid wrap in a parcel, and would not come.

The days passed, and Flora was never aware of them. She swam below the surface of consciousness in a half-light and turbulent dreams, out of reach, out of touch with her own self.

The bells rang out the old year to a world bound in iron cold.

Miss Pinkney wrote letters to explain that she must be absent as long as necessary, into the new term, appointing her deputy and making detailed arrangements. Flora was more important than school or her own immediate future now.

Snow fell for two days and nights. Miss Pinkney was disturbed from her sleep by the immense silence. And perhaps it was the same silence that woke Flora to some awareness, for the first time, of her surroundings and of Miss Pinkney's presence with her, and she struggled and flailed weakly, trying to sit up. Her eyes were wild, bright and staring. She took a sip of water and then lay back, and there seemed nothing to her but frailty and exhaustion.

But it is a beginning, Miss Pinkney thought.

The following afternoon, Leila Watson arrived, come from Surrey and across London through the snow and cold, with some books once borrowed from Flora. (Which were an excuse, for Christmas had been hard, without her husband, but among his family, to whom she belonged and yet, now, somehow did not. She had longed for talk, an outing, companionship with Flora, who was so reserved and self-sufficient, clever, aware, and undemanding.)

She stood, horrified, just inside the room.

'You are Miss Pinkney?'

'And you are Leila Watson,' Miss Pinkney said, before they both turned, to look with love and distress and infinite concern, at Flora.

Thirty

They were married three months after the day Molloy had first come into the shop. It could have been sooner, except that too short a time would not have been seemly, Elizabeth's mother had said. There would be talk.

The church was the one in which she had been christened, but she had never been there since, and so it was quite strange, and added to the whole strangeness of the day. There were steep steps up to the porch, and she had tripped and almost fallen in the unfamiliar shoes.

It had been decided from the beginning that things were to be very quiet and she had not disagreed, because in some odd way the decision seemed to have nothing to do with her. It was only years later, after her illness and the change in everything, that she would change. Now, they agreed things between them, her father and mother and Molloy, and she had not minded, not wanting a grand occasion herself, or any sort of show. (But sometimes, in a fantasy, she saw herself arriving at the Cathedral in a great splendour of organza and flowers and attendants.)

None of it had been important because she was quite happy, as she had been since he had returned to the chemist's shop and said that it was her, and not her father, that he was there to see. The happiness was contained and cautious, but none the less clear to her.

They had ridden out on bicycles to the Greel Lake, where there were wild swans nesting, he had told her, and other beautiful birds whose names she did not know wading about the shore. It had been a cool, steely bright day, the lake very still. They had eaten a picnic sitting on the low dunes beside the water, and watching the scurrying movements of the birds in the gleaming shallows. She had never spent time alone with such a person, who listened to her, and paid attention to her for herself.

Calmly and privately, each of them had made their decision.

Molloy had arrived at his quite easily. Elizabeth did not in the least resemble his mother. There would never be any possibility of her disturbing or obscuring that memory. (Though perhaps there was a similar reserve, and a self-knowledge about them both which he failed to identify.) They did not look alike. She had been tall and very fair. Elizabeth was small, her hair dark, her colour high.

They settled at once into a companionable way of things which to Molloy was right and satisfying, and touched no depth in him. He guarded himself, held what mattered to him as closely private as before, and yet was a good enough husband, considerate and amiable, and if his slight distance from her was puzzling and even a disappointment, Elizabeth came to terms with it, and settled herself to make the best of their daily life.

But of all things it was her new home which gave her pleasure.

He had found it, and the particulars of another house, in the evening paper. It had seemed right to offer her a choice. They had visited the tall house first.

It had stood on a corner, with a sitting room looking up the street from two windows. There was a bright wallpaper and varnished doors, and she had walked in and out of the empty rooms after him in something like despair. Perhaps it was that she was not happy after all, she thought, and, with this viewing of a house, feared to do the wrong thing by marrying.

But it was not that.

'It's a good size.'

'Yes.'

'The rooms airy.'

'Yes.'

'All suitable.'

'Yes.'

'Do you not care for it, Elizabeth?'

How could she have said that there was a sadness, as well as something makeshift and false about the house? That it smelled wrong to her. That she felt threatened by the houses opposite that jutted towards it. That the colour of the red bricks made her feel unsafe. She did not have words to phrase and express such feelings in any way that she thought might make sense or be acceptable to him.

'There is another house.'

He knew, then. There was no need for her to say anything. She felt she might cry, with gratitude.

'There is another house.'

She did not have to go in or walk around. She knew, without any question, as they turned into the street. She would not have been able to say anything about her longings and imagining beforehand, because she had none. They would be married, and, so, live somewhere, in a house together. She had thought no further.

It was a short terrace with identical, small, plain-fronted houses on either side.

Their house was the last of the row.

'I shall live here,' she thought, and, at once, a latch dropped down, with a click, resolving things.

She had stood at the window of the small back bedroom in a patch of sunlight that slanted across the bare floorboards, and had looked down the long strip of grass and nettles and brambles high as a man that was the garden, and led to a gate in the fence and, beyond that, to the embankment. The hawthorn blossom was clotted all along the hedgerow. In the kitchen, a tap dripped into the stone sink. There was no other sound.

But, opening the window, she heard a multitude of birds.

114

Thirty-One

She remembered. Remembering became easier all the time. She sat at the window, watching the blackbird in the pear tree, and the pleasure of her days here, in the calm, still, silent house, brought back the happiness of the first years, the first house.

She had left at eight each morning, and cycled along the canal path, to the chemist's shop, and nothing at all had changed there, and yet, since her marriage, everything was different. She sensed a power that she had not had. They took notice of her. She made changes in the arrangement of the shop, and her father allowed them, and said nothing, though in the past when she had made suggestions he had always rejected them. It was as if the status of being the doctor's wife had made her altogether more important in their eyes. Until now, she had had the feeling that they were not very interested in her. They had been kind enough, and yet as a couple they had been self-sufficient, so absorbed in one another, that she had felt superfluous, an intruder. Now, with her own home, her own life, she was their equal at last and no longer any threat to them.

But it was in the house and garden at Linney Street that she was happiest. She would never have left it if that had been possible. He had remarked about it, but did not seem to mind. It had not troubled him.

She remembered that, on her slow, stiff, painful way to the

sunlit kitchen, to make tea. That quietness had been the same, and her own contentment in it.

Because of it she had quickly come to terms with his reserve and separateness from her in certain respects. He scarcely spoke of his childhood, and she learned, from a hardness and wariness that came over him, not to question. If she did, his eyes changed, his face seeming to stiffen and close. He drew back behind a shutter. She neither understood nor referred to his passion for attending upon a death. He would return late, or go out in the middle of the night, to sit with the dying. 'I must be there,' and that, too, had been a withdrawal from her. Gradually, she had learned to absorb herself in other things.

The house was small and, when they moved into it, neglected and dirty, and so she had cleaned it, scrubbing out each room, washing down each wall and window and, having cleaned, painted, whitewashing with a wide brush, out of an old bucket she had found half-buried in the weeds of the garden. She loved the slap of paint against the plaster, the soft rasp of the bristles up and down, up and down the wall. Slowly the house had been transfigured, to reflect the light that came into it, at the front in the morning, the back through the afternoon and evening.

She did not ask him to help her. He worked hard, she said, she would make their home. But the truth was that from the very beginning, she had preferred to be alone there.

The spring and summer were hot, the year of their marriage. She cycled through snowfalls of blossom and fresh, pricking green. The leaves of every tree seemed transparent, dancing in the sunlight, and the door of the chemist's shop stood open all day, though inside it was dark and cool and antiseptic, beyond the barricade of counter and cash till and shelves.

'Good morning to you, Mrs Molloy.'

Even those who had known her since childhood accorded her this respect now when they came into the shop. She was not only a married woman, she was the wife of a doctor. She could not get used to it. She felt spied upon, an object of interest to them in a way she had never been, and, sometimes, she hid in the dispensary, finding some job among the shelves or at the sink, so

116

that her father was obliged to serve them. And even then, she would hear.

'Is Mrs Molloy not in today? Is she quite *well*?'

At the end of the afternoon, the streets were dusty. But the house in Linney Street was flooded with sunlight, and welcoming to her. She sat on the back doorstep and drank tea and revelled in the quietness and the possession of her own walls and doors and floors and windows. Her own rooms, and the garden.

When Molloy returned she greeted him very gladly. She was happy to have him with her because in some curious way they were quite detached from one another and gathered their individual privacy like cloaks around them. They were suited.

Spring opened out into high summer, the days drifting down. Blackbirds and thrushes and tits of all kinds hatched in the tangle of old trees and rubbish at the end of the garden and, at dawn and every evening, sang and sang. Hearing them, she wanted nothing at all to change and was entirely content.

Once, rooting about in the broken-down greenhouse that leaned against the privy wall, she broke off the stem of a red geranium by accident, and stuck the dry twiggy remnant in a pot of soil. When she returned, weeks later, the plant had struck, thrown out shoots and begun to grow, all unregarded.

In a year she had a line of geraniums, bright along the window-sill, and brought the garden to life again, a place of order and fruitfulness and beauty – though, at the bottom, by the gate to the embankment, the order gave way to a tumbling wilderness, for birds.

Now, this garden she looked at from her window, beyond the terrace and the stone wall and the pear tree, had only birds to enliven it.

No one would have understood how he and she had been happy, living such separate lives, together, for so many years.

They had been suited. It was only lately that fear had come to each of them, fear of age and change, and of being thrown too much together, strangers, still, as they were. She feared her own

117

weakness and dependence, and, then, she longed more than ever for the days at Linney Street, when the house and garden had been hers and his presence only occasional and, as such, welcome.

The house would no longer be empty and tranquil and silent, day after day.

No one else would have understood.

She sensed his profound unhappiness, his fear. He was losing his life and she wondered how he would bear it, but could not ask, as neither of them had ever asked such questions.

There were chaffinches, walking prissily on the grass. The branches of the bushes and tree were full of little hanging things to hold crumbs and crusts and nuts. On the kitchen window-sill, there were red geraniums.

But she had not been able to do anything to this garden. It was small and neat, there was grass and paving, and a man came to attend to the tidying of it once a week. But it was still hers, she thought, in a sudden spurt of anger, and longing and possessiveness. Hers, as the house was hers, though both were shells now and yielded no love or delight, no companionship or consolation. Her own, hollow places.

But the blackbird pinked and scuttled, bright-eyed, beneath the pear tree, and the robin was expectant for crumbs. She had her tea tray and the sun was on her face and the dust motes danced up and down its bright ladder, the clock ticked to soothe her and she was again content.

No one would have understood.

PART TWO

One

The room was quiet. But there were birds singing beneath the open window and somewhere, faintly, the soft rasp of the sea.

Flora woke, untroubled, no longer in the grip of the terrible dreams in which she had suffocated underground among squat shapes.

A patch of sunlight was falling like dappled water on to the white wall, and a pale curtain blew a little now and then gently towards her.

She was alone, and the room was strange, and in her odd state, half-detached from her body, it seemed to her that she might not be part of real life at all. But the hand that lay on the coverlet was her own hand. The skin was almost transparent over the blue veins, the pale bones gleaming just below.

She moved her fingers a little.

'Flora Hennessy.' She spoke her own name, aloud into the room, and knew her own voice.

She had come back from death and knew it and felt utterly changed by it. She had no fear, nor even apprehension. She would survive now. Her body was weak as vapour, her thoughts unfocused, fluttering and light, but that would pass, and then she would walk about again strongly, among people, anywhere, think and talk and make preparations for the future.

But now, like a revenant, she drifted on the tide that was

floating her back, and fragments of the journey floated alongside her, and she recognised them.

They had come here over roads that had jarred through her body, and her bones had ground together between broken glass. Miss Pinkney had pulled the blanket closely around her, her face soft with concern, and given her sips of water and sweetened milk out of a flask. She had slept, a tense, restless sleep, and woken, sore from the car's movement, sick and damp with sweat and her own weakness.

But it had been safe for her to travel; the young doctor had been firm, and reassuring. She would rest, and begin to recover.

Miss Marchesa had shovelled them with obvious relief out of her house.

'You will never go back,' Miss Pinkney had said.

But the sound of the washbasins draining above, and the footsteps of the women morning and evening, the cracks at the ceiling corners, were impressed on her forever.

The house she was to go to belonged to people known to the doctor. Miss Pinkney had travelled down alone first to see it, and then it had all been decided.

'You will be healed there,' she had said.

The fever and nightmares returned; for a week after the journey from London, she had been ill. But it was the last skeins of the illness that threaded around her and they were unravelling, and losing their strength, they could not grip her.

They had travelled for the whole of a day, from early morning, stopping often so that Flora could have rest from the motion. She was coughing again, and the cough grated painfully in her chest.

She had a recollection of their arrival, of the hiss of water over pebbles, and the clear coolness of the night air on her face, and the way in which those things had eased her, and softened and soothed her sleeping.

Miss Pinkney had been with her sometimes, and others, too, coming and going quietly. A dog had barked, there had been the cry of some night animal in the distance, and, in the silver dawn, of seagulls. Days and nights had passed calmly, her fever had evaporated, her cough lessened. She had sat up, propped on her pillows, to drink soup from a cup held by Miss Pinkney because her own hands were unsteady again. But the next day, she had been able to walk across her room and sit in a chair beside the window, and eat potatoes whipped up with milk and butter.

'Healing,' Miss Pinkney said. And Flora had felt sudden pure happiness burst like a shower of sparks from coals that had been dead and black for months within her.

Two

'If you have a child of your own you will know,' May Hennessy wrote. 'The childless cannot understand.'

It was raining, soft spring rain, sifting through the tree-tops, and the sound was a relief and a balm for the feelings that her mother's words aroused.

'I have nothing but worry, and no means of doing what I would wish, to come and be a mother to you there. It is left to strangers, and you do not understand how distressing that is to me, how much worry it has caused. Your Miss Pinkney has been very good. Yet it seems peculiar. She is not family.

'You were always a hard child, and closed against me. There has not been any understanding. If you have children, it will be clearer to you.

'It would be better if you came home now. Olga needs the right companion. She is so quick and bright, and very popular, but headstrong, and causes worry to me.

'Being ill among strangers cannot be good for you.'

Yet strangers love me, as I have not been loved, Flora thought, letting the letter rest on the plaid rug that covered her knees.

(But the picture of the boy Hugh came to her then, sitting pale and eager, in the back of the Lagonda car – for there had been love.)

She was not angry at the letter – anger had just flared momentarily, and been extinguished, perhaps by the rain. She was puzzled. It was true, as May Hennessy said, that she did not understand. Was it only worry and distress, then, that tied mothers and their children? Had there been no delight or softness or understanding? She remembered none, but did not know how far she was herself to blame for it. She felt no warmth towards her mother, no desire to touch or to be held by her, no affinity at all between their bodies.

(But when the boy Hugh had crept on to her knees or raced across the grass, to fling himself up at her, she had felt the joy of it, and an intense delight in his small limbs, and the particular smell of his skin.)

The rain fell and she closed her eyes and let the sound of it rinse over her. She felt brittle and frail; when she walked, she wondered how she remained on the ground, her body seemed so moth-like and insubstantial. The surface of her brain was made raw and painful by too much depth or intensity of thought or feeling.

She would not go home – for what was 'home'? There was no such place. And she needed none. Only, for now, there was this house, in which she sat at a wide bay window, down which the rain softly ran. It would serve; there was kindness here, infinite, patient kindness and a sort of love, if love was concern, the answering of need, an absence of questioning.

They were nuns. (Whom Flora had been brought up to fear and to suspect. Girls from families they 'did not know' had sometimes become nuns and, in doing so, entered at once, May Hennessy said, into prisons of superstition and false belief.)

Within a few days, Flora had lost any fear or mistrust, in response to the peace and the gentleness, to the laughter, the rain in the trees and the sound of the sea below. The acceptance.

She had been allowed downstairs for three days, and now the letter had come and she felt pierced by the outside world, by reality, and the reminder of her old self, her past life. But she had shed those, she thought, walked away from them long ago, they lay at her feet, transparent, colourless, ghostly as a chrysalis.

Of course it was the house, she knew that perfectly well. But why, she asked a dozen times a day. Why do houses tie our hearts, in a way people do not? What are 'houses'?

It was because of Carbery. She knew that, too, and this light, in the early mornings; because they both faced the sea, and were close to the sounds the sea made. So was this merely a reflection of that happiness, then, a reminder, at high tide and low tide, dawn and dusk, and no more?

'Why are we at ease in one place and not in another?' she asked Leila Watson, who was with her.

'We feel secure.'

'Yes.'

'With me it always has to do with the light.'

'Yes.'

'And airiness.'

'Yes.'

'Otherwise ... '

'Quietness. Some places have a friendliness.'

'Yes, those things too.'

They looked at one another.

'You are much better.'

'But I am afraid.'

(For she realised suddenly that she could say anything to Leila Watson, in a way she was unused to.)

'I am afraid of everything. Of noises and suddenness. I startle at anything – the leaves shifting about ... the cat racing suddenly across the grass.'

'Because you have been so very ill – everything is shocking.'

'Yes.'

'That will ease, I think. You will be quite calm again.'

It was comforting, to be told definitely.

They sat in the sunken garden, in a shelter plaited from willow that grew like a living roof over their heads. The air was as clear as a glass dome around them, as brittle-seeming, but blurred, and paler, over the sea.

And abruptly, the boy Hugh was there, running towards her, arms outstretched, bright-faced.

'Do you see ghosts?'

126

'I used to see Edwin. He was always there. When I turned round, or at the corner of a street. Then – he was nowhere.' Her voice was clear and bleak and desolate, so that Flora reached out a hand, and the day was held for them, saved, in friendship, and this unspoken understanding; and the ghosts retreated from the garden.

But there was no calm, because of the sudden, terrible cry, that came again, as it came through the day, always without warning, sometimes once, sometimes a dozen times, so that Flora started recoiling, as if the sound had flayed her bare skin. 'He is not mad,' she said to herself, 'he is suffering.' But she turned to Leila Watson for reassurance, as the cries came again.

'He suffers so much. It is all in his poor head still.'

He had been almost burned alive they had been told. His ship had exploded, and the surface of the sea had caught fire and blazed all around him. He had drifted, half-dead, for days and nights on a life-raft crammed with others. They had been found, but all corpses, save for him.

The cry came again, rose to a scream and then died, quite suddenly.

Flora saw him every day, walking round the garden, and along the beach, head bent, and sometimes with his hands clutched to either side of it, embedded deep in his own fear, unreachable. But at other times, he sat, reading or working a tapestry on a frame, beside the lily pool, and smiled at her gently as she went by. The skin was stretched thinly, taut and shining over the bones of his nose and cheeks and jaw.

'You should not stay here too long,' Leila Watson had said, 'once you are stronger.'

They had gone into the sitting room to collect her book, where the old woman, Miss Feeney, peered at them out of her bundle of shawls and rugs, like a pupa, with tallow transparent hair and skin, as though there were neither flesh on her bones nor blood in her veins. 'As if she were not alive at all,' Leila had said, half-laughing. But then again, 'It will not be good for you to stay here very long.'

She put out her arm to help Flora up the staircase. Tiredness came on her suddenly, a total, deadening exhaustion of body and brain, confusing her speech, crumbling her thoughts.

'But you are so much better – so much stronger. I never thought to see it.'

'No.' Flora steadied herself, resting against the rail.

'I am only afraid of how much the others may distress you.'

'Yes.'

But they do not touch me, Flora would have said, for nothing touches me. I am miles away.

In her room, Leila held the bowl for her to wash her hands and face.

'You need to be looked after, and have the comfort of it all … until you are perfectly strong. Only then …'

'Then.'

Flora lay back on the pillows, her head light enough to float from her shoulders. Then where will I go? There is nowhere, because I do not dare. I cannot imagine the world beyond this house. I am safe. I hear the sound of the sea. This is far enough.

It did not matter to her that she was among damaged people and the near-dead.

'A healing place,' Miss Pinkney had said.

(Miss Pinkney had returned home quite abruptly, to her own life, and, in time, Flora would question the fact, piece together an answer to her questions, and be angry. But her letters came regularly, full of good reasons and of her unchanged concern.)

'When you are stronger,' Leila Watson drew the curtains softly against the late evening sun, 'we will talk about it all. Not now. Not yet.'

She would have answered, but could not make the words come together, and then the Sister came rustling into the calm and shaded room.

Flora slept.

And the song of a late thrush poured into the garden from the lilac tree, to soothe the poor, burned, half-crazed man sitting beneath it, and the tide sighed up and back over the shingle; and the sounds rinsed Flora's sleep. (And in her sleep, she cried out: Where would I go. Where would I go? But silently, disturbing no one, and, in the morning, did not remember.)

Three

'The last time ... last ... last ... last.'

His footsteps sounded down the hollow corridor, in and out of the abandoned rooms.

'Last ... last, last ... last ... '

There was a hole in the corner of a ceiling showing through to the sky. Clouds. He had a key to the padlocks. He came again and again. Walked through these corridors, trying to come to terms with the emptiness.

He knew what would be said of him. 'A madman now, that Dr Molloy, going in there still, walking about.'

One afternoon, with the frail winter sunlight finding a way somehow through the smeared and shuttered windows, he found himself weeping alone there. His face when he touched it was wet with tears.

'Then I am mad,' he said, and struggled to remember the textbooks. 'Mad. Insane. Deranged. Crazed.'

He wiped his face, but the tears were like a spring spouting, or blood from a wound that would not be staunched, flowing down his face.

The building was full of echoes. Voices. Ghosts.

He should see someone. Visit a doctor?

'Doctor Molloy?'

Voices. Ghosts.

But she was real. Her cardigan had a slight egg stain, beside the top button.

'I saw your car turn in. I was on my way shopping.'

She looked up and around her. What did she remember?

'But it is done with,' she said. Her voice was gentle to him. 'It is nothing now. Not to me, not to you. The old place.'

He felt like a child with the tears running down. He was surprised not to feel any shame, in front of her.

'Don't come again. It isn't good. Not on your own, wandering about. No one knowing.'

He let her lead him, holding his arm, as if he were an old, blind man, out of the doors. 'The last time,' she said. The padlock clicked.

But I am not an old man, he thought, not blind.

'Then what am I?'

'We must both make new lives for ourselves. That has to be the way of it.'

He turned, and looking back, saw at last only a half-derelict building, the window panes broken here and there and weeds growing up out of cracks between the paving stones. Nothing to him. But he searched his mind for another place, another time, for he had mislaid them.

'Nothing,' he said.

'Not now.'

He saw a woman with a square jaw, heavy, plain. Generous to him. What would she do after this? He did not know. He realised that he knew nothing about any of them, and had not cared, absorbed in himself. He put a hand briefly on her shoulder. What did she feel? Where was her life to be?

'Goodnight, Sister.'

She watched him go slowly to his car, saw him safely away, out of concern, before looking once behind her, at the grey barracks of a place, with the clouds gathering and darkening around it.

Molloy went straight to the shore, and walked there, close to the water's edge, as the small waves pleated over and over, and felt a great relief as at the lightening of a burden, and a sudden astonishing exhilaration, so that he wanted to shout to the

131

expanse of sky and sea. But only walked on to the headland, turned, and walked back, as the rain fell out of banked clouds, softly, on to the sea.

Four

The blow did not fall in the expected way. She had prepared for the blow of illness. Life dealt that often enough; she was familiar with it from her work in her father's shop, for people told things to the chemist, fearing to go to the doctor, hoping to have their fears dismissed by someone who was, after all, medical. And then she had married Molloy.

She thought about it sometimes, sitting on the back step looking down the garden on fine evenings. Tumours. Tremors. Paralysis. Parkinson's disease. Strokes. The long catalogue of Latin names. She was prepared, not being confident or trusting of life.

They had been married and at the house in Linney Street for almost five years and the garden had come into itself, the new hedge growing up, borders and bushes plumped out. The birds had their hiding places.

The blow came from behind; and even as it felled her, she felt betrayed, cheated by it because it was different.

He walked in the front door and through the house, to find her. It was the first week of May. She had noticed that the swifts were back, soaring above the market clock.

'You like the sea, Elizabeth,' he said. His shadow fell across her book. 'The sea and the country quietness.'

She did not understand him. In a moment, she would take a colander and pick the early gooseberries.

'You would like a bigger garden.'

'Oh, I've as much as I can do with. There isn't a deal of time, after work.'

'But you'd not have to work there.'

There?

'Unless it suited you. I'd never stand in your way, if you wanted.'

'I'll make tea.'

She would make tea to give herself time, trying to sort out his meaning. But he followed her, standing in the doorway, blocking out the sun.

'St. Andrew's. It's a fine, small hospital. I'm to be the Consultant. To specialise there.'

She stared.

'Gowan Bay.'

'That's a hundred miles away. To the west.'

'A hundred and thirty miles.'

She could not imagine it.

'The hospital is on the edge of the little town and the sea is ten minutes only.'

'I don't know the sea.'

The Greel Lakes had been her watering places.

'You'll come to know it.'

'We're to move? Is that what you're saying?'

'It's a very good place, a very good chance – the best. The best chance for me, to do what's important, and give up the rest.' He made a movement of his hand and she followed it, and saw the young and the infectious, those who were only ill in passing, fly from him, and the shadows of the old and dying gather round him close as a cloak.

But this small house was everything. She looked out desperately to the garden and had a crazy, panicking thought of somehow taking it with her there. There.

'Is it decided then?'

'You wouldn't prevent me, Elizabeth? You would surely not want ever to do that?'

She looked up into his face then, and saw his purpose, and saw, too, that there was no unkindness.

'The sea,' she said, trying out the word.

As so often, he ate quickly, and went back, to a patient. And after he had gone, there was the space, in which she could stay quietly.

The blow, falling as it did, had confused her, so that now she did feel ill, as if it had been that that had come to her after all; her limbs were heavy and oddly weak, when she walked to the bottom of the garden and the little wild patch beside the fence, she felt as if she had never done this thing, put one foot in front of the other and moved behind them. The whole place looked strange, altered, the light and the shadows fell in a different way, troubling her. It was as if the garden and house were distorted, dream images of their real selves.

The swifts were high in the sky, swerving madly. On the ground, beside a pockmarked stone, a snail lumbered for a moment within its shell, before gliding forwards down the smooth path.

It was cool. She should go in and make a fire to sit beside.

Her childhood rooted her in the town, but something else clove her to this house and garden. She was not certain what, or why it should be so powerful.

She must sever it then. If she let her thoughts burrow down like worms they would destroy her. She would accept, and experience the pain as terrible, once, and be done.

When he came back, at first light, as the birdsong filled the garden, she was awake, waiting.

'What month would we leave?'

August. And so there was the whole summer to get through, the soft pale mornings and evenings when the shadows lay long on the grass.

She tended the garden still, most carefully, keeping the flowerbeds neat, tidying and clipping, setting every blade and leaf in place, in a sort of frenzy. And it was hard, there was rain

135

throughout June, billowing and heavy, blurring the line of everything, weighing the bushes down, and making the growth lax and soft. She simply worked harder in the face of it.

The house was soon emptied and cleaned, and no longer hers.

'Here's a toast to your brand new life, Elizabeth,' her father said, lifting his sherry glass, at the end of her last day. They seemed glad to have her go, bustling her away into her future, anxious to settle back in contentment with one another.

August, and the sky had dried out, hardened and brightened, the grass was brittle and bleached as hay. The harvest moon rose, huge and melon ripe. In the light of it, she took a flame-torch to the garden.

Five

The blankets had writing across them, and the sheets, the pillowcases and towels too: 'Property of St. Andrew's Hospital' in bold, bright blue.

So they were a part of the hospital, in a hospital flat, in a hospital building. It was as if they had no life, no independent existence at all. She might have been given, or sold to it. 'Property of St. Andrew's Hospital.'

He had watched her, for weeks after coming here, after the fire, though he had said little, and asked no questions. She knew only that he had understood, at last, the power of her feelings.

'Would you want to go away somewhere for a while?'

'Away?'

'On a holiday. I've time owed to me. We could go ... '

'Where?'

'Wherever you would like. The mountains. Or to Paris.'

'We've a move to make.'

'You've not been in an aeroplane.'

'There's the sea to get used to.'

'Well ... '

But she knew that he would give up easily enough, and with relief, anxious to begin his work, and was glad of that, never finding it easy to go against him or to argue; she could not muster thoughts and words sufficiently well for argument.

They would not go on a holiday. There was enough strangeness

137

already, enough change and difficulty and difference, and lack of ease.

'We'll take on the flat until we find a house you like.'

'You.'

'I know how it is, Elizabeth.' There was a softness then in his way of speaking.

He had come in very late and seen the smouldering garden, smelled the paraffin and scorched grass, and doused it with cans of water, until the smoke blackened and the smell turned to a stench, sickening her. In the morning, the sight had been terrible, the bushes dripping and blackened, plants twisted in death, and all the birds frantic.

The hospital flat was above a canteen and offices, in a building set behind the main building. There was no garden, nor even any grass to be seen, though a few trees grew beyond the perimeter fence, and an old hedge of blackthorn and quickthorn and elder. She felt released from the past and from her old self, and suspended here, in a time that was out of the real stream of her life. It was very quiet, but there were people to watch going about along the asphalt paths below. The windows were large and cloud-filled, as autumn blew in from the sea.

To her surprise, she was not unhappy. Sometimes she went down to the wards and helped them serve lunch, or change water jugs and arrange vases of flowers and they treated her very politely, and cautiously; there was an invisible space between them, but no unfriendliness.

They said: 'He is a wonderful man,' almost every day to her, and she believed it. He belonged to them, though they, like her, could not know him.

Someone had scratched across the base of all the saucepans 'St. A. H.' and marked every piece of china, with nail varnish.

There was an old black bicycle which the handyman spruced up for her to use, and that was marked too, in white letters along the mudguard. But she was grateful, and went out on it for hours alone across the scoured countryside, where the bushes were bent

138

low, grown that way from flattening themselves against the wind. She liked the sand dunes and the little mounds of gleaming rock, and the smell of the seaweed at low water. But by October, it was wet and the wind blew too strongly for her to ride against it, and she retreated to the flat, and the hospital wards, and felt very safe there, and quite useful, and the old life was safe, too, sealed off and protected in her memory. She rarely thought about it. But in dreams sometimes, she wandered around the old garden at Linney Street, and sat on the step in the darkness, smelling the grass and the damp night air, before the fire took them.

The stiffness began that winter, with the endless days of seeping damp and cold, the wind that always blew. She felt it in her joints and her limbs each morning on waking; a stiffness at first, and lack of ease, but not pain. She spent longer in the wards, reading to old men and women from the newspaper, giving help in the pharmacy. She found that she was very happy indeed here, sheltered and safe. It was as if no harm could come to her there, nothing touch her at all. She ate with them at lunch time and if there was nothing at all for her to do, and even the cupboards had been tidied beyond tidiness, she simply sat in a corner reading.

And it was a great help, they said, she was very useful, there was always room, wasn't there, for an extra pair of hands? Though they often looked at her questioningly, uncertain of her, not quite relaxed when she was among them.

January was clamped in iron cold, the wind pierced every crack, fog and damp wreathed about outside the windows trying to insinuate themselves.

There was a morning when the stiffness burned into her like a brand, and he prescribed tablets. She remained in bed. But the pain scarcely eased, and the stiffness paralysed her a little more each day, she could barely move from one room to the other. He sent for a colleague and, later, for a specialist from St. Edmund's Hospital, in the city. One of the nurses brought up flowers, and later, lunches and dinners came on trays from the canteen.

The branches of the trees beside the perimeter fence were bare and twisted. As she looked out of the window at them, hour after hour, they seemed like her own limbs, sapless and blackened.

Nevertheless a strange peace came to her, in the grey hours, and a contentment like that she had known sitting on the back step looking down her garden at Linney Street, and she gathered it gratefully around her. But those other mornings and evenings might have been a hundred years ago, and certainly in her youth – for she felt old now.

He drove her to the city, for another consultation, with another doctor, for X-rays and examinations and tests. She saw him conferring with them, at the end of a corridor, or in an empty cubicle, but she felt quite detached and calm, unafraid of anything they might know or discover about her.

But they knew nothing, and nothing was discovered.

He drove her back in silence, and on the way she felt the stiffness tightening, as if something that until now had still been warm, pliable, fluid, was setting hard, turning to steel or stone. She could barely shuffle from the car.

They must move then, he said, the stairs were quite impossible now, and there were no other hospital flats. He took a day off, and another. On the third, he found the old, single-storey, clapboard house, facing the sea. Someone had made a small garden, of shells and stones and bits of bleached driftwood, bone-pale, whitened by the wind and the sea-salt, not dark, as the tree trunks were dark. Steely blue, globular thistles and sea-peas grew like bristles.

He had chosen it for the wide windows, he said. Living room and dining room and bedroom faced the sea.

'The sea is everywhere.'

'It is.'

'Look at the sky, at the light changing. And the little garden.'

'Yes.'

He got all the help to move, unpacked everything and set it out. She had to do nothing.

'In summer, you will have the beach and the dunes to walk on.'

He was anxious to get back to the wards.

140

*

It did not feel right to have the old things from Linney Street around her here, familiar and yet belonging entirely to that other place, the other life. The blankets were her own; there were no scratch marks and letterings on the pans and the china.

From every window, she saw the huge sea, moving heavily about within itself, pressing forwards, cutting off her escape.

Six

'This!'

Leila Watson said, letting the door swing open, and standing back, as if in triumph.

And so they paused for a moment on the threshold, looking, at the sunshine splashed on to the bare boards from the skylight – looking, but not yet going in, and Flora felt the moment to be important, and the start of something. And then they stepped into the flat, and that was the end of something else, her past, she thought, her youth, even.

The rooms were at the top of one of the tall, plain-fronted houses in a Bloomsbury square, with iron railings and two steps to the front door.

'This!'

The ceilings sloped. They were on a level with the clouds. London sailed, far below.

(Leila Watson's house in Surrey had been let very advantageously, so that she had been able to take the lease. She wanted to live in London, she said. 'Surrey was the past. This is now, and the future.')

Flora stood looking out, as she had looked out of the window at Miss Marchesa's; but that looking had not been in happiness. The houses on the opposite side of the square matched this house exactly. Pigeons were settled in the groin of the roof. She felt as if she were floating, suspended so high. But the roots of the house ran down firmly into the ground, and she was rooted with them, in touch with the life of the square, and the surrounding streets, the whole of London.

She turned, smiling, to Leila Watson.

The arrangement was this. That Leila was to teach at a small school in Cavendish Street, from which pupils would also come at times, individually, to be coached by Flora, who had infinite patience; and she would continue her own study of art, but privately. She could not have faced returning to the Institute.

'We shall manage quite nicely,' Leila Watson said. And when Flora had written to tell about it all in one of her letters to Miss Pinkney, there had been a reply at once, containing a considerable amount of money, by cheque. 'I have savings,' she had written. 'Quite enough for my needs and the rest are of no use to me. It is what I long intended to do for you.'

She had wanted to return the money, at once.

'But you cannot,' Leila Watson had said. 'You must not.'

'You think that it would offend her?'

'I know that it would hurt her.'

Now, Flora went about the rooms, picturing them furnished, lamp- and fire-lit. It was September. She had completely recovered. But the illness had cut her off from something, some place, as well as changed her, and she could not go back.

She opened the window, and a street seller's cry came up from the corner of the square.

'We shall make new friends, and have them in. We shall have suppers and discussions. Life will begin properly again.'

Life. Flora looked around her in a moment's panic, wondering what life was.

Seven

It was now.

For there came a time of great happiness, a settled time, fulfilled, expansive, serene. Life promised and life paid, so that, looking back, she saw it as vibrantly coloured, like the Blooms-bury sitting room, plum-dark, glowing, rich, intense, with a ruby and earth-brown rug and Turkish cushions bought from a junk stall, and two silk shawls with glittering threads woven here and there, that caught the light of the gas fire. The room became the heart of their lives.

Yet they saw little of one another. Leila was all day at the school, Flora at lectures, in the galleries, or teaching and studying at home. They worked. The new friends and the discussion groups did not materialise, were never missed.

Flora had begun to set down her analyses of certain paintings, in short paragraphs, and then, her confidence increasing as the ideas came together, at greater length, until finally, meticulously, she copied out the ten pages she had written, in a storm of excited recollection, on the pictures in the Rotunda gallery. She had no need to see them again, for she carried them vividly with her; it was her own passion, first aroused, that she was desperate to convey.

After more than a month, the letter came.

'Your article interests me greatly. You write with delightful

144

freshness and conviction. The paintings brought to life and re-created, in your words ... '

She held the sheet of paper, engraved with the letterhead of the journal, shaking in her hand.

There are moments, pure as fire, which we experience and which we do not forget, and sometimes, when they come, we know them for what they are, as Flora knew, standing in the small Bloomsbury sitting room with the letter in her hand. 'I shall remember this,' she said. And was to do so, through everything that came later, for it was lit as brightly as any of her other beacons, and would light her to her grave. But before she had time to savour the joy of the letter, there was another, telling her that Miss Pinkney was dead, and she was plunged into the middle of the journey home, giddy with the swiftness of it all, knowing there must be her mother and Olga to visit, to stand before, and to placate.

Leila would remain, to preserve their daily contentment and industriousness, their room, and the circles of light within it, the books and papers, and pleasant, quiet exchanges about this and that, until her return. Flora thought that the satisfaction of the past weeks might, surely, sustain her through those to come.

She felt sadness at the death of Miss Pinkney, bound up confusedly with regret for those things that had never been spoken between them, knowing the strength of the kindness and the affection she had received. She owed Miss Pinkney every-thing, and knew it – owed her education, her escape, her present life. Life itself even.

Death. She held the word in her head, in her mouth, to taste and make sense of.

But after the funeral, she walked away, and found herself, out of past habit, taking her old route through the streets of the town towards the park, and the streets had not changed, so that she felt confused, as if she had stepped back into a dream world. She had changed. She had been a child then. Staring at the tall, cream-painted houses, the pillars, the flights of shallow steps, the half-moon fans above each door and the lace of wrought-iron railings

145

and balconies, she felt that she was looking into the past through a mirror.

It was cold, a brilliant day, the trees pricked clear against the sky. She walked on, and sometimes looked down in amazement at the paving stones beneath her feet, and they were the same stones, rubbed and scored in the same way, she remembered the marks upon each one, from time after time of stepping, looking down. The park gates were wide, as if the place waited for her.

At the funeral, there had been faces she knew, and which recognised and wanted to know her, but she had sat apart and not acknowledged anyone. They had been changed, as the brick and stone were not, strangers, now as then; but she could not be concerned about them, not out of aloofness, or even the simple difficulty of knowing in what way she might relate to them again. She was aware of nothing but grief.

The news of Miss Pinkney's death had shaken her; on the journey, she had thought of her, remembered her words, her kindnesses, her presence – though, strangely, without being able to bring her face to mind. She had, she thought, been mourning, been moved, affected, distressed.

But, in truth, she had felt nothing. But, sitting in the hard, dark pew, seeing the coffin brought in and carried past her so closely that the arm of a bearer brushed her shoulder, a wave of realisation, and pain, had surged through her, knocking the breath from her body. She saw Miss Pinkney, her face, the set of the hair on her head, the odd way she often held out her hand as she spoke, all was as clear as day. But the woman she saw was here, on the stone step before her, she saw the face, the hair, the hands, tallow, stiff, still, cold, shrouded, lidded. Dead.

The words of the service came to her as though distorted, from deep under water, down a tunnel, or spoken in some obscure language. Her mouth was puckered and dry, so that she could neither pray nor sing.

She had not loved Miss Pinkney, in any sense she could make of that word, but she understood now that Miss Pinkney had loved her, unreservedly, generously, but almost impersonally, without desire, or thought of response or reward, and that the love had been all-knowing, all-seeing; she had been able to rely upon it, without heed.

No one else, perhaps, would love her in such a way again.

As she walked from the church she wept and her weeping was for the death and for herself, and the terrible realisation.

She went through the gates of the park, and walked on, more slowly now, down the path, between grass and flowerbeds, under the formal trees, towards the water. A nurse pushed a pram. A grey woman sat hunched on a bench. In a lance of sunlight, a little wet dog stood, shivering, and they were apart, each contained within a bubble, separate, and separating.

The last section of the path bent round between great, dense laurel and holly bushes, so that the water was not visible, might not have been there, and coming upon it was always a surprise, every time she had always anticipated her own start of pleasure at the sudden reflection of the lake, curving so beautifully away.

Then, as with the rush of grief, so came the next thing, a devastating, split-second of presence, and awareness.

She was between the high, dark shrubs, out of the sunlight. A blackbird scuttled in the soil at the holly root, after fallen berries. The sky was bright, above her head. Somewhere, on the other side of the water perhaps, a child laughed. And in that second, Miss Pinkney was beside her, or just ahead, or at her shoulder, was all around, was close enough to touch, enveloping her, unseen but sensed and so absolutely that mere sight was quite unnecessary. The sense of her, the simple presence, made Flora stop dead, her hand flying to her mouth, made her say aloud, 'Oh. Oh, so you are … ' And then, for a time out of time, they stood together, speaking what was not spoken. The vividness, the certainty and clarity of the moment which was less than a moment and was a lifetime, was absolute and imprinted on her heart and mind and memory forever, so that she never questioned or doubted it afterwards – nor spoke of it, save once. She did not look for meaning, reason, explanation, and neither understood nor tried to understand. That it had been was sufficient, then, and later.

147

After that, she stepped out of the shadow of the bushes and there was the lake before her, brimming with light, its water reflecting the clouds that sailed across the surface of the sky, its beauty piercing her heart ...

Eight

… strengthening her when she most needed it. For her mother
had aged a hundred years, it seemed, aged beyond age, and
shrunken down into herself. Her hair was sparser, the skin of her
hands taut over the bones. Her face seemed dingier, dotted with
tiny blackheads, as if she did not always wash. She was clean and
now she is dirty, Flora thought, she was genteel and fastidious
and now she has given up hope; she is an old woman.

She was repelled by the sight, and at the same time burned
with shame at herself, rage and guilt and distress turbulent within
her.

The house seemed shrunken, and dimmer, smaller, shabbier.
There was a smell of something coldly rancid in the kitchen. But it
was not the house that mattered.

She stood, looking at May Hennessy, who held on to the
chairback, as if to steady herself, and all was unspoken between
them, too, there were things thought, palpable on the air, that
could never be said.

As, you are old. You are strange. You are not very clean. You
have lost all heart, all courage, all hope. I am ashamed. It is my
fault. I cannot bear to be here.

You are a young woman, and stranger than you ever were. I do
not know you. I cannot love you. You are tall and cold. I need
you. I am afraid of you.

149

'Your room is just as you left it. But I daresay it will not suit. Things are very different for you now.'

'Oh, no.'

'In London.'

'Olga ought to have had the room.'

'Olga ... '

'It has the view over to the hill and it is so much larger.'

'If she is here, Olga likes to look out on to the road. To see who is coming. To see life.'

Life?

'She spends so much of her time with others. Friends who live at East Side, and Tillcool. They are what matter to her. And the dancing.'

Yes. Smartness. Houses with maids and gates and gravel drives. She knew it.

'It was in the paper. Your Miss Pinkney.'

'Yes.'

'You would come back for that.'

'Miss Pinkney was my friend.'

'For a stranger.'

The grate was cold, the cinders and ashes of an old fire scattered there.

'You've known nothing of how it has been here.'

The words were the old words, but the spirit had gone out of them, her voice was merely querulous.

'When you were ill, I could not have come to you, it was too difficult. It was not possible. Strangers came. I had Olga, and you have gone too far away. I still blame myself.'

'No.'

'Perhaps it has changed you.'

'Yes.'

'Such illness.'

'Yes.'

She looked into her mother's eyes, and saw tears there, and the tears were the most terrible of all.

'I shall die here.'

She wanted to run from the room, and from everything said

150

and unsaid, everything that was meant, and from her own guilt pressing so hard upon her. May Hennessy was old and perhaps ill, and alone and in need of her, without spirit to find friends, courage to live, or any purpose in living. Flora could scarcely breathe, for dread of what might be demanded of her. She could not stay, and when she went, she must bear the shame of having betrayed them.

They heard the sound of the car from miles away down the quiet road, and the wheels turning in the grit, the brief voices, so that there were moments of silence in which they waited for Olga to come in, banging through the doors, and stand, bright, pert-faced, plumply fresh, and defiant, before them, and Olga's presence shifted the balance in the room so that, briefly, Flora and May Hennessy seemed ranked together against her, and the shabbiness and dinginess were merely background to the girl's boldness and hard-paintedness and noise.

But then she saw her mother's face, turned to Olga as if to the sun, soft with indulgence and uncritical pride and the old, besotted love, which had begun on the night that Flora had been brought home from the house of strangers to find them there together in the wide bed.

She felt no envy, as she had not then. Then, there had merely been a sense of her own exclusion from the charmed circle, and bewilderment at her mother's displeasure, her own apparent unsatisfactoriness. She had grown aloof, and come to rely entirely upon herself and her own steely determination. They had served her. Now, seeing her mother and sister again, and the truth of everything, their whole future together in this place, she felt a clean, simple, final severing of the thread attaching the weight of guilt and duty to her. It lightened and lifted, and then soared from her, so that, in the close, cold, dismal little back parlour, she almost lifted her head to look up and see it vanish into the high, high clouds above her.

One thing was left to do before she began the journey back to London and the anticipation of it was so intense that she scarcely slept and, when she slept, dreamed of it.

She sat at the top of the flight of steps that led up to the Rotunda before the doors were opened, glad of the time, for the early morning sun was up, shining into her face, and there was still warmth in it. She looked down over the leafy square and the morning streets, and the anticipation of pleasure was part of pleasure itself.

There had been no meaning left for her in her old bedroom. She had looked around it without either delight or distaste. It was the front parlour in which the uprush of memory had come to her. She had stood holding the china door handle, looking ahead, as she had done that other time, and the chair in which her father had been dead might never have been moved or disturbed in all the years since. She saw him there still, his arm hanging down, the sallow skin of his long fingers, and the silence was as dense, as absolute now as then. There had been love, she thought, and understanding. If he had lived, what would I be? But it occurred to her then that because Olga had not known him in any way at all, her father was hers only, and she held the realisation to her, and gained warmth and purpose and pride from it.

Above the rooftops and the trees, in the distance she saw the line of the hills, violet against the pale sky, and an unexpected love of this place, and an understanding of its beauty filled her. The days since the news of Miss Pinkney's death had been powerful, with new thoughts and feelings, memories and realisations. She felt herself changing again, starting forward into new awareness.

And then the bolts were being drawn back and the key turned in the lock, and the heavy doors of the Rotunda were opened to admit her.

She did not run. The cases of flints and fossils were delightful to her now, as she passed between them. She stopped here and there, to look at them, strange, gnarled, coiled, and at the rocks in which seams of precious metal and chips and fragments of crystal glinted, and their strange, solemn, satisfying beauty touched her.

But it was not for their own sake that they were delightful, but as pointers and she began to walk more and more swiftly along the empty, tiled corridors, towards the beautiful round hall, and up the staircase that spiralled from it to the dome above, and she began to climb towards it, and towards the sky, the daylight. All was as before, as she had remembered and so often dreamed. She had climbed this staircase, her hand felt familiar on the cold, slender rail, the frieze against the white plasterwork was miraculously the same. The last curve of the staircase threw a line of shadows elegantly on to the white wall.

She reached the top. The upper landing was set evenly about with the doors through which she would go, into the long, high, clear space of the gallery. Her heart was racing, but lightly, pattering like rain, and for a few seconds she felt faint. This building, these rooms, and her first sight of the painting, of the woman beside the open window, had changed her life, directed it and given it purpose, had formed her. What she was now and would become seemed to have begun from here, and the rest, the prelude of home and childhood, had been irrelevant. She was almost afraid of going on into the empty, airy rooms and coming face to face with the reality of the picture again, for perhaps it could not bear the weight of meaning and importance she had attached to it and would wither before them.

And then, she walked quickly through the open doorway, and into the room. Her body felt light, as if it floated an inch above the ground. The sunlight was piercing through the rooflights in long slim shafts before breaking softly to spill out on to the floor, and in the beams the dust motes danced. And suddenly, the dead were all around her again, her father, the boy Hugh, Miss Pinkney, and closer to her than they had ever been in life. There was a brilliant, intense, eternal present in which all was luminous and rapture, and, in that moment, she saw that the gallery was quite empty and the white walls bare, the pictures gone, there was only light and space and silence. She went on carefully, as if she might break it open, shatter and fragment this new beauty, and as she did so, the momentary shock and sense of loss dissolved into the air around her, into nothing. The picture was not here. Yet it was everywhere, it was hers, she carried it within her, nothing could destroy or remove or change it. It had been her vision, and would be.

Her joy, standing in a lance of the sunlight, facing the white wall, was inexpressible.

Nine

It had a rhythm of its own. Some days, she was barely able to creep from her bed to her chair at the window and the bones of her hips and ankles were riven with rusted nails, and grated together. There were half a dozen bottles of tablets, fat as bolsters, to be swallowed.

Then, waking one morning with the sun slanting on to her pillow, she would realise that the stiffness and pain binding her had been loosened, softened, eased and smoothed, so that she walked freely.

For weeks, during the first winter and late, bitter spring she had sat in the bay window looking out across the scrubby gardens to the sea; and after a time, those who passed by, striding in the teeth of the wind for health, or with dogs, or to break the winter boredom, grew accustomed to the sight of her and would nod, and raise a hand. Nurses came sometimes, cycling out on a half-day, carrying cards and messages, flowers and fruit. But they treated her differently now, brightly, as if she were one of their patients, one of the very old.

'You're looking fine, you're getting well now, mind, you're to come back soon and give us a hand. We've all the little jobs you used to do just lying waiting. We tell the Doctor so.'

She did not know how to deal with them, who she should pretend to be.

Alone afterwards, sitting at the window, she looked back and

155

then she saw Elizabeth, at school, at home, behind the counter in the chemist's shop, in the house at Linney Street, watering the garden, slicing beans into a bowl, on the back step. Elizabeth Molloy, 'Property of St. Andrew's Hospital.'

When the pain eased, she walked along the rough path beside the dunes, past other houses, though very slowly, not trusting, for there was no reason why this day she should be well, and the next and the next, for a week or a month, nothing within her, no change in the sky or the sea or the shape of the days and his absence. She was used to that. She walked as far as the butcher's shop and the corner grocer, and they called her by name and were polite, but there was nothing more because so little was known of her.

The evening sun would break between streaks of sullen, violet cloud and strike like fire on to the sea and the gulls would rake about the sky and the cormorants dive. She listened to the wireless a good deal, for company, and dozed in the afternoons and read and was not unhappy. But she thought of asking him if she might learn to drive a car, missing the hospital wards, and the safety and shelter she had known there, and the idea was an excitement; she dreamed of a small black car of her own drawn up outside the house.

Gales roared through February and March, whipping the sea to a frenzy, booming and battering against the house. There was a spray always on the windows, smearing the view.

She could not find the right words to talk about the car, the right time to speak them. Influenza and pneumonia and death were rife among the old and he spent nights on end at the hospital, sleeping when he could, on a mattress in their old flat. 'Property of St. Andrew's Hospital.'

She looked at the sea, boiling coldly beyond the windows, and the racing sky. For days no one passed by and even the dogs were not walked.

And where would she drive to in any car? She would not have the courage to go a hundred and fifty miles, to visit her mother and father. In the spring, he said, then he would take her, he

156

might be spared for a holiday then, there would not be so much sickness and death once the weather warmed and the days lengthened.

'You should go out a little, Elizabeth, into the town, find a friend or two there maybe. Now things are better.'

The pain was lying in wait for her the following morning, as she got out of bed. She took an hour to go to the bathroom and dress herself.

The tablets he brought home this time were different, sulphur yellow bullets with a fungoid smell. They burned her stomach, but blurred the pain and stiffness.

The weather calmed and brightened, though it was still cold. She could not have gone outside. The dogs were walked again. She recognised some of them now as they snuffled about the gate. There were people to greet. She began to smile at them, and, after a while, it was by her smile that she came to be known, and remarked upon.

Ten

It had begun in this way all those years ago, with Elizabeth at home in her pain, yet not unhappy, not in need of him. Or so it seemed.

The epidemic of death was easing; the previous night they had not called him, he had slept through, on the mattress in their old flat. So many of the old were tough as leather, only strengthened not outworn by the hard life, surviving and sitting up now bright-eyed in their beds, sharp-witted and triumphant at having skipped nimbly out of the way of death.

He had been standing in the corridor, pausing outside the swing doors, and the life of the place seemed renewed and reinvigorated, it hummed like electricity around him, he heard the voices, the footsteps, purposeful, cheerful, and felt pleasure and satisfaction in it and a sense of belonging.

Then, from within a cubicle, a single voice sharp with impatience and with another note, too, of something like cruelty, something like pleasure.

'You'll lie down again there.'

Nothing more. 'You'll lie down again there.' But spoken with finality and with malice.

Molloy stepped forward a few paces quietly into the little curtained space. Bare bed, bare walls and the light glaring in. The old woman had fallen back, cowed and silent on to the thin pillow. Her eyes were tear-pricked, glittering, afraid.

'Nurse?'

A young girl, loosely fat, pasty from laziness and self-indulgence, hair ill-combed beneath the cap. He moved up to the bed and saw the frightened, darting eyes on his face searching for reassurance.

'Are you not comfortable?' And he put out his hand to her, and after a moment she drew hers out from beneath the bedcover and first touched, then clutched at him.

'We were wanting to sit up, would you believe? In such a state!'

'Fetch another pillow. Help me with the backrest.' He was angry, scarcely able to look into the girl's bold face, spoke to her as he did not often speak to any staff, and she was all aware of it.

The woman was dying, would die, of a carcinoma but the disease moved slowly through her as it will through the tissues of the very old, she was weakening and failing not suffering aggressive pain. She would take her time over her dying which he believed to be her privilege but the girl was impatient, had thought there was nothing left, no human being worth bothering with, no point in prolonging matters. A stupid girl; but others were stupid and yet had gentleness and sensitivity. She had none. He noted it.

The woman was named Ettie Marshall. He had propped her up on three pillows and sponged her hands and face, drawn the blind a little against the glare.

'But I like to know what is going on in the world out there, I don't like to be all shut in and dark,' she said.

She had had a husband, long ago, but no children, a father and mother and five brothers and all were dead. She had locked her own front door for the last time, she said.

In the sluice room the nurse talked to herself under cover of the running tap. Where was the point of dragging it out, she'd no one, she'd be more comfortable dead, best off, she'd a body like an old scrawny hen, she'd lost her teeth, she was the sort of old woman like the witches of her childhood who had screamed at her for being a slut, fatherless and dirty, for any reason and none, because they came from the wrong side of the track. But she was

159

better than any of them now, young still and with some authority. The water ran round and round in the bedpan she was holding. She watched it idly, not caring to move. 'Witch,' she said.

It had begun in that way. He sat with Ettie Marshall for an hour and returned late that night and through the weeks that followed – for her life extended into weeks after all and she sparkled with it, with the enjoyment and the laughter and the remembering. He let her remember and the memories flowed through her veins and refreshed and strengthened her so that the sickness shrank back a little, and was quieted like an animal cowering and tamed for a while, and slept in its cave. He gave her what no one had given to her since childhood, for she had had happiness then, and love and running riot with her brothers, health and gaiety and company. But then a bad marriage to a morose man and only loneliness after. So she told him. What he gave her was time in which to tell, quietness in which to remember. He prompted her with a question now and then and his questions stirred the memories so that sparks shot up through them and they blazed.

And he realised the satisfaction of it, listening to Ettie Marshall hour after hour and the time he took and his presence beside her were his atonement, for he would have sat in this way with his mother when she lay dying. He had not but only because she had kept her dying from him, out of her fierce, passionate love and protectiveness and ambition for him. He had been taking the first-year examinations. But in sitting with Ettie Marshall he sat with her, in giving life back to this old woman even as she was dying he could begin to forgive that other, most terrible betrayal.

Ettie Marshall spoke of childhood happiness and married misery, of joy and cruelty, freedom and love, bitter isolation and disappointment. Every day there was something freshly, vividly remembered and so restored to her, before being in its turn laid to rest and he in his turn told her his own stories, his own truth, told everything that he remembered together with his most dark and private feelings in a way he had never told any other soul nor ever would again. When she received what he had to say, as a gift given, she took it without remark and so he felt that she had

160

buried it and that it was safe. He had carried secrets, hurt, dark matters, and they had been a burden and the telling of them eased him so that now he had no need ever to speak of those things again, they were his but no longer only and painfully his.

When the time came for her to die – for the beast was only sleeping, after all, and stirred and woke and sprang eventually – he remained with her day and night and would have no one else near her. He eased her, kept company with her, tended to her, and she asked him the questions about death that were unanswerable. It was the first dying that he took upon himself of hundreds and he learned everything from it but most of all that this was home to him at last, his true vocation.

'Shall I close my eyes?'

'Or they will be closed for you.'

'Will you be the one to close them?'

'I will.'

'No other?'

'No other.'

'Shall I see my brothers?'

'I believe it.'

'Here in this room?' Her eyes were hungry on his face.

'Do you want it?'

'I'm afraid of it not being so. Will it be so?'

'Your brothers – tell me.'

She told him through hour after hour, night after night, all the time he could spare to her, which became all the time that he had, and as she told him of her brothers and her childhood days with them like wild things in the hills, fetching the horses down bareback holding on to their manes, driving the sheep in and fishing the waters, she was born again and lived it anew. The marriage had been endurance and hard grey years, but the man had died in the end, a sudden death, shocking, brutal and then over, releasing her to make the best of things. And as Molloy sat listening, wiping her face now and then as she talked to him, he saw the procession of all the people she had once been pass through her again in turn, saw them in her face and on the flush of her skin, the brightness of her eye. This sallow husk had been a

161

firm-fleshed, bounding child and a young girl and a grown, vigorous woman and all were here packed into her small, brittle frame, the room was full of spirits; she was dying and yet fully, blindingly alive here with him. He was drawn back and back to her, absorbed, attentive, wrapt; in giving to her he paid what for so long he believed that he had owed.

He sat with her until her death and after it, closed her eyes and went with her through the corridors to the morgue, and abandoned her there. Afterwards he drove to the sea and walked alone beside it and knew and cared nothing that at the hospital, they talked of him, whispering among themselves.

Eleven

'I wonder that you wanted us to be married. I do often wonder that now.'

She had never mentioned such a thought. But on this early morning, after the night of Ettie Marshall's death, she had been up at first light and in the kitchen, sitting at the table in her dressing gown and waiting for him.

'Are you not happy, Elizabeth?'

He had asked it of her before.

'I often wonder it now – just what would have been your reason.'

'Do we not do well enough together?'

'Well enough.'

He set a pot of fresh tea on the table between them.

'But it seems that you have no need of me – of anyone at all, that you need only your work to satisfy you, day and night.'

'An old woman was dying.'

'Yes.'

'Died.'

'Yes.'

'I was with her.'

'Oh and there is good in that, all the good. I could not do it.'

'You might.'

'No.'

He felt restless and awkward under her questioning.

163

'You are closed against me. Shut away from me. Well, I suppose there is nothing more to be said.'

'Then you are unhappy.'

'I am ... ' She stared ahead and he saw now that she was searching as she often searched but could never find an answer.

'I will do as you ask, whatever you want.'

'But it is not a case of that – of doing.'

'I cannot change.'

'I would not ask it.'

He stood, drained suddenly and exhausted after the hours of watching beside Ettie Marshall, his limbs weak as water.

'Go to bed!' Elizabeth said.

'It troubles me. What you say.'

'It need not.'

He felt helpless. Things were as they were. He did not want talk such as this and questions, probing, disturbance, had never had those things, he needed her as she was, self-contained and quiet, needed the equilibrium.

'There is nothing to be done,' she said.

They were silent for a moment. He saw that her hair was dry as a bird's nest, as though starved of some essential nourishment that once had given life to it.

'I have never wanted things otherwise.'

'Well then.'

'You should know that. We do what we do and live with it afterwards. I did not ask for you without thought or caring.'

'No.'

'I would have you content too, Elizabeth.'

'Am I to believe it?'

'Yes. What else would you do?'

'Nothing. Nothing else.'

He left her then, sitting in front of the china teapot with the birds patterned on the rim and the kitchen walls watery with early morning sunlight and knew that she would continue to sit there, separated from him by her thoughts and questionings for a long while as he slept.

But he did not sleep at once, for her questionings had entered

164

his head and they fluttered there, disturbing him, and he asked them of himself now over and over without lighting upon the answers, and in the end had to leave them. He had married Elizabeth and told the truth that it had not been without thought or caring. It had been right, but there were no reasons that he could have named to her and reasons did not signify. They were as they were and life went on. His fulfilment, his satisfaction and purpose were elsewhere, as she knew and had always known, in the past and with the dying and all of it lay like a chasm between them.

The following week he took her home to her mother and father and to the shop, where nothing had changed in the least detail so that she felt faint at the sight of it and at the old familiar smell as she walked through the door, the past rushed up and knocked the breath from her.

It was such a little time ago, her life here and her growing up, and all the neatness and order of it before she had met Molloy, yet she felt so changed, so far removed from it in age and time and distance, as though she were altogether a stranger.

When he had told her that they would come – for the death of Ettie Marshall had released something in him, earthed him somehow so that he was able to give this time easily and freely to her – she had not slept for the pleasure and anticipation.

Yet sitting across the hearth from her mother and father she felt the old disappointment, and the sense of being even more excluded. They were content, locked into their tight little world, governed by the absolute and regular pattern of their days, harmonious, inward-turned, wanting no other. They asked kindly about her home, her life and his, the hospital, the small differences there must be of weather or habits, the lie of their land, the sea, that might be of some interest, yet she saw that they were not interested. They cared for her, loved her, dutifully and honestly; if she had ceased to exist she thought that they would mind it for a while but then scarcely notice it or remember her after.

165

*

They stayed for three nights and on the first she dreamed of the house in Linney Street, walked in the door and through each of the rooms, sat on the back step and, looking down the garden, saw every bush, every plant in place just as they had been, and woke in tears for the happiness she had known there and would not go near that side of the town.

On the second evening, pinning up the hem of a dress she was altering for her, kneeling in front of her on the floor, her mother said abruptly, 'Have you felt no need of children, Elizabeth?'

The question was shocking because her mother had never spoken intimately, never, even in her girlhood, asked such private things and Elizabeth recognised that she had been able to do it now only under the pressure of her own need.

She did not reply and after a long time of silence in which her mother knelt and pinned and moved and pinned again, the question which had lain heavily between them was simply no longer there, though the void left by it was unbridgeable.

That night she did not dream, and scarcely slept, but lay silent and still, searching about for the truth of her own feelings. Children had not been born to them, that was the fact, children had never been in any way referred to, and after the first year of their marriage there had not been the opportunity made for them. She did not know why, could not have asked, and when she tried to bring them to mind now the visions were altogether strange, of the white, bland babies in cribs and small children with jerky movements, she saw them as if in the far distance, walking about and calling and now and again turning to her to stare. They were not hers, she felt no interest in them and knew quite certainly that he would not. Instead she simply saw the two of them and their lives that were parallel and inseparable and which ran ahead of her on and on until they became faint and finally invisible. The lines seemed to have no interruption in their smoothness, no bends or breaks and neither point nor purpose.

166

Twelve

London. The summer, but only fitfully hot. Clouds like mushrooms billow up over the black river and behind the domes and spires, the roofs and towers.

Flora, writing her papers, meticulously and with growing confidence, able to express and articulate, to justify, Flora, sitting, receptive, quiet and contained for hours in the galleries and afterwards in front of book after book. Flora walking in the wind and fleeting sun beside the river.

Flora is beautiful. The illness has done that for her, carved out her bones and tautened the flesh, paled and refined her.

Flora, one Sunday afternoon, suddenly, bewilderingly, blindingly dissatisfied, made angry by the pictures, as though she were starving and they were mirages of food that dissolved to an airy nothingness before her.

[She had gone restlessly, hungrily about the galleries, frantic, feverish, snatching at this one or that, a red, a stroke of white on white, a blue, a shadow, a cloud, a shape, a reflection, a line, longing to be fed, to cram this beauty, this treasure into her for sustenance until she should be satisfied. But they remained as pictures only, hard and inanimate upon the grey walls, giving her nothing, leaving her ravenous.]

Flora running, shocked and full of fear, down the steps and along the pavements and across the wide road to lean on the wall looking down at the black water, the river flowing away from her.

Thirteen

'Something has happened,' Leila Watson said. They had not yet lit the lamp. The setting sun splashed scarlet across the sky above the roofs of the square and the room was briefly on fire around them.

They sat opposite one another at the table, books spread. Flora did not speak, could not have told what had happened. That day was packed tight painfully within her: she did not understand it, was unable to clear her thoughts, but only sat mute and pale in the small sitting room among the drapes and cushions. She had returned to find Leila working quietly at marking her pupils' books and the sight of her and her stillness had calmed her and taken the edge off her fear. They had had tea. She had made a show of working.

'Something has happened.'

Leila Watson seemed suddenly older and infinitely wise, knowing her own mind calmly, seeing her own way ahead.

The sky darkened and the walls of the room closed in upon them. There were clouds, gunmetal grey, bramble black, where the sun had been and, for a moment, desperately, Flora looked at the sky as on a picture in the frame of the window. But it was not a picture, the flaring beauty had left no trace and panic filled her.

'The pictures are dead,' she said, and turned to Leila at last, her face white and streaming now with tears.

Leila did not move to comfort her or speak bland and easy

words, but only sat gravely waiting for Flora to ask for what she might need. But she needed nothing; Leila's calm and quiet acceptance were sufficient to steady her, so that at last she was able simply to set the thing aside until she could bear to face it again.

Something has happened.

The pictures are dead.

The facts were like small hard stones in some bleak and sunless landscape.

And so they sat as the room grew quite dark except for the faint lightness of Leila Watson's pale grey dress and the whiteness of Flora's face, turned towards the window. But after a time Leila got up and turned on the lamp and the pools of dim light seemed in some way to unite them and re-kindle their first intimacy. The books were cleared, the table laid for supper. The curtains were left undrawn, so that the half-moon, when it rose, was clear in the sky over the rooftops on the far side of the square.

'How confident you are,' Flora said suddenly, 'how surely you move. As if you had the answers to things. As if you knew.'

Leila Watson looked up with amusement from laying out segments and quarters of fruit in a pattern on her plate.

'Knew?'

'Knew everything. What life is. Death. Yes – knew everything.'

Flora watched the meticulous peeling of the apple, heard the soft moist sound as the blade moved through the flesh.

'Perhaps you have come up against a terrible truth. Is it terrible? That what you had nailed your colours to is not enough, after all.'

'That the pictures are dead?'

'Or if not dead, at any rate no substitute for life.'

'But you,' Flora said urgently, 'what do you have? What is enough for you? What is your secret?'

'Oh, it is no secret.'

'Then what? Whatever it is, I envy you.'

'I learned,' Leila Watson said at last, 'to settle for just enough. It gets me through the days sufficiently well.'

Flora looked into her broad-browed face with the hair plaited

169

around it, and the heavy-lidded eyes, and realised with shame then how little she had cared to know of her, for fear of disturbing the equilibrium of their friendship, provoking confessions, emotions, revealing some chasm of need and longing and loss and distress.

'How bleak then,' she said.

'Not at all bleak. But what has happened – what is happening – to you is important. Or at any rate to be taken as –' She held up a segment of orange but did not eat it.

'As?'

'Oh ... ' Leila Watson shrugged.

'You must say.'

'Well then, as a sign. A message. At any rate, something with meaning.'

'What meaning? To have taken away what has been – everything. Yes, yes, it has been everything, that is the simple truth. To have all certainty and assurance thrown about anyhow. To have lost all meaning. What "meaning" has that?'

She felt passionately, ragingly angry.

'What is left? What is there now for me?'

'Everything, still,' Leila Watson said quietly after a moment. 'Yes. I think – everything.'

The moon was curved and bright as a blade in the sky beyond the window and they remained in silence for a long time, looking out at it.

Fourteen

'We will go together – or rather, you will take me and show me through your eyes. I am going to learn everything from you.'

Leila Watson wore her brown hat and the coat with the seal collar and an expression, Flora thought, altogether middle-aged, as a governess, a nanny, an aunt. But they were going to one of the galleries – she herself was to choose which – and there, she would be the guide and the teacher, Leila the pupil. But she could not shake off the feeling of a great disparity between them in age and assurance. Leila Watson knew her place in the world.

'But you,' she said, 'know pictures. Your eyes are open. Mine have never been.'

Flora dared not say again, 'The pictures are dead.' She knew that she should be grateful for the chance Leila wanted to give to her, and her optimism. But, instead, she felt both nervous and in some odd way patronised.

She chose what she knew would distress her least, a gallery she rarely visited because nothing at all within it had ever pierced her heart; yet about everything there would be plenty to say, narrative and substance and history, myths and legends that could be explained very satisfactorily and interpreted, stories re-told. There were formal, heavy, solemn, dark pictures, grave and distant pictures, about which she could be didactic and towards which she felt simply dutiful. She could shelter behind them. It

171

was crowded, with other dutiful people. They walked slowly and in silence from room to room before the gilded frames.

Dido's Lament before Carthage. The Muse Apollo. Sisyphus. Eurydice. Actaeon. The Flight into Egypt. The Annunciation. The Martyrdom of St. Stephen. Strong, rocky, desert landscapes full of caves and little stunted trees and serpents.

But after a time, in a remote room which few of the Sunday crowds had penetrated, Leila Watson stopped. The walls were magnificent with cardinals and popes.

'No,' she said quietly. 'Not here.'

At once, Flora felt herself close like some mollusc retreating into its shell when touched. She would not be followed there. For Leila had seen through her perfectly well.

'Not in this place. Whatever has been alive for you, whatever you could show me, is not here.'

'No.'

'Well then, I understand.' She looked round in sudden amusement at the draped prelates with proud, sharp faces, thin lips, cold eyes, mean mouths. 'Would it be here for anyone do you suppose? And if so whatever kind of a person would they be!'

They left quickly, pushing their way through the crowds, to walk, arms linked, through the Sunday streets of London, and Flora felt both relieved of her burden and of any need to speak about it to Leila Watson again.

Fifteen

Children were playing with kites that rose, sailed, soared about in a hundred colours, and the children ran with them laughing, faces upturned, pushing into the wind. Flora saw them as a picture, the habit she could not lose, and from where she sat, at the top of the Hill, London lay at her feet and the air between was blue as smoke. A great happiness seized her, making her want to run in the wind, soar up and dance with the kites. It had happened so often before, that life seemed to be waiting for her, at any moment she would be borne away on it.

But it had happened, too, that she had been deceived before. She had asked, 'Life – what is "life" to be?'

Life is this. Kites swooping crazily in the wind and the upturned faces of the children.

Their cries were blown back to her across the heath. She saw the old picture then, the boy Hugh, sloe-eyed and solemn in the back of the Lagonda car.

Life, she said.

Death.

The tail of a kite snaked to and fro, streaming its little coloured bows.

On the previous day she had visited the magazine offices, at the request of the proprietor, whom she had thought of as her benefactor. He had stood, huge, dome-headed, blocking out the little light from the street behind him, and looked at her with interest, benignly – yet she had been made uncomfortable by his stare. 'And I am not a child. I am not even so very young now,' she had thought. For it was only the truth. (Yet she felt herself a small, scrubby thing, nevertheless, in this great mahogany room.) There were piles of books on the table, volumes of his magazines and journals bound up in green leather. Solid things.

'The pictures are dead.' But she could not have said it.

He would pay for her to visit Venice and Florence and Rome, and later Bruges and Ghent. He had said as much before, she thought, watching a pigeon strut about, cooing fatly, on the blackened ledge; and before him Miss Pinkney – there had been so many plans, so much excited talk.

The sky was opalescent between the chimneys and she had a sudden picture of sunlight gilding stone, of carved Renaissance faces, warmth like peach flesh, high-ceilinged galleries and domed churches, and for a few seconds went spinning into it, seized and caught.

'I could not go,' she said aloud. (For the pictures were dead.)

'It is not charity.'

She was silent.

'You would be going to work, on my behalf, at my commission.'

'Why?'

'Because I believe that you have a talent.'

'But I am no one. I am almost untrained.'

'You have what is worth everything.'

(But the pictures are dead.)

'An instinct, an eye ... without those ... ' His hand fluttered and then fell.

Flora had not answered. Tea was brought. He had talked to her of Vermeer and van Eyck, the cool, dim cathedrals of the Low Countries, his own particular passion.

174

'I long to have it re-created by you, seen as if for the first time, seen afresh. That too is worth everything.'

She had felt sudden gratitude, and sadness for him, too, that she was to let him down, and to be a disappointment. The mahogany room and the heavy curtains, the soft cooing pigeon on the window ledge, the blade of sky, oppressed her as she had sat on, mutely, watching the gold signet ring on his thick finger as he stirred the tea around and around.

The kite swooped and dived madly down, then was stayed again, then snaked back up, and all around it the others bobbed like boats with the little white clouds behind. And as she had dived down into a numb misery, so now she soared suddenly into happiness, as if she too were being blown about lightly, freely, on the same breeze. The Hill was crowded. It was Saturday afternoon. But only the children's faces were open and eager. How dull, how fretful the adults, how strained and worn and drawn and grey, she thought, how the light fades and the life seeps away, how quickly, it seems it is all soured.

The children ran about anyhow, their kites and their laughter streaming behind them in the bright air.

Looking up, she saw him. He stood with his back to her a dozen yards away. The bones of his neck stood out with the same fragility and bareness as she had once seen in the boy Hugh.

He wore the uniform of some foreign country, with an odd stand-up collar.

Afterwards it remained quite untarnished, unaltered, the momentary picture before he turned and looked towards her. No one else ever saw it and she told no one. The picture was hers only, of the young man standing with kites and clouds and children patterned behind.

And then the kaleidoscope was shaken.

His name was Henrjyk Tadeusz. He was on sick leave, he told her, to see some specialist in London and waiting to be

175

pronounced fit or unfit, to be recalled or else discharged. He had bowed a quick little, stiff bow from the neck.

'I like to walk here. To be in the air.'

'Yes.'

'To see … ' He looked up, gesturing to the kites, making the shape of them with his hands.

'The kites.'

'Kites. Kites. Kites.' He had laughed, perhaps at the word, at the kites themselves, at the scene around them, she could not tell.

'Kites,' and they had watched one that was higher than the rest, tugging on its string to get away. A small boy clung to it. His face as he looked at it soaring above him was rapturous.

'Oh, it must not go,' Flora said. 'It must not break.'

'It will not.'

She believed it, as a word from God.

'It will not.'

He asked permission to sit beside her on the bench and they watched in silence as the kite flew, and, gradually, others were watching, other kites were ignored, and only this kite was the focus. She could not have told how long the time lasted. (Though in the end, the kite dipped as the wind veered. Others overtook it. People began to drift away.)

The afternoon was mild. They walked slowly to the other side of the Hill where they could look down on the great Ponds and the spring-fresh trees hazed green. She had had no thought of a companion, solitude was her natural state, and satisfying. But she neither resented his presence nor found it strange.

He was twenty-three and had been almost two years a soldier, under the usual State obligation. He neither liked nor disliked it. 'You must do it,' he shrugged.

The small town from which he came bordered hundreds of miles of woods. He hunted there with his brothers.

They stood quietly together at the top of the slope. 'No hunting.' He looked to where the elegant, civilised trees were

176

grouped in their parkland. Yet he liked London, he said, the river, the bridges, the buildings, liked the churches and squares and the faces of the people, he had walked for miles from the barracks where he was lodged, quite alone. As she did.

Leila Watson was with her dead husband's family in Surrey, to which she went more and more now, and each time for longer, returning, perhaps, to familiar safety.

She must go, she said, at the gates where the Heath ran down to the ordinary street. (The kites and the children running were in her head, pictured forever.) He had bowed again, the odd quick little bow from the neck, and turned away.

Sixteen

His father had only one good leg – the other he dragged behind him, a dead weight, useless, after a wild boar had gored him. Henrjyk had been six years old – he had been sent home for help. His eyes had blazed in remembering the terror of it, as he told the story to her. (For of course they met again, on the following day, it had been all arranged, hastily, in a second just on parting.)

She had returned to the flat, running, and sat for the rest of the afternoon and into the dark, going over the meeting with Tadeusz carefully apart in her mind, and scrutinising each fragment, piecing the whole together again.

She had never talked so to any stranger, yet he was not a stranger and nothing about it was in any way surprising. She closed her eyes, and saw the trees that stood together at the bottom of the slope below them, saw their individual trunks and branches, dusted pale green, and the shadows below.

His family were all farmers, his father managed the whole of a great estate. His mother's family had been professional and 'higher-born', he said. But they lived well, their house was good, he and his brothers had been to a good school in the university city.

'What happened to the boar?'

178

'Oh, my brother shot it of course. And I have never run too fast again!'

'So fast.'

'So fast. So fast,' he repeated obediently.

They sat again on the Hill high above the trees, high above London. But there was cloud and a haze, little was visible. There were no children.

'No kites.'

He spoke in great detail about his family so that she learned everything, names, animals, the ways of this or that neighbour, their daily routine, though he saw quickly that she did not like to be told of hunting.

It seemed to Flora, listening, that he came from a fairy story, a world of deep forests and wild boar and huntsmen and, it might be, witches and talking cats and gingerbread houses.

Tadeusz laughed. 'Yes,' he said, 'perhaps. Those tales come out of these lives, these countries.'

Once or twice he asked about her own family, but she deflected the questions immediately with one of her own, so that in the end he looked at her with concern, his eyes grave upon her. But her life, and everything that had filled it until now, had no substance, no interest, she turned from it impatiently and towards him.

One day they did not meet because he had to spend it on temporary duty at the barracks, another because he was being seen by the specialist at the hospital, and those days were a blank landscape to her, and endless.

If there was nothing at all she wished him to know about her own past, her home, her family, she delighted in showing London and her knowledge of it off to him, telling what she knew, of martyrs at Tyburn and Princes in the Tower, of Kings crowned and statesmen and prelates and great soldiers on plinths, and ancient surrounding walls and pigeons wheeling; the river, the wharves, the dark alleyways and handsome squares, parks, playgrounds. The High Heath.

It rained and then they went to the galleries; she showed him

179

the pictures. They stood before the mighty Turner canvas of boiling spray and whirling cloud and brilliant light that streamed out towards them, and she saw with what respect he looked at it, his face absorbing the power and energy of the painting as he clenched and unclenched his fist.

When they came out, it was into sunshine. They sat on a bench and ate oranges he bought from a barrow. And she began to speak to him of the Rotunda Gallery, the white rooms, the picture of the woman on the couch before the open window. It was like the opening of a door, back into a place that had been closed to her.

She told him everything then.

Seventeen

Leila Watson mended stockings, the needle flicking neatly, evenly, in and out, in and out. The air beyond the open window was soft with spring. Men had mown the grass in the square.

'It is new to you,' she said, looking up. 'It is all new.'

Flora turned.

'Your face has changed. Everything shows in the face does it not? Love ... grief.' She smiled.

They had not met, Leila Watson and Henrjyk Tadeusz, Flora had not yet seen a way of bringing them together. But, suddenly, it seemed urgent, because life would change. Leila was returning to live in Surrey. She had a teaching post near her husband's family, sisters and brothers-in-law, their little children. But being away alone in London had been very necessary, she said, she had been lost and needing to find herself again in her own way.

'But now ... '

It would have been a blow to her, a disaster, the thought of struggling all over again would not have been bearable.

'But now ... '

Leila Watson rolled up a stocking deftly. 'Now you should go to Italy, and then to Bruges and Ghent. You owe it that.'

'It?'

'The past. Your commitment to those things. For the pictures have come to life again, have they not?'

Flora tried to imagine then how she might indeed go, saw herself in cobbled streets and vaulted churches, saw altar panels glowing, gilded, and yearned briefly to be amongst them, to drink from what they had to offer her. The past was a state infinitely to be desired then, because she had been alone in it, expectant and entirely free. 'Life,' she had thought, 'what is it?' But had not yet known. Life had still waited for her, somewhere safely in the far distance.

From this time, the past and that state of being were irrecoverable; she recognised that she was changed utterly, and the future was forever altered and, in some strange way, the thought was terrifying to her and gave her no joy. When she walked about among the pictures Tadeusz walked with her. His not doing so was unimaginable now.

There had not been such a spring for forty years, everyone said so, when the blossom came crowding in, profligate, hard upon the daffodils, and the hedgerows were like snow.

Sitting on the Hill, on the top of the world, looking up at the spinning sky, he began to teach her his language. 'So that you will be a little ready.'

And so it was settled and natural and inevitable as her next breath, that she would be with him. There was so little likelihood of anything else that they scarcely needed to speak of it.

The world was shot through with a beauty and a translucence that dazzled her and, in her head, she composed the letter to her mother. But the writing of it was postponed day after day because, every minute, they must be together. They left London, and ate a picnic, resting on the flat slabs of tombstones in a churchyard, and the grass and the creamy heads of the cow parsley drowned them. The sky was pierced by spiralling larks.

He talked more and more about his country, his village, his house, the city in which he had gone to school, but she could not begin to picture them as real, as existing, solidly, now, at this hour, and merely not here but 'there'. She must simply go there to discover it.

She would settle there. That was what her life would be. None of it was in question. He had written his letter, he said, and it was posted.

She looked at him, shocked with love. And then, turning from him, looked at the waves of blossom like the surf of a tide out of which the grey stones rose, and the tower of the church soaring to heaven. She thought, it is decided then. And went on looking, to seal the memory of tower, tombs, foaming blossom, this picture, along with those others that were hers forever.

'There was nothing at all,' she said later to Leila Watson, 'and now there is everything. But how can that be?'

'It cannot.' She spoke gravely.

'Everything, everything is changed.'

A pigeon pecked with little hard, darting pecks at the crumbs they had scattered on the ground around them. It was cooler with steel grey cloud. They were sitting in the square.

'You are changed.'

'Were you? You never speak of it.' She looked into her friend's calm, thoughtful face.

'I think it was not – the same. You are overtaken by it. Yes, it is a sort of possession.'

'It is all I know now. Nothing else exists. He is what I think of. He is what I am.'

'No! You are Flora and not lost.'

Flora laughed, startling the pigeon with clapping wings into the air.

'Lost. Oh, yes.'

'A marriage is a very different thing.'

'So solemn!'

Leila Watson smiled, a smile of something recalled. 'No.' She pulled her coat closer around her neck, and, in doing so, reminded Flora of a much older woman.

'When Edwin died I thought that I would die. Would have preferred to die. But you see, one does not.'

'If … ' The sky lurched sickeningly for a split second. 'I *would* die.'

'No.'

'I shall belong to another country, another family, another language, another past. Everything.' And she saw it all ahead of her. But the strangeness was not strange and she was quite unafraid of it.

They were to leave the flat. They had one more week only of this life. Already the rooms had begun to draw back into themselves, to revert to strangeness, and anonymity.

'I am afraid for you,' Leila Watson said. 'I must say this. I could not forgive myself.' She reached out and took Flora's hand between her own. 'I am so happy that you have this, that you have known love. It is not all, I have never been able to believe that. There is so much else. But it is at the heart of things. Yet you cannot know – how can you? How can you take all this on trust?'

'I do.'

'Then keep something back.'

'No. It is a new life. It is everything.'

So that, after a moment, Leila Watson let her hand go.

They sat, still together, still in friendship, until it was too cold to sit longer and they left the square. But the ease and the amity had gone from between them, and when they reached the flat again it was merely poky, dark, and the cushions and drapes and lamps dusty, lacking the old glow their sense of brave conspiracy had lent to them.

She had tossed everything on to the pile, to be disposed of anyhow.

Her father's death. The house called Carbery and the boy Hugh. His life. His death. Miss Pinkney's hopes for her. Her life. Her death. The Rotunda Gallery and the streets and squares through which she had walked and walked, learning the beauty of the buildings. And the terrible things. The cold and her own absolute loneliness in the boarding house of Miss Marchesa, which had defined her then. The illness, from which she had nearly died and the miracle of her recovery into a world prepared for her so lovingly by Miss Pinkney and by Leila Watson. The

184

pictures. The old future. She dismissed them. Tadeusz obliterated everything.

He was to be seen at the hospital once more, and any treatment decided upon. But it seemed probable that he would be discharged the army.

'Then?'

'Home then. We shall be at home. That is all.'

But the all was unimaginable.

'And now they will have read the letter. Now they know of Flora.'

She looked into his face and saw everything she might need there.

'They know of me.'

'Yet you love London I think.'

'London does not matter.'

'I love London. We will come back, I think?'

But she was impatient to leap ahead, could not imagine returning and had no interest in the suggestion of it.

She held both her hands to his face, carving his expression at this moment into her memory.

He had given her a book, small, bound in rough grey cloth. When he had taught her more of his language, she would understand it and she would like it, he said (and already they could talk a little together, several sentences to and fro).

It was called *The Lady with the White Hat*.

'Write in it.'

He held the pen for a long time over the page, but in the end wrote only her name and his own in black, with the thick nib, the letters striking out boldly across the page.

She slept with the book on her pillow, touching her face.

Eighteen

There was something wrong. He had smelled it, like a fear, as he opened the door.

'Elizabeth?'

She was crouched against the wall in the living room. Her back was to him. (They had left the house facing the sea, the sound and sight of it troubled her, she said, she felt trapped behind the grey wall of it. They had come here, to the small, clean, silent bungalow, with the pear tree beyond the kitchen window, and her invalid life.)

'Elizabeth.'

It was always the same. He had called her name from the first, coming into the little house in Linney Street, to find her on the back step or at the bottom of the garden there, and to the hospital flat, and the house facing the sea. And so, now.

'Elizabeth.'

But then there had always been a going away from her and a return, his life elsewhere and their life together, a reason to call her name on returning.

Now there seemed none. He had no longer any other life. The grass and thistles and nettles grew up around the hospital and the doors banged loose in the wind. There was barbed wire and a dangerous chimney waiting to topple. Even the ghosts were gone. He had this, now, here.

'Elizabeth.'

There had been a dreadful heaviness about the way she had fallen and a greyness to her skin. He had been able neither to rouse nor lift her but in the end knelt beside her, chafing her hands and speaking her name again and again. 'Elizabeth. Elizabeth.' But he knew that she heard him.

The room was bitterly cold.

'Elizabeth.'

And perhaps for the first time, kneeling there, he felt love for her, though it was a dilute and pitying love and soured by fear.

Once she would have been taken to his hospital. Now it was to the City General thirty miles away, where he was scarcely known and not at all regarded. The ward was full. He sat on the chair beside her and felt out of place.

The stroke had twisted her mouth oddly and deadened the left side of her face so that she looked strange to him, a distortion of herself.

There was no one he should tell. Her parents were dead. They had been found together in the flat over the chemist's shop, side by side of the fire in a room filled with gas. Downstairs, everything had been neatly arranged, the shelves in the pharmacy tidied, the sink cleaned. The door had been locked and the CLOSED sign swung across, and there was a letter to Elizabeth on the sideboard. It had been about old age, she had said, and illness and pain and the impossibility of separation. She had read it and burned it and afterwards retreated into herself, dry-eyed and far from him.

(But he himself had always been similarly alone and both of them knew it.)

'Elizabeth.'

And then her eyes had opened and she saw him and for a few seconds everything was clear and revealed between them, the whole of their marriage and the past seemed balanced on this steady eye-beam, and everything forgiven.

That was all. Elizabeth slept. He took the first bus home in the early light of the morning, not trusting himself to the car, and sat at the table in the white kitchen listening to the ticking clock, his limbs heavy, and prepared himself for the future here, whatever life was left. But later, through the afternoon, he slept, and dreamed vividly of his mother, so that he woke bathed in bliss at the sight of her and the sound of her voice and at the evening light filling the room.

All that he thought, with a passion he might have felt if he had been drowning and clinging on to a spar, was that he must cling to the dream and not surface from it, not wake, and for a moment he succeeded. But then the dream fragmented and pieces broke away like a cobweb torn open by a probing finger, which was his consciousness.

He had never until now been given sight of her face but in his dream it had been as clear as his own in a mirror would be to him, and every feature distinct. She had wild hair that sprang anyhow away from her head when she loosed it from the restraining plait and comb, and in the frame of it her face was a young girl's face. She had been speaking to him, saying something, though of no consequence, turning towards him as he sat over his schoolbooks at the parlour table. The oil cloth was as he remembered it, green and cream check, and the lamp was lit. The corners of the room flickered in shadow.

The skeins of the dream drifted from him, as he snatched at them they dissolved. He woke, to the powdery bedroom in the evening light, hearing his own voice calling out.

But did not catch the word.

He had never wept and would not now.

In the garden the late blackbird in the pear tree suddenly burst out singing.

It was the dream that sustained him. He fed off it for the rest of his life, though it never returned to him; for all his craving, he never saw his mother in such a way again, waking or sleeping.

He sat beside Elizabeth on the flimsy hospital chair as it seemed he had sat for a thousand days and nights and at first he held himself in readiness. He waited, because she was dying. Her skin was soft and silken as a child's skin and faintly damp, not the moth-dry skin of the old. (She was not old.)

188

They were not concerned that he was a doctor, the fact was simply brushed aside, irrelevant to them. He had no status here. He was next-of-kin of the patient Elizabeth Molloy, and the rest counted for nothing. He counted for nothing. They came to attend to her and chivvied him out of the way. He went down a white-lit corridor towards a waiting room where old cigarette smoke was stale upon the air. It was square as a stamp, and windowless. The place was noisy with lifts and doors and the scraping trolley wheels, the familiar noises, and no one thought to hush their voices. He wandered out and down other corridors and no one paid him heed. He lost his bearings almost at once but, at last, came to a sluice room with a window and opened it wide.

It was raining, evenly, steadily, softly on to the roof and falling into the yard below and the sound steadied him, when he returned to her, he felt quieted.

'Elizabeth.'

Her eyes opened at once, but then fluttered anxiously about the cubicle like bright moths caught in the still, pale, heaviness of her flesh. But when at last they did rest on him, it was blankly, with fear but without any recognition.

All night it rained, until the pattering drops seemed to fall inside his head, as he sat beside her.

That morning, he drove to the sea, and walked, as he had so often walked, following the whole curve of the bay as far as the point over the rasping shingle. It was still and empty and cold. The seagulls rawked and wheeled above him in the silver sky. He tried over and over again by some means to reach his dream, or else the waking memory of it, but there was no trace of it given to him. Instead, he saw Elizabeth crumpled against the wall, and heavy and motionless on the hospital bed. But she too was far away from him, and quite unreachable.

Nineteen

After a time, there was nothing left but the silence, which seemed to creep out from them over the room in which they sat, over the whole house and out into the air beyond, to fall like a spell upon the square, the street, the whole of London. It was an absolute silence and terrible at first, but after a time they were soothed by it.

They had waited for footsteps and none had come, for a voice but no one had called out to them, a knock but there had been no knock. So that, in the end, they simply sat on in the midst of the spell of silence, frozen, like figures caught in the instant in sleep for a hundred years. One lamp was lit. The wine on the small table glowed ruby red in the light of it. The plates gleamed white as bone. The soup bowls and the fruit dishes were hollow, empty.

There was to have been a chilled soup, delicately pale with cream and cucumber, a dish of hot lamb, a pyramid of fruit, an ice, a Stilton cheese.

Unhappiness Flora had known and the chill of sadness, shock, loneliness and fear, but a disappointment such as this she had not known. It was disappointment and it was betrayal of all expectations, all hope, and she felt it as a physical pain, sharp at first but soon gnawing, dull, relentless. It affected the passage of her thoughts, paralysed her speech and her movement, froze her brain, so that she could not have told the time or the day of the week, scarcely even her own name, could not have fled from a fire or the violence of an assailant. She had gone down the stairs three times and out of the house, to pace along the street, looking, looking, and to return in distress and agitation, yet, strangely, she had not in her heart ever believed that there might have been some plausible reason for his absence. Once the moment had gone beyond which mere lateness was possible she had known absolutely that Tadeusz would not come. She might have screamed and cried, flailed out in anger and in disappointment, but she did not, her response was, as it had always been, to shrink back into a cold, stony place within herself and into which Leila Watson could not reach.

A cat yowled suddenly from the rooftops on the other side of the square, yowled again and the noise should have startled them into movement or words but strangely it did not, they merely heard it and sat on, frozen to stone. But after a time Leila Watson realised that she herself was crying, slow, silent tears of distress and misery for her friend. But the tears fell unnoticed and so in the end they stopped and because there were no words and could be none, she broke free of the spell, stood and began to clear the untouched, unsoiled dishes and uneaten food from the table. After a while, automatically, Flora helped her and when things were dull and usual again and every sign of the evening's expectation gone she left the room and went into her own and lay on her bed in the darkness, fully dressed, eyes open, still as death.

But at three in the morning, with the cold moonlight to see by, Leila Watson came from her own bed, weeping to her, and lay on the covers beside her, wanting to give her comfort, find words that might explain or reassure. But there was no comfort, no explanation, no reassurance, and they both knew it, and so merely lay in silence, and the moon slid off their faces, over the floor, watered the mirror, before gliding away, leaving them in the still darkness.

The dawn was hours in coming. But at last, fitfully, both of them slept.

Why Tadeusz did not come she never discovered. That was

191

something she learned from the experience of those weeks; that to some questions there are no answers, to some puzzles no solutions. Ends may remain loose and matters unresolved, forever.

He did not come then, or ever. He did not write.

Flora wrote to him, a single, anguished, raging letter of remembrance and love and bitter blame that concealed nothing.

His face was between her and the paper as she wrote.

But after a time she realised that, as much as Tadeusz himself, she missed the future that he was to have given her, the new country, the farmhouse in the village close to the woods, another language, the strangers who would have become her family. She dreamed of them and of their horses and dogs and forests, she smelled that life as she would have lived it, smelled woodsmoke and pine needles trampled underfoot; she knew how the mattresses would have felt to her body when she lay on them, coarse and uneven and thick, saw the grain of the scrubbed surface of the wood tables. That new life had been a story, begun but abandoned. The book was closed and thrown away, the ending of it denied to her, along with the life.

Of Tadeusz she dared not think because he carried so much of her away with him into the silence and emptiness that had closed round him like the sea, because of the trust and the confidences he held. Tough in waking she could exclude all thought of him by a simple act of will, but her dreams she could not control and he came to her in dreams, until she woke in bitter, furious tears and beat her fists against her skull to drive him away.

In the dreams he was his true self; there was nothing strange or surreal about them, no distortion. They were ordinary dreams, in which over and over again they walked away from the Hill and down the sloping path towards the clustered trees below and behind and above them in the sky trailed a multitude of kites. In the dreams, she spoke his language fluently. But once he got up from the bench on which they sat and walked away. She called to him and he turned and looked back, but in looking, he was not Henrjyk Tadeusz but the boy, Hugh.

*

The book he had given to her lay on the bedcover, beneath her hand.

In the last days, knowing that this life was quite over and that it was the end of their friendship, she and Leila Watson talked, swam in streams of talk, of questions and recollection, of revelations, as if talk were to be used up now or never allowed to either of them again. Which in a sense, was so.

She had told Tadeusz everything of herself and might have wondered if there were anything left to tell, that somehow the well might be dry and the bucket light and empty as it rose. But these were different wells, it seemed, there was more in them of detail and of feeling, that she had not remembered before. What she had shared with him remained his, given freely away, but what she and Leila Watson told made a quite different telling.

She wanted to weep but could not, there was only a dry pain burning in her stomach and in her throat. What she felt was a confusion of something like shame, for that she was in some way to blame for her situation and her own abandonment she had no doubt, though she could not properly decipher nor at all understand it. He had betrayed and punished her because he had found her wanting, though in what ways she did not know.

No one else had been told anything, no one but Leila Watson knew. But she thought, once or twice, about the letter he had written home. His plans, her coming to them, their future, had been in the pages of the letter; she imagined the black strokes of his curious handwriting, upon the white paper.

If there had ever been such a letter. If they had known of her existence, after all.

Twenty

'No.'

Leila Watson had turned, in the very moment of leaving. She had on her coat with the fur collar, her hat and gloves. She was a middle-aged young woman. But still she turned, her arms out to Flora, and her face poured tears. She was the one to need comfort.

'No. No.'

And so Flora comforted her, as if she were a child being torn away from her.

'This is wrong. You should not be staying here, you should not.'

'I will not be here.'

For she was to go to her new life the following day.

'Come with me. They will welcome you, there is a place for you with us. It is so good, so sheltering there. You need shelter.'

For a moment, she saw it as it would be, the small house Leila was to go to, next to that of her sister-in-law and in the same village as almost all the rest of her husband's family. Everyone was related to her or knew her, there were the nephews and nieces, she would be the Aunt. The village sat in the shelter of the Downs among trees and pastureland and comfortable farms, protection, welcome, shelter – the words she had used – calm, an ordered life. Matins on Sunday morning, tea on Sunday afternoon. It held its arms out to her, this life, she might retreat into

194

them. The fields would be greener than any fields, the skies softer, the birdsong sweeter, the contentment absolute.

'There is time to send a telegram, change the labels on the cases. It is quite easy.' Leila Watson clicked her fingers. 'It would be done. I cannot bear you to go to strangers.'

But looking into her friend's face, gentle, tender, infinitely loving, Flora saw to the heart of the matter: that such a life would cloy and suffocate, might ease for a time but could never satisfy. She did not know what there would be for her, she only trusted in herself, in her own inner strength and in the place where she was quite alone and infinitely self-reliant, the place she must nurture, not muffle and soften and stifle with the kindness and company of others.

She kissed Leila Watson on both cheeks and turned her round by the shoulders, gently, towards the waiting cab.

And then, in the midst of her own desolation, there came to her a new sense of infinite possibility. It blew into her face with the breeze that came across the square. It was a moment in which she felt that life was being breathed into her anew, and without condition, and that she must seize it.

She had not gone with Leila Watson to Surrey. (And indeed, she was never to see Leila Watson again.)

The pain of Tadeusz's betrayal had probed below the surface and into her bones and settled deeply there, and like a parasite would grow, fed by the silence and darkness, she would never dislodge it. Yet still, with the breeze blowing into her face, she felt this hope and turned to it, joyfully and in gratitude.

Twenty-One

Thistles grew tall as trees beside the railway track and, now and then, the seed heads blew and floated down on the air like tiny ghostly parasols. There was a mustard-coloured weed and bone-dry grasses that keened in the wind.

The train had stopped, she did not know where, nor how much further she had to travel. The journey seemed long. It was also very beautiful, the train riding high over the open country that had become bleaker and barer as they went. Now and again, it had curved, following the line of the coast, so that she had looked back from the open window of her compartment to see the coaches like segments of a caterpillar, curving round.

She had left London without looking back – and not just London, it seemed, but that part of her life and of herself which had belonged there. They had snapped and broken away from the Flora who now travelled on and she felt light without them, as if, when she stood, she might leave the ground. Leila Watson, the flat in the Bloomsbury square, the few weeks with Tadeusz, might not have been.

A cloud of little sky-blue butterflies fluttered up from the dry grasses beside the train. She had replied to an advertisement for a companion. She would be required to read aloud, to have conversation, and to take dictation for the writing of a memoir. Nothing more. The house, the town, this part of the country, were entirely strange to her.

'Write often,' Leila Watson had said, 'and of course I shall write, and if things are not right for you, you are to leave and come to Surrey. Do not even bother to tell us in advance. Come.'

But you will be settled, Flora had thought, into the comforting shelter of that place, that family, you will take root and put out first shoots and then strong branches there, you will grow old among them. She had an image of rich foliage parting briefly to let in Leila Watson, and falling back at once, a curtain to envelop and conceal her. She would grow moss, like the slates on her cottage roof.

'Write often.'

Her bones felt scraped bare, but infinitely strong and able to support her without need of any other. She believed passionately now that there was no hope or salvation for her save from her own self.

Creaking, the train began to move and, all along the track, the butterflies fluttered up again in panic and for a second unnerved her, too, so that her heart pattered in her breast.

Where am I, she thought, and why, and what will happen to me? To be lonely again among strangers might be both unbearable and inescapable. Pride had made her refuse to go to Surrey, and comfortable shelter. Pride and her own aloof independence were hard and bitter food.

But the station roof had an elaborate canopy, scalloped at the edge, and the railings were freshly painted and, most pleasing of all to her, the air smelled of the sea. She was to be met. But once the platform was empty of people again, once the train had gone, she was glad to be left for a time to herself, to sit on the green bench beside her suitcases in the sun, and the old feeling of being suspended in time and space came back to her; she might have rested there for five minutes or five hours, it did not matter, she needed nothing, nothing troubled her.

There were dozens of sparrows in the iron guttering above her head. Somewhere in the distance was a sense of the ending of land and the beginning of water, a pale brightness.

197

The signal clanged down, but still, for a long time, the hour hung heavy, nothing moved, no one came to her.

The sparrows went on squabbling and chattering in the dust.

PART THREE

One

Once, she said that she had been led to the place, by a star or an angel, and for all that she was so ill by then, weakened and with an intermittent fever that laid waste her body and confused her mind, for all that, she believed it to be so. In her last months, she had taken to reading the Bible, seeing its stories not in terms of their message, or indeed, of their words at all, but as a series of pictures, tableaux, which she was able to look at in her mind's eyes. There, in pictures of angels and stars, prophetic messengers, she had found her confirmation.

'For how else,' she had said, 'would I have come here?'

From the beginning, on the station platform, the first realisation that she was indeed completely alone, she had felt a sense of home-coming deeper than any in her life. She loved the small town as she might have loved a person, and better than she had loved any save that one. (If there were another, it was not Henrjyk Tadeusz, after all, but the other boy, the first boy Hugh. She did not speak of the brief, flaring up of love with Henrjyk Tadeusz, and the ending, in betrayal.)

The town, set behind the long shingle beach and then the sea, was perfect to her, then, and ever afterwards, and she left it once only, to travel to her mother's funeral. She did not believe that such settled happiness, such a sense of an ending, and of a rightness, could have come about by chance, the casual finding of an advertisement in a newspaper for a lady's companion, and so

201

the idea of the angel or the star, her fate and destiny, grew in significance with her, the only superstition and irrationality she had ever entertained.

It was laid out in regular lines of houses running from the hill down to the sea. The high street was surprisingly broad, with the back of the shops and houses on its east side to the sea and the winds that blew off it for most of the year. Every few yards, between the buildings, a narrow lane ran up to the seafront road.

Flora spent her days at work in the shelter of the high street and her nights in the cottage that faced the sea. But at the beginning, she had been obliged to take a room in The Ship Private Hotel, a genteel, cheerless place. She had been panic-stricken, feeling like a bark at first cut adrift from its moorings and then cast up on this unfamiliar shore. (Though even in the midst of her panic and bewilderment on the empty station platform, waiting, waiting, she had felt a curious happiness, and the relief that comes on arriving home after a long journey.)

She had sat and waited on the bench at the railway station and no one had come to meet her, as had been arranged; then, someone, a boy, red-faced, straw-haired, with a scribbled message. Miss Judaker had died the previous night, so that, until just now, Flora's arrival had been forgotten, overlooked, scarcely known or thought of. She must return. She would have no employment here after all. (And the house and its domestics were in confusion, Miss Judaker having had no family, perhaps not a single relative.)

She must remain one night, then, for there was no further train, and return to London the following day. But return to where? And she would not go to Surrey, to Leila Watson – she would not give in to that easy, comfortable solution.

She was tired. Her head ached. The boy had carried her trunk to The Ship Private Hotel.

That evening, the sky over the sea had been silken and pale. Flora had walked beside it along the path and then climbed the wall and jumped down on to the deep shingle and walked there, her face to the sea and sky until the light left it and there was only a soft, still, violet dark on the surface of the water. Then, she had turned and looked back to the lights that shone from the huddle of houses that marked out the town. Here then, she had said. For why not? Where else? Whatever had brought her, what chance, what accident, what betrayal (as she thought of things then) was not relevant. Here.

And all the pieces fell into place.

That night she slept as she had not slept for weeks, and in the course of it she seemed to travel, travel a thousand miles for a thousand years, for when she woke, she was another person, and the rest of her life, the old life, was over and half-forgotten. She could scarcely remember the faces of Leila Watson and even of Tadeusz. The people she had known, the places in which she had lived, seemed to have fragmented and blown away in pieces on the wind that came from the sea.

The sensation of having no past, or constraints, and of the infinite possibility and reassurance of this present, made her light-headed. She went out early, to walk again along the sea's edge, seeing the gulls wheel and turn and drop suddenly through the pale clouds, and even her own name, Flora Hennessy, seemed strange and unrelated to her.

Later that same day she had taken her job, fallen upon the work, the place, the people, with the rapture of a new discovery, and of a solution to her emptiness, and had remained there, through her mother's death, through her own move to the cottage, through day after orderly settled day, for years. Until now. Until now.

It was the shop that she had fallen in love with. Later, even her son understood that.

On the first morning, she had come into the back room of the hotel from her walk along the shingle and asked, knowing quite certainly that she wanted to stay here, about the possibility of work. The woman behind the counter and the woman polishing the tables had stood, looking at her, looking at one another. Looking.

'There's Desmond's,' one said at last, 'Miss Desmond has been wanting.'

And so it came about.

The shop was the only double-fronted one, on the south side of the street; there were blinds to be drawn down on many afternoons, against the sun, but the shop itself was set back, dark and cool within.

It was the orderliness and the pattern of it that so pleased her, the way things were arranged. The materials were on rolls laid beside one another in order of type, of weight, of colour, patterned, plaid, plain, linings and outers, the silks and cottons in glass-fronted drawers that rattled as they were pulled, the balls of wool fitted into triangular spaces. Below the counters were the buttons, the pins, the needles, the fasteners and hooks, and those drawers were lifted up and set on top of the counter for their contents to be displayed. On the other side of the shop, the drawers contained gloves, collars and cuffs, belts, tray cloths, and, in the cardboard boxes discreetly racked beneath them, under-wear. Further back, in an ante-room, were the furs and the millinery, with which only Miss Desmond herself had to do.

'You have a good sense of colour,' Miss Desmond said, after only a single day, and then, 'You have a tidy mind.'

There were Miss Desmond and Miss Lea, one tall, one very short, both thin, spare, colourless, immaculate, deferential to customers, and yet retaining a pride and a dignity which was pleasing to Flora. She loved the place and her work there from the moment she began and might have been there forever and the old life lived by another person whose memory she had by chance inherited. But she did not look back. She had decided something, and quietly closed the door.

She arrived at the shop at five minutes to nine and left at five past six. They closed for lunch between one and two fifteen.

Sometimes during the day she would look out of the long windows on to the triangle of sky and see a gull sail and wheel around and sometimes, opening the door for a customer, she caught, behind the sounds of the street, beyond the to-ings and fro-ings and everyday life of it, the smell or boom of the sea, and was happy.

'We knew Miss Judaker,' Miss Desmond had said. 'You would scarcely have been happy there.'

The house had been pointed out to her, red brick, heavy, ugly, on the hill past the church.

They asked no impertinent questions. She suited them. They told her little about themselves. (At six fifteen, Miss Lea caught the bus to a village four miles inland and her infirm mother. Miss Desmond walked along the high street and turned left and out of sight, to a narrow, tall house pressed between two much larger ones, in a thin dark street.)

They were the only store of its kind, and had a reputation – people travelled miles to them, orders were despatched. There was a boy, Lennie Cheat, who worked in the back room, packing, and taught Flora how to tie the string in a little handle around a brown paper parcel.

After a month she felt that she had been here forever, and lived in her dim room in the hotel, and walked over the shingle and down to the edge of the water, and took down the heavy fabrics, the silks and the cottons and the tweeds, and unrolled them skilfully across the counter just so far, and slit them with the points of sharp shears, and re-arranged the reels of thread in exact order in the shallow drawers. Recognising her worth, Miss Desmond improved her starting wage within three months, so that she could afford to rent the tiny cottage and believed that she would indeed live here forever. For in this life she felt safe; things were ordered, within her control and predictable. Her ambitions had left her. It seemed she had no need, now, for the wild dreams and hopes, for the longings that the paintings had stirred in her; she was wary of friendships or involvements, anything at all outside the boundaries of the ordinary day. For a long time she did not even take the bus out into the countryside around the town to discover what it might be like there. Sometimes, visiting the lending library for books, she looked at the little museum attached to the reading room, with its relics from ships and fossils

205

and shells, stones and preserved sea-creatures and dark, varnished pictures of terrible sea-wrecks and bearded mariners. The
wood-panelled room with its high schoolroom windows and
wooden floor, its oak tables and chairs and the cupola up to
which she could look to see the sky above, reminded her just
sufficiently of the Rotunda Gallery to comfort her in the
knowledge that, should she need it, the past was still there, still in
place.

There were glass cases containing papers and charts and maps,
complicated weather instruments and tide tables, and she learned
from them slowly, as if she were learning a foreign language and
came gradually to love it. No one troubled her there. Only from
time to time some old man came in to read a newspaper, or
simply to sit, and peer at her oddly.

Summer went, and autumn, in soft golden light off the sea, before
winter came raging in with storms and gales. The gulls were
tossed about the sky like paper scraps and the cold air and spray
lashed her skin, the booming of the wind and the sea at night
were terrifying. The shop smelled of the oil stove, as well as of its
silks and tweeds and wool and threads.

In November, the telegram came from Olga, about her mother's
stroke.

She would travel, Miss Desmond gave her leave at once, she
was to stay until matters were resolved one way or another. She
dreaded it. The thought of the journey back into the past and her
childhood, the old life, froze her heart. But before she could even
set out the second telegram came. Without opening it, she knew,
and knew that she should weep, feel grief, pain, regret, shock, but
she could not, only relief. She must still go but the journey would
not be terrible now, and she would be free to return at once,
without ties or duties.

She left wearily on the first morning train and the countryside
was scoured and raw and colourless, with a thin, mean, bitter rain
that stung her as she waited on the platform beneath the
scalloped shelter of the roof, where the sparrows had once
squabbled in the warm dust.

206

Two

When the telegram came, she had known without opening it that May Hennessy was either dying or dead but as she held it in her hand her first thought was that she had kept the shame to herself – for that she worked behind the counter of a draper's shop would have been shame to her mother, who had believed even the position of private governess to be a humiliation. But a tutor, the teacher of a child, although still a domestic servant in her eyes, was one of a superior kind. There was no superiority that could be claimed for any form of shop work.

But she had never known. The few letters Flora wrote to her had been at first full of careful lies about Miss Judaker and the position she held as her companion, and later, merely evasive. She had wanted to protect her mother from the truth, protect the last of her dignity and her sense of their standing and importance, perhaps out of guilt, because she was so distant from her, and had gone her own chosen way so wilfully, without any regret or a single glance backwards.

As she arrived the rain greeted her, the old familiar, sodden, billowing clouds and wind, the waterlogged fields, the dull, poor, dark little villages, their roofs shining with rain. Her childhood had been lived under these skies, in this greyness, this rain.

To return was terrible because she so disliked her home, but more, because of her dread, dread at what she would find, and at the memories which would rise up within her, dread at being trapped and sucked back into the confinement and narrowness of the old life.

There was nothing for her here. There had never been anything. She knew it, riding on the bus out of town and down the endless, dull country road. Only her past awaited her and she was done with that and wanted none of it. (But in her dreams the previous night she had walked down Lord's Parade and gazed and gazed in joy into the glittering shop windows, until she saw that out of the window of every one she herself gazed back.)

She walked into the dark, damp-smelling, frowsty back parlour of the house.

'I'll go up,' she said to Olga, who was so much older, was adult now, and yet still the spoilt-faced, ringleted child to her. 'When I've had tea. If there's tea?'

'Yes. Oh, of course there is tea. There's anything you want.'

'Upstairs?'

'Oh, no. No, she's not here. Not upstairs. She's at Flynn's, the undertaker, you know? And later this evening to the church. The body rests all night in the church, you know. It's usual. She went back to it all you see, Flora, did you not know? Did she not tell you? She was very religious these last years. It was all she'd left to her.'

For you left too, Flora thought, looking at her sister, you could not bear to stay here any more than I.

The kitchen was cold and smelled fungoid, of damp wooden sills and draining board and stale food. Beyond the window the road, the flickering light of a single car. Then darkness again. Rain.

Olga had gone to the city to work in a dancing school. Soon now, she might try for America, she said. Why not? She had a pouting, old-young face, the same bland eyes, the same willingness to sing and dance and perform her way through life and into favour.

'Should you want to go down later? To Flynn's?'

'Yes.' Though she did not wish it.

208

'Yes, I said so. I asked Macey's car to come for us at seven o'clock.'

'Yes.'

At the window of her old room she stood and stared at the darkness and was cold and the house seemed to put out tendrils that wound around her and suckers that clung to her, threatened to absorb her and drain her new life from her, and succeeded for a while, so that she could not remember it, could not picture the sea, the cottage, the inside of the shop, but instead, only had before her a picture of the garden of the house called Carbery, on the day they buried the boy Hugh. Her new life had ceased to exist, then, the place was not there, or else, worse, it was there but had no knowledge of her, and she did not belong there and could not reach it.

Olga came to the door. She wore the short jacket with the beaver collar. Flora felt awkward, foolish, beside her. Younger.

'Macey's is here.' Olga's lipstick was dark and thick as blood.

But she took Flora's arm out of the front door and down the path and held it even in the taxi on the dark journey to Flynn's.

The undertaker's had frosted windows, lettered in gold like a saloon bar, and leather benches in a cold front parlour, and the whey-faced, ingratiating Mr Flynn. A terrible place, it seemed to her.

Only the sight of May Hennessy was not terrible at all.

'She is young,' Flora said, and felt her eyes swim. 'She is ... '

Not soured, puckered, yellowed, shrivelled, as she had looked in life, not disappointed and thin, with all the life and hope and pleasure, such as there had ever been, gone out of her. Not old and stained and lonely, as she had become. Not a dead-looking thing. Seeing her now, Flora saw death and that it was nothing but a healing and a great mercy. She was young, her brow smooth as a girl's, her hair brushed freshly back from her face. Then, guilt and remorse and shame drained from her, for whatever had gone before, for all was resolved.

They stood for a long time, side by side, and she smelled the sweet sickly smell of Olga's perfume mingling with the heavy, perfumed smell of death, and reached suddenly for her sister's hand and pressed it to her. Then, they went out together, over the polished linoleum floor, out of the polished parlour, into the evening rain and, on an impulse, she directed Macey's taxi not back to the house but on into the town, to Brom's Hotel. They drank gin, and then ate in the dining room, a good meal, mussels and lamb chops, and had wine, and for the first time in their lives, it seemed, were friends, and strangely close, though of her new life, as of so much that belonged only to her own past, Flora did not talk, for those things were buried and private to her and never to be shared. She let Olga talk, laugh, tell, confide, for Olga had no inner life, and nothing hidden about her at all. So that, in the warmth of the soft red-shaded lamp that was set on their table, and of the food, and the wine they had drunk, Flora looked into her sister's bright, open face, and envied her.

The house was sold and the contents easily, quickly disposed of. What little money would come from it they were to share. Flora felt no flicker of affection for it all, nothing but relief and freedom, after the clearing up, after the bleak funeral. They worked together but spoke little, the brief time of closeness over, as they accepted, though they felt the effects of it still and so were gentle and friendly towards one another. For moments on end, Flora would stop still to look at her sister, watch her, study her, as though this time between them had to be learned like a lesson and stored away in memory, to be fed off for the rest of her life – as indeed was the truth. She will succeed, Flora thought, she will blossom, and her energy and openness will be rewarded, she will attract love and friendship and success and the generosity of others. She will win.

The thought pleased her, not for her own sake, nor even for Olga's, but for May Hennessy's, as some sort of a recompense.

Three

She had returned expecting to be content. And she was, content with the shop and her work there, the pleasing daily routine, the calm and orderliness, content with the sky, the sea, the neatness of the houses, her own cottage, her walks beside the sea, morning and evening.

Yet in walking, a week after her return, she knew suddenly, in a moment of absolute revelation, that content was not enough; and knowing it, remembered Olga, vibrant, confident, easy with life, and eager for it. I am young, Flora said, whatever youth is I have it now. Content should not be enough. Must not be. What I must have is ... she looked about her, searching. Rapture. And recognising that, within minutes she recognised more, as if she had opened a flood-gate within herself, and swirling, seething waters had poured in, overwhelming her.

Her reaction to the betrayal of Tadeusz, which she also thought of now as in some part a betrayal of herself by her own feelings and impulses, had been to close those gates, to drop down a portcullis against all feeling, all life, anything from the world outside which might disturb her. She had believed in Tadeusz and her responses to him, surrendered to them, loved, hoped, and given herself up to that hope, of the new life to which she believed he would take her. She had only allowed her defences to be lowered once before in such a way, in her love for the boy Hugh. Twice, she had been dealt the worst of all blows.

She had not allowed herself to wonder about Tadeusz's betrayal, to speculate as to its possible cause or whose fault it might be – if indeed there was fault and not another terrible accident. She had frozen, some time during that night following his absence, frozen all feeling, all reaction, all thought, and only acted, calmly, coldly, decisively, to distance herself from him and what he had done, and from all memory of it.

But her mother's death and the sight of her body, the visit to the dismal house and the disposal of their old life, above all, Olga, had thawed her, and she felt the upsurge of a warmth and a confused return of feeling.

She sat on a breakwater in the weak sunlight.

She was content. That was sure. That would not change. She loved this small strange town full of unknown people, and the glory of this setting, day after day. She would not leave it, partly just because of the content, but more because she saw that she must not run away again, as she had run before; from where she had run had always been clear – but to what? She had run here, and this must suffice.

Except that she felt the lack of something which she had seen for the first time in her younger sister, a vibrancy, an urgency, a carelessness, an openness to feeling. She lacked Olga's courage for life, she thought now. And, thinking it, turned her face instinctively to the sun. But it did not warm her.

She would not run again. She must make her life, embrace everything it might offer her, out of what she found to hand. It was only that she did not yet know how. But having been granted this revelation, she did not doubt that she would succeed, knew, quite surely, that something, some way, some solution, lay ahead, and that she would reach it and recognise it.

Then she was able to turn and look back, without trembling, at Henrjyk Tadeusz, and, for the first time, his face came clearly to mind and she looked into it. There had been no change. She had loved him and trusted in him without reservation, and she did so still.

The memory of her time with him was painful, the memory of his betrayal infinitely worse. Above all, she was bewildered. Yet his absence and the suddenness of the change, from hope to despair, were like a death. Their effect upon her was the same as if he had indeed died, as the boy Hugh died, so much so that she wondered if he were indeed dead and she knew it in some subliminal way not open to reason or explanation. She must deal with what had happened, then, in the same way as she must with a death. She had been shocked, and angry in its aftermath, and had acted precipitately, as was her way. But she had not grieved or mourned the loss of love and of hope, nor the absence of his person. She did so now, crystallising the grief into moments of pure sorrow as hard and clear as drops of resin wept from the bark of a tree. Her tears were inner tears and did not moisten her eyes or her face. They were all the more bitterly wrung from her for that. She would not love in such a way, with such grave openness and trust again, or in such commitment. So she resolved. It did not occur to her that a repetition of such feeling were possible in any one human lifetime. The brief, sharp business of mourning and the acknowledgment of it, was gone through, and followed by forgiveness, though she was unsure what she must forgive. Later, she realised that, with her grief and forgiveness, went a leavetaking.

The process cleansed her, so that in the shop for the rest of the day she felt as if she were somehow beginning her life again, and that another attachment to her past, her old self, had been broken.

She thought of Olga, and when she had a short, bright letter from her, was surprised at the pleasure she felt, and replied at once, in the same open, free tone, revealing both everything and nothing at all. She did not want to see her sister, would never deliberately invite her here, and yet if she had appeared that day might have welcomed her with genuine pleasure and fondness, and without resentment.

But Olga did not visit, nor write again for many months, and so she, like May Hennessy, the old house at Dorne, the rest of her old life and those who had peopled it, receded from her, joining Miss Pinkney, the fat Belgian sisters she had once taught, Leila Watson, Tadeusz even, in some untouchable, distant and strangely perfect place. Only the boy Hugh seemed closer to her, and more real, the boy Hugh and the white picture in the Rotunda Gallery of the woman before the open window.

Thinking of the picture, she began to visit the small library to look for books on art and, then, finding little of interest, to cycle inland or take the bus into the next town.

The town itself was hateful to her, dull, dirty, lying low on either side of a flat river plain with brick chimneys at its heart, and she fled from it with her books, to ride the long straight road towards the sea with joy in her heart at the first thin silver line of it ahead. But the books did not satisfy her as they had once done, and even the beauty of the paintings seemed dead, cold and separate on the pages, the life at their heart sealed up and unreachable, a life that had once been lived but was far remote and over. She respected the pictures dutifully, but they did not excite her; she would have had only formal dead words in which to write of them now.

She took greater pleasure from the arrangement of folds in silk or damask or the drape of muslin on a stand, the pattern of colours, scarlet to shell pink, pale sky to indigo, mushroom to earth and chestnut brown on the reels of thread. The harmony and quiet order of the shop delighted her in the way the paintings had once done, the symmetry and order and formality of its patterns satisfied, so that at times she caught herself standing at the counter or in the doorway and looking back at it as if it in itself were a picture, art not life.

But still she was restless, still she lacked. This is satisfaction, she said, this is contentment, this is evenness and quiet and inner prosperity. This. This is not enough. There was a hollow at the heart of things. It was in part an isolation, her own self-chosen separateness, but also an urge to be as unidentifiable, unnoticed and unremarkable as a single stone on the shingle beach, a mere fragment of the ordinary world – for she thought that she had never truly been that, never known how. But even more, what she felt was an emptiness, a desire for completion, a need for a focus to the sense of urgency within herself.

*

Seven months were to pass, months in which she glided over the surface of things, not unhappy, not restless, not in any way distraught, months in which she knew herself to be simply waiting, though for what she did not know. Seven months, before it came to her.

Four

For the rest of her life, she always said, 'What was to happen, did,' and believed that the pattern had been laid out, and she had only to follow it. It was one with her belief in the angel or the star, this conviction that she had somehow only to fulfil her destiny. The Bible she found crammed with prophecies fulfilled. She did not for a moment inflate her own importance, or believe that she was singled out, merely that what was to happen would.

Did.

It was so clear and straightforward she might have laughed at it, had it not seemed such a solemn, even a momentous business, as did the whole of life to her; she had sometimes been light-hearted and joyous, but had never understood frivolity. Even laughter was to be taken seriously.

It was to happen.

Did.

She walked back into Desmond's shop after her lunch, to find a man sitting on the chair kept for customers, an open suitcase beside him on the counter. Miss Desmond had looked up at her.

'Flora.'

Flora had stopped. The hand, up to unbutton her coat, had frozen near her collar.

'This is Mr Molloy, Mr Tigh's successor, from Farradew's. I am going over the order with him myself today.'

216

He had half-stood. He was very thin, with the whitest skin she had ever seen on a man, but shadowed on his lower cheeks and jaw by a grape-ish blueness where a beard might break through. His hair was a rich, reddened brown, thick as a woman's hair at the neck, luxuriant, springing, shocking hair. And seeing him, seeing the white skin, the grape-blue shadow, the rich hair, Flora had not seen some young man, a Mr Molloy, the new traveller from Farradew's, Silks, Haberdashery, Drapery, with whom she had no business to do. She had seen, had heard herself say with an inner conviction, 'Then this is the man I am to marry.' For she had also seen at once the way he had looked at her, coming through the door of the shop. 'This must do, then. What is to happen will.'

After Henrjyk Tadeusz, there would be no more love, no possibility of giving herself up, whole and entire, past and present and future, to anyone or to a new life. There would simply be a man to marry, to conclude some sort of unfinished business and end a time of waiting. More than this, she did not know, simply because more was not yet vouchsafed to her. But that it would be she was in no doubt.

She was obliged to turn away quickly, going into the lobby and pulling the curtain to conceal the fearful trembling of her hands as she finished unbuttoning her coat.

Five

Why did she marry? Why had the idea that she must do so come to her with such urgency?

Because of what came next, as it always would. Because of the boy Hugh.

She did not love Lawrence Molloy, because love of a man in that way was not an option for her now, she had closed herself to it, after Tadeusz. But she needed Molloy. She was grown tired of her own isolation. She thought that she wanted to swim in the stream of ordinary life, wanted what others had, though she did not need status, or respectability, concepts she neither acknowledged nor understood.

But even more, she felt herself, quite simply, to be in the grip of her fate. She would marry Lawrence Molloy, because the moment she had seen him, she had known that it would be so, and because of what would follow. Did.

That day, she had come out of the lobby after hanging up her coat, and crosssed the shop, going behind him to the window, where she was in the middle of changing the display of scarves and gloves, and as she had passed him, he had stood again and moved his chair out of her way, though it was scarcely in her way. She had murmured her thanks.

She liked dressing the window, arranging, then standing back, re-arranging before going outside to judge the effect until she was satisfied, as she did so remembering those windows endlessly passed and viewed and admired on the Saturday afternoons in Lord's Parade. She liked to create a tableau, or a pattern, some slightly unusual effect that would draw the eye. Once, she had put a single pair of champagne-coloured kid gloves in the bare window, one glove pulled on to a display hand, the other on the floor beside it, and, for two days, Miss Desmond had allowed the window to remain, perhaps merely to please her, before giving in to her anxiety that it looked uninviting, bare.

Now, she was aware of Mr Molloy from Farradew's in the shop behind her, aware that he was prolonging his visit. When Miss Desmond called for a tray of tea he drank his slowly, deliberately, not watching her, but conscious of nothing else.

Flora left at four minutes past six. It was winter, already quite dark. He was waiting for her a few yards down the high street. He wore a hat on the luxuriant hair and raised it.

He was staying at The Ship Hotel, he said, perhaps she would take supper with him?

Closing the door of the cottage, she felt weak with shock that this was happening as she had known, planned even. Yet the plan was not hers, she was merely following one that had been pre-ordained, recognising the future as she had seen it ahead of her. Washing and changing carefully then, before going out to meet the young man, Lawrence Molloy, at The Ship Hotel, she felt both a sense of inevitability and of relief, and of panic, too, as if she were powerless in the face of what was to happen. Yet she was no more powerless than she had ever been, was willingly acquiescent, eager, even, for this new future. For the bad had already come about, a sequence of miseries, wrong turnings, accidents, mistakes and betrayals. What had she to fear?

She was neither vain nor artful. But she took care over her appearance.

He was thirty-one years old. He had suffered a nervous illness after leaving school and spent some time in a hospital. Now, more fortunate than many, he had this job, which gave him a salary

219

and freedom, an interest. He liked it, he said, for the things he sold as much as for any of those he met, loved as she did the colours and patterns of the materials and the silken threads.

'Yes,' Flora had cried in recognition. 'Oh yes!' It seemed very important, this sharing, a joke between them at once, and a secret too, for whoever else would understand?

'And the places,' he had said, pouring out a tumbler of water for her slowly from the carafe on the table between them. 'I like the different places I go to. More than the people. I've often been troubled by people.'

'Yes.'

'Well, until now.'

Flora had looked up at once, directly into his face.

'Now, I feel the need to have a settled place to come back to.'

He had come back, appearing in the shop four days later, and again the following week. He invited her to drive with him on that Saturday to Brodie Veagh Castle, thirty miles away.

They had climbed a hundred and seventy stairs, to the top of the tower, counting as they went, and when they came out on to the parapet it was like being above the clouds. He had pointed out the distant silver rim where the sea met the sky. There was a lightness, an airiness and a softness about everything above the heavy grey stone tower.

'We should be married,' Lawrence Molloy said, and it was quite plain, quite obvious.

Flora had turned away from him, to look all around. What was to happen would, then. Had.

Yet she recognised a split second in which she had a free choice and could have turned away and refused her fate. There was no obligation. Only if she acquiesced and accepted would everything afterwards take an inevitable course. She knew herself to be in the second, the eternal now. It lasted forever, her whole lifetime, from birth to death.

'Yes,' she said gravely, turning away from the sky and the clouds and the distant silver line of the sea, towards Lawrence

220

Molloy, and the white of his skin and the ruddiness of his luxuriant hair set as they were against the stone behind him.

'Yes.'

The split second had been not so much a measurement of time as a place in which she had been standing, an open space like a chasm, between her past and her future.

'Yes.'

She stepped aside, and the space closed together, like the line of light beneath a closing door.

Six

It is April. There is no reason for any of them to think of Flora Hennessy, at one moment or another in the course of this day, scattered as they are and most of them unknown to one another.

But they do think of her, in passing, perhaps reminded by this or that, by chance, and their thoughts of her, however fleeting, are a link between them, although they do not know it, and their thoughts, if one is to be sentimental, form an invisible aura about her, of friendship, of kindness, of memory. Were she aware of it, as possibly she is, it will strengthen her.

April. But cold in London, icy cold, and the outlines of things sharply cut under a brittle sky, the pavement scoured and whitened by a bitter wind.

In his dark, important rooms, among the heavy pictures, the draped blinds, the leather-bound volumes, the magazine proprietor, lifting his tea-cup to his lips, thinks of her, her face comes to him, he is reminded perhaps by this act of lifting the tea-cup, of a day, any day, when she sat before him here. He sees her pale face, gravely beautiful, in the dim room.

If she were to know his thoughts she might be surprised, encouraged, flattered. (Or else no longer interested.) For he remembers her young, fresh, untutored, unspoilt talent, her eye, her vision, her clarity of response, her earnest words, and with regret, as he drinks his tea, as the pigeons coo fatly on the ledge outside the window.

Flora Hennessy, he remembers, and stops as if to look at her, calm, proud, pale, young. Unknowable. A puzzle to him.

Flora Hennessy. And wonders, before he is interrupted by a knock, disturbed by business, pressed to make some decision or other. And so forgets. Though her presence in his room still lingers. And in his mind.

In another place by the sea, another tall, lodging house, grey and gaunt as an old stick of a woman, Miss Marchesa, overseeing some domestic activity, simply looking up as a door closes, and for no reason at all, recalls Flora Hennessy (but whose last name she does not, in fact, quite remember). The girl in the corner of the dining room, eating alone, aloof, proud, strange. Not entirely welcome. Disturbing. Something happened. Some illness? Something untoward.

Miss Marchesa frowns, turning back to chastise, for a job carelessly done, in this lodging house which is much the same as the London house, except that there are no working women, no typists running water in all the basins of the house at seven in the morning, and again every evening at seven. Instead there are old women, faded, forgetful, trembling women, who go nowhere, but stare into space, or sometimes, unseeingly, out at the grey, heaving sea, all day, all day.

The soft closing of a baize door has brought Flora Hennessy to mind. It is April. She scarcely pays the memory any attention, for it is of no significance to her in her new lodging house, her new life, any more than it was in the old. (Though in feverish dreams much later, the lodging house and her own meals, taken alone at the dismal corner table, near to the swinging kitchen door, the sound of the water, running at seven in a dozen washbasins, will come back to Flora, swirling and receding, mingling with the pursed lips of the respectable Miss Marchesa.)

How often do such thoughts of another person coincide, if it could be known? How often do they each recall Flora Hennessy, her face, her manner, her graveness, her strange pride, reminded fleetingly by this or that?

But on this day in April there is nothing at all unusual in the parents of the boy Hugh thinking of her, at the house called Carbery, for she is linked, inextricably, it seems, with their last memories of him, she is forever about the house, as he is, in a doorway, hurrying behind him down the stairs, running across the lawn towards the silver sea. She and the boy are always laughing, their laughter rings silently through the silent house. His room and the schoolroom are as they were, exactly as they were, on the day of his death. (Though Flora's room is bare, dust-sheeted, closed. There are in any case far too many rooms in this house, hers will never be needed.) In the schoolroom are the exercise books in which Flora has written, the timetable of lessons on the wall. And so she is always here with them, with him, and will never leave. Her face, her voice, her laughter, the sight of her in the straw hat, sitting with him under the cedar tree, their books spread about them, is as clear as any of the pictures on the walls. On this day in April, when it is unusually cold, the sea glazed and still, as if it were varnished on to board, on this day, waking they think of her, because their first thought, separately and unspoken, is the same, is their dead boy, he bright-faced, solemn, and Flora Hennessy, pale and grave. But at once, crowding out the thought, the picture that follows in their minds is of another child, not yet born. They are uncertain about it, guilty even, trying to keep the picture of the boy, and that of Flora, most vividly in mind. For if they had loved him with such passion, they had come to love her, too, a little for herself, most because of her love for him, and the fact that he had loved her, so fully and freely and devotedly in return.

And so it is that Flora walks invisibly before them, smiling through the house, with its view beyond the tall windows and the green lawns, of the silver sea under the thin cold April sun.

In Surrey the sun is cold, but less so, for it is never truly cold here in this sheltered village tucked beneath the Downs, always sheltered, from the worst of any wind or winter. There is a

224

greenness over everything here, a green lichen veiling every churchyard stone and creeping over every wall, a leafiness and a softness of green meadow and ferny banks unfolding to the little brook. But still, pale smoke coils up out of a dozen cottage chimneys where fires are lit, stoves warm kitchens and parlours. As with the parents of the boy Hugh, so with Leila Watson, no day ever passes in which she does not think of Flora, and with sadness and a sense of loss (for she has had no letter, no word, has written but her envelope was returned to her, after months, as addressee unknown).

Her small, square house is neat and warm and comfortable; it shelters her. It is next to that of her late husband's sister and across the green from that of his mother and along the lane from that of his second sister, she is in the heart of an enclosing, loving, sheltering family and will never lack for love or company or concern. They have not altogether understood her absence from them in London, yet saw that somehow it was necessary to her, and, besides, it does not matter at all now, that time is a dream and quite forgotten, now that she is here with them again.

Flora, she wonders, opening her bedroom window and letting in the cold, sweet-smelling, green-smelling April air, shaking out her pillows, stroking the little black cat before it streaks thinly down the narrow stairs.

The kitchen smells of apples and woodsmoke and the sun comes in through the green tracery of plants in pots on the ledge. Leila Watson will grow old here. She is already, somehow, grown into the old woman she will one day become, that person is curled, dormant within her, like a flower within a bulb, waiting to emerge at the appropriate time. Her house is the house of a neat, contented old woman, aunt, great-aunt, curiously sexless.

Flora. She wonders what she might do, how to obtain the forgiveness she vaguely still feels that she needs, how to re-make their old friendship. For her family please and comfort and shelter her, but somehow are not enough.

Flora. And suddenly a memory of walking with her, arm in arm, and laughing, through the streets of London, on the way back from some cool, high gallery to the flat at the top of the

225

Bloomsbury house, returns, achingly to her, and she longs to be there, among the buses and hurrying footsteps, under the street lamps, close to the cooing pigeons on the ledge.

Flora, whom she could not protect, or save from the ultimate cruelty of love. (Though Leila Watson has never been angry with the memory of Henrjyk Tadeusz, believing him to have been quite helpless and blameless, to have been simply ordered abruptly elsewhere by his regiment, by doctors, by his own family, or else to have had some appalling accident – for she understands about accidents, after the shocking death of her husband, expects, indeed, that they will happen, for years to come she assumes that everyone she knows will die some sudden and terrible and quite unforeseen death.)

Flora.

But after all, she thinks, turning to greet one of her late husband's nieces who has come running in, after all, I never understood her. Never really knew.

April cannot come and go quickly enough for Olga Hennessy, nor May either, for on the first of June she is to sail to America, where she will dance in a musical comedy, and have success, sufficient to be asked to dance again and again, until she leaves the line for a leading part, small enough – but enough to be noted all the same. For now, she is resting and practising and teaching dancing to small girls and seeing her friends in the town, where she is happy, pretty and happy, but not conceited, not thoughtless.

She thinks of her sister, not all the time, not every day, but often enough and with affection; but above all, with bewilderment and a sort of awe. 'Florence is deep,' their mother had said, 'Florence is clever. Wilful. But clever. People will hear of her. One day people will talk of her. You should respect your sister. You should look up to her.' Though her tone had always been puzzled. And Flora has puzzled Olga almost from the beginning, there has always seemed to her an aura about her, like a freezing zone through which she might never penetrate. But she has loved her in spite of it, and rather more as she has grown up – which she did very early, without the usual struggles and pain; she loves

226

Flora because she senses a fragility within the frozen zone, a lack of human knowledge and strength, which will lead, must lead, to her ultimate unhappiness. She would like to protect her, for she herself is at ease with and in the world, has had the measure of it from birth; the world will never catch her unawares. But they will not coincide, these sisters, the paths they take will never converge, because they are so unlike, as is so often the way.

She prays for her (for Olga is very devout and that is never to change), though in general terms, uncertain what her sister's real needs might be, prays regularly, and remembers from time to time, as on this day in April, for no particular reason, and is glad of the thought, and turns warmly towards it, gives it her time and her full attention, as the sunlight slices a blade through the shadow at the corner of the building. Flora's picture and presence fill her head.

And then there are the dead, so many dead, too many for one who is, after all, very young. Perhaps these dead too call her to mind on this day – if there are days, for the dead.

John Joseph Hennessy. The boy Hugh. Miss Pinkney. The woman who brought her to this place, the Miss Judaker she never met. The dead crowd round her and into her consciousness, as she may already be in theirs.

227

Seven

On that day, then, Flora Hennessy was married to Lawrence Molloy, so that perhaps the thoughts of the others clustered about her by some telepathy, attracted by the simple force of her emotion.

The emotion, below a calm and measured happiness, was fear, fear of her own power, that things had fallen out in just this way, as she had foreseen and planned. She was afraid of how straightforwardly and swiftly it had come about.

They had eaten a plain supper warily together on that first evening after their meeting, in the dining room of The Ship Hotel, and afterwards he had walked with her to her cottage, watched her go inside, and then returned to his lodging.

'This is the man I am to marry,' Flora had thought every so often, and looked up with surprise at him, sitting opposite to her, carefully taking the skin off his fish, carefully cleaning the butter from his knife on a roll of bread, carefully stirring the sugar into his coffee.

'This is the man I am to marry.'

It was as though she had been making her way for years through a maze of confusing paths up to a particular door and here the door was now before her, the door of the house she must enter.

He was courteous to her and careful in his manner. He was, she saw immediately, a nondescript man, dull even, with only a remarkable appearance that attracted and was unusual. He said little of interest, his horizons did not extend far. After his illness he had retreated into this found safety and would not venture beyond it again. Nevertheless, she was to marry him. He would give her what she needed. What was to happen, would.

Did. For he had looked at her, too, as she had come through the door of Miss Desmond's shop, and seen what he needed there, and recognised the acknowledgment in her eyes, the corresponding need, interest. What more should there be? He was looking to marry, needing to feel safe, but saw at once that she was extraordinary, and that in marrying her he would not marry in any way that he might have anticipated. She had a grave calm which reassured him, and an intelligence that alarmed, an air of foreignness; he had been in awe of her at once. She was younger than he was and yet understood things he did not, had seen and known far more, yet she had no flirtatiousness about her, no cleverness. She had a stillness, and composure, a self-containment, that drew him.

They were not especially well matched, yet no worse matched than many. Perhaps his expectations were greater, his hopes more vibrant. Flora had only the clear assurance of following fate. This was to happen. Did.

And the wedding on that particular brittle, brilliant day in April had a frivolity and a dancing sort of happiness about it, after all, though only a few came. The fear had all been in advance of things, Flora thought, the trepidation at having taken this step, hesitation at the way she must go. Yet she had walked alone into a new life often enough before now, her inner strength was not in doubt. Things might go well. She felt relieved to be with Lawrence Molloy, who was so easily, so readily known, in whom there were no depths or dangerous waters.

She did not love him. She had loved Henrjyk Tadeusz. Such love was not repeatable. But the promises she made now to Molloy were truly made and meant, there were no reservations in her heart (save the essential one, always, which was the reservation of herself).

Lawrence Molloy was in awe of her still, awed by her beauty, and her assurance, by her seriousness, and he sensed the reservation of herself, the aura through which he could never break, and was accepting.

And so they began well together and happily enough, neither having too great an expectation of marriage or of one another, things settled, things ran along quite easily. Things would do.

Eight

He said, 'I brought them for you,' and opened one of the leather sample cases and began to pull out ribbons, broad bands and reels of silk, satin, grosgrain, taffeta and unroll them anyhow on the table top before her; scarlet, emerald, indigo, gold, cerise, lemon, ink blue, cream, white spilled out and lay heaped in the light of the lamp. 'You've such a liking for them.'

She reached out and touched her finger to the soft silken colours.

It was a kindness of a sort he had not shown – though he was never harsh nor dismissive of her – for she thought that she missed her life at Desmond's as much for this as for anything, the colours, the patterns and the brightness spilling out in front of her, and by bringing the samples for her, oddments he had collected and kept back, he revealed an understanding of how she felt that she had come not to expect. His thoughtfulness moved her.

She kept the ribbons beside her and laid her hand on them or slipped them through her fingers now and then.

He left again very early the next morning.

It was November, and scarcely light all day, the sky packed and dense with cloud, lowering over the sullen sea. At night the wind raced up the beach dragging a furious tide in its wake. Flora lay in bed for hours in the room facing the sea, silent, listening to the

231

wind, and feeling the weight of the child beneath her hands as they rested upon it. The days were long and dark and silent and she saw no one. The coming child anchored her and filled her with uncertainty and dread.

The year burrowed deep into winter and blackness and went out in storms and boiling, terrifying seas. She felt as if she were islanded in the midst of them as the wind and water hurled themselves towards her. The child was restless. Who are you? She asked the question aloud, but could answer neither for it nor for herself now.

The first year of her marriage had not been unhappy. The spring and summer had seemed long, even, calm, quiet. When he was home he had sometimes walked on the beach with her, or else they had gone out in his car to the countryside, to the villages that lay on the watery flat lands and, once, back to Brodie Veagh Castle, with a picnic which they had eaten on the grassy mounds below the rearing stone walls, and thrown their crumbs to a little dog.

He was absorbed in his own thoughts, troubled sometimes, his face shadowed by past confusions, past distress. He left her to her own thoughts and she saw that occasionally he looked at her as if she were a stranger, as indeed perhaps she was. But there was a large enough part of their life in which they were companionable together to suit them. He was restless, never settled for long. He travelled miles. He needed his own company, set his own routes and calls, knew a great many people by name and face and place in the order book, knew their choices, their special dislikes, the taste of their customers. Otherwise, knew them not at all, as to them he was courteous enough, and amiable and also quite unknown.

He had not returned to his home town for years. In their rejection of their roots and their need to be free and separate, they were alike.

Flora had not considered the question of love again. Now, sitting at the window watching the mutinous face of the sea, she understood that this was not only because of Tadeusz. For she sensed that a different and infinitely greater love was to come.

*

He had seemed startled by the idea of a child, and went away at once, and for longer than usual. She scarcely noticed his absence, for it seemed that there could be no absence that mattered to her now, that her present and future were full.

She felt well but slow, and suspended in a twilight and dream-like state, waiting, not speculating or looking ahead, trusting. The old sense of following her destiny never left her. It seemed patterned in the sky and on the surface of the sea, and in the arrangement of the stones on the shingle beach. She had only to follow.

She had continued to work in the shop with Miss Desmond and Miss Lea only for a short time. It would not be suitable, Miss Desmond said, not seemly. Her place was not behind a shop counter now, nor in public sight.

She was saddened, and for some time afterwards both regretful and rebellious, and unsettled, walking the streets and the beach four or five times each day, uncertain of things all over again. She did not know this child. Her own body was suddenly strange to her and grew each day more so, seeming to belong to her no longer but wholly to this other.

But as the weeks passed she settled into herself again and was happy, rooted and content to mark time, to wait.

She began to draw at that time. By chance, sitting in the window one morning she had seen a gull on the breakwater, and began to make pencil strokes of the pattern of its wing feathers in the margin of her book. That afternoon she bought paper and drew the pattern made by the shingle. She saw that what she drew was something produced as if by an earnest, meticulous schoolchild. Her critical eye did not fail her. But the activity was satisfying to her, the sound of her pencil scratching softly over the surface of the paper induced pleasure. After that, she drew every day, patterns and shapes in intricate, detailed cross-hatching, and her pleasure increased, and with it a small measure of skill. She saw the world differently, saw pattern everywhere, on the skin of

233

the sea, in the night sky, in clouds. After a time, it was the clouds that claimed her. Her pages were cloud-filled, looking at them and into them took her beyond herself, her condition, her past and whatever might be her future. She did not pull the curtains together, so that whenever she glanced up, whichever way she chanced to turn, she saw a portion of the sky framed there, some formation of clouds.

Her husband did not trouble her. He seemed wary of her, anxious to let her be. Flora saw no harm in the way things were. Lawrence Molloy went away, returned, seemed to find her presence a reassurance, but he was abstracted, concerned always with leavetaking, moving on, travelling about, as the constant change itself, it seemed, made a pattern on which he could rely. She understood that he had been rootless, unhappy and unanchored in his single life, needed to know simply that she was where she was.

Once she found him standing at the table going carefully through a sheaf of her drawings, examining each one minutely, frowning in concentration. Seeing her in the doorway he went on looking until the last sheet and then set them down and turned away and said nothing. That was the night on which he returned with the ribbons. But to introduce some colour into her patterns of stone and sea and cloud was beyond her. Instead she simply enjoyed the heaps of brightness for themselves, and took to pinning a different one to her sleeve or draping one across the corner of the mirror or over the cushions. To catch sight of them on coming into the room lifted her heart, yet always, after a few moments, she turned back to the paleness of the clouds beyond the windows.

December blew out in raging seas and great-bellied, blue-black, flailing skies. The new year came in with bitter cold, scouring her skin when she walked, though it was only along the paths now, she was no longer able to plough through the heavy shingle.

Looking at her, sitting beside the lamp, Molloy said, 'I'll not go tomorrow. It seems best,' and she was glad of it and, going up the stairs slowly that night, felt a spurt of fear.

She had written to her sister with news of the child and waited weeks for a reply, but that morning the letter had come, short, breathless, the words streaming out in excitement anyhow across the page. It was from America. Olga was dancing, acting, poised for popularity, acclaim, success, her good humour filled the letter. Reading it again after she had undressed, Flora wept suddenly for love of her sister, and also for a seemingly irrational dread for her, as well as for the past and their strange separate childhoods.

Beyond the window, the sky seemed oddly softened, muffled and heavy, the sea quite still. There were no stars. The moon was blanked out.

In the early hours of the morning she woke to a sense of absolute strangeness and an eerie light. The air was warmer.

She went to the window and watched the snow come tumbling from a vast, pale, quilt of sky, and the pains began as she stood there, bare-footed, shivering, transfixed.

Nine

And so it began, the rest of Flora's life.

The snow fell, on the day of his birth and for a week afterwards, so that it seemed they were both caught up in it and held, cocooned in this whiteness. Even the sea was quieted.

She had known that there would be delight in the child, sensed that with this she was to take a final step, to her arrival in a new world. But the reality she could never have anticipated.

Where such love as she knew came from she could not fathom. She lay in the high bed and the boy slept in the crib beside her, or else in the crook of her arm and, bathed in this bliss, needed no other. The room was brilliant with snow-filled light. She scarcely lifted her eyes from his features, her mind was crammed full of his every limb and lash, blotting out the past and all memory.

The sight of them together filled Lawrence Molloy with fear. His banishment was absolute so that he knew it would only be a short time before, her protection having been withdrawn, the demons would crowd in upon him again. He escaped to the world outside, driving through the snow-filled lanes as the voices began to whisper, goading him on. He must concentrate fiercely on his counting, trees, fence posts, mile posts, crows, to placate and silence them. Only sitting in the room of the cottage with her and their son on the edge of the charmed circle of blinding light was he at ease and for the time being held by their force for good.

236

There was no unkindness about her, simply an absence from him, her withdrawal as she was caught up and held fast in the radiance of the child. He looked on, bemused, awed, fearful, and did not intrude, but fetched her things she wanted, spoke little, respected her state of possession.

She wanted this time never to end, the snow never to melt, the year never to move on, the child to remain as bound up with her as this, coiled away from the world. She lay awake as he slept to hold to the time, to feel its every moment of passing, and prayed for him never to leave her.

He did not. In the town it was always remarked upon, and with disapproval, that never had there been such a mother and son, never any so close, so inseparable. Unhealthy they said, unnatural. She held herself aloof, uninterested in what was said or in those who said it, and kept him aloof also. The truth was that they were inexpressibly happy, that the joy they had in one another's company strengthened each day, that they were all in all to one another; and she saw nothing but good, it was as though her life had been a progress only towards this.

Her horizons had been closing in and her world had shrunk, but now, for all that she was in the same place, the same closed circle, all things seemed hers and all to be marvelled and wondered at, with him and through his eyes.

He was a quiet, steady child, alert and aware from birth, and yet, like her, quite contained. Everything interested him, everything he saw, learned, touched, tasted, fascinated him, he was eager for life, but if he felt any excitement or impulsiveness, restrained it. He was easy and even tempered, slept, ate, played, walked, talked with her or at the least in her company, scarcely cried or expressed impatience or frustration.

The bubble in which they were held during the days after his birth never burst, it sheltered them, sealing them off from the rest of life. Often, years afterwards, she was transported back to that time in dreams and recollections. In her last weeks the memory sustained her, as a balm to all pain, all distress. She forgot

237

nothing, every detail was hers, to return to freely and dwell upon. Closing her eyes, night or day, she was back in her bedroom overlooking the sea in the brilliant light, surrounded by the softly falling snow, and he beside her. Every hair on his head was numbered. It was in those first days, too, that at last she understood May Hennessy and, in understanding, forgave. With her son's birth she had crossed a one-way bridge and on the other side of it now was knowledge of the love and concern and anxiety her mother had had for her. There was nothing sentimental about her new-found knowledge. She had no longing for her mother, felt no further grief and scarcely ever spoke to her son about that time, that place; nor did she ever regret her own independence. Only now, in place of resentment and bitterness, there was healing and an understanding of the truth about the way things had been. If she had been haunted, the ghosts now had been laid to rest by his birth. If there were anxiety, guilt, fear, it was her husband who was at the heart of them, for she saw clearly that he was absorbed in some inner turmoil, withdrawn from her, preoccupied. He returned home less and less, and always without warning, but on seeing her, sitting with the child in her arms or sleeping close beside her, he seemed momentarily quieted. He would eat and talk a little and, always, he brought a gift for her pleasure, some scrap of colour, and brightness.

Once, he brought a silk-lined lidded basket in which she might keep every ribbon and piece of silk, and he felt that he had brought her a delight which was only his to give.

He continued to be nervous of the boy, and distant from him out of anxiety, as if, it seemed, he feared that he might damage him by his very presence and the proximity of the things that troubled him.

If Flora did not love him, had no love to spare for any other living thing, she was nevertheless intensely protective towards him, and always kind, perhaps out of a feeling of guilt (though no guilt attached to her, for in truth in marrying Lawrence Molloy she had granted him a reprieve, had held back the voices and the madness, so that he had known for the first time in his life an absence of fear, before the tide rose up again and came racing in to drown him).

Ten

The rest of her life, lived out in absolute love, absolute peace and pleasure with her son, might have been eternity, so slow, so crammed, so intense were the days, and yet it was the blinking of an eye, there, now, gone. Everything progressed, as it would, as life does, and all was orderly and nothing disturbed the even surface (save for her husband's distress and illness and final terror, lost to the voices and their punishments).

After his death, when Hugh was four years old, the final, never-ending battle was simply to survive, for there was no money, quite plainly no money at all. She faced that sitting alone one autumn night after the funeral, with the boy asleep in the room above. She must support them, and they must remain here, this was her final resting place, where all things had come together. She took pen and paper and made a list of work she might do and the list was only a few lines long. She would not go back to Miss Desmond's shop, even if a place were available, because she needed to be with the boy so much of the time, even after he began to attend school. There was no one she might teach, and any work she might once have found writing for journals of art she would have no confidence or authority to attempt now. She had been different then. For the rest, there might be housekeeping jobs, in private homes or at the hotels. Well, she must do those, anything at all to provide for him, she would have counted the stones on the shingle beach, if it had contributed to his welfare and growth and happiness.

Then, walking slowly with him one day past Desmond's, she saw a hat on a stand in the window, trimmed with braid, and at once, in her mind's eye, saw a better, the trim more elaborate and fine, the colours iridescent.

She returned home and made it, almost to her satisfaction, from an old plain straw of her own that was little worn, sitting over it until the early hours of the morning, the basket of coloured silks spilling out over the table, on to the floor, pinning, turning, cutting, folding, re-working, until what she had imagined was before her. Then, looking at the pillaged heap of ribbon, tumbled anyhow, she remembered the evening her husband had brought the first scraps of it home for her, saw him as he had been then, white-skinned, with the luxuriant red-brown hair, anxious to please her. He had passed through her life and scarcely belonged in it, scarcely made a mark and yet she owed him everything because she owed him her son, the brief marriage had been because of him, but she saw now that perhaps it had been for other reasons, too, that she had, for a short time, been able to hold back the tide of voices and give him a steadiness and an ordinary calm in this bright room, to which he had always returned for shelter and safety. She had not understood. The voices and the terrible shadows had been there from the beginning, disguised and concealed from her, but there none the less. They had claimed him; there had never been any possibility of his escape. They had crowded finally into his head, to overwhelm him and he could neither turn aside from nor silence them. In the end, she had been powerless to save him. But sitting before the silks and skeins of colour in the quiet of the night, she was touched by love for him, and a tenderness, more than at any time during their marriage or in his living presence, so that when she went upstairs to lie beside her sleeping son, looking at him she saw for the first time the image of his dead father imprinted on his features, and in the paleness of his skin and the red-brown hair, and was glad of it.

241

Eleven

A good name is rather to be chosen than great riches,
And loving favour rather than silver or gold.

Rain beaded the windows of the car, blurring his view of the
church. It was a dull church, the stone spire weather-darkened.
But Elizabeth found comfort there, had friends.

To every thing there is a season and a time to every purpose
under the heavens.

He waited at home and then here, reading. His mother had
read the Bible to him, the Psalms and from the Prayer Book. It
was all in her head, she had said, she read the words until she
knew them by heart and then turned them over in her mind, like
pebbles. Sometimes, coming upon a particular phrase, he heard
her voice so clearly that he turned towards her.

I will lift up mine eyes unto the hills
From whence cometh my help.

But now the doors of the church were opened and they were
running down the steps, rapping urgently on the window. Molloy
got out of the car and the wind took their voices from him,

242

scattering them, they were mouthing and he could not understand them, standing there in the gale and the pouring rain, but only followed them, as they directed, back into the church.

They had made her comfortable, lain her on a pew with her head on a prayer hassock wrapped in someone's coat, with another strange coat to cover her. Molloy knelt. The stones beneath him were cold as graves.

She could neither move nor speak. Only her eyes were open and looked into his, wide with fear. Her face was puckered oddly, her mouth twisted.

He put his hand over hers, as it lay on top of the stranger's coat. 'Elizabeth.'

But she made no response.

Most of them left, quickly, out of tact. But a few stayed, a little knot of them in the aisle a yard away.

'Elizabeth.'

Ahead of him, he saw the great candles guttering on the altar in the wind that blew in from the open door. The smell was pungent to his nostrils.

> Purge me with hyssop and I shall be clean.
> Wash me and I shall be whiter than snow.

There was nothing he could do for her here. He waited with his hand remaining on hers, and the gale battered at the high windows.

She would not live, they said, not this time (but he was one of them, after all, and knew, they did not need to speak to him of it).

He sat beside her in the dim cubicle.

'Elizabeth.' Perhaps she heard him say her own name over and over again. Perhaps she heard.

Perhaps, when he began to speak about the rest, she heard. For he told her everything, over the days and weeks, and as he told more, more was remembered, scenes, places, pictures, their talk, the smallest details crowded, pushing one another in their urgency, into his mind.

243

He described their house, took her from room to room, into the parlour with the lamp, and the front bedroom facing the sea, in which for years he had slept close beside his mother: as the sun rose it shone into their faces. The room in which she had pinned and stitched the hats, turning them slowly round in her hands against the light so that she could judge them precisely and he could admire. He remembered them now, when he closed his eyes they were before him and he described them to her. Straw, golden straw, and a straw so pale it seemed bleached as bone, black gleaming felt. Braids and ribbons. Feathers, silk roses and violets, with intricate, soft petals. She had a wooden stand shaped like a head and she moulded and trimmed the hats on that. They had been dampened and then steamed, with the hot iron held close but not touching the straw and felt. He could hear the hiss of it, smell the strange, yeasty smell and another, sharper, like varnish, see the ribbons coiled and stretched, tied and folded.

'She would make one to perfection, just the one, no two were ever the same, and it would stand there, on the table, on the ledge, as if she wanted it to herself for a day, just hers – ours – to admire, before it went off and another was begun.'

He had loved to watch her, to see the slow, careful transformation of this plain shape of grey or black or blonde into a wonderful thing, an adornment, unique. Every evening he sat looking up now and then from his books, or with his head resting on his hands at the table, his eyes following the deft, intricate movements of her fingers, seeing the concentration tautening her face.

It amazed him that he remembered so much, that there was so much left to tell. The days they had taken the bus out and walked through the reed-beds beside the snaking, inland river that ran across the flat marshes, the shoals of little pale blue butterflies, the sound of the bittern and the curlew and the larks, the immensity of the sky and the pale land stretching away to the sea, the heat of the sun on his head and neck, the pine forest, its dark, cool, curious smell. The bristles on the undulating back of a caterpillar he had let trail across his hand. He told her. He went back, taking her with him. They had climbed up the steps of a castle to the tower and he had felt the world turn beneath them, seen the bright heavens spin. He had thought that he might easily leap and fly.

He told her of the rock pools and the suck of the fronded waving sea anemone gripping his finger. He smelled the pungent salt-brine. There had been seaweed, he remembered, thick as leather beneath the pads of his fingers pressing the blisters, and weed like green silken tresses laid over the jutting rocks, slippery, treacherous. Beautiful. Day after day, in this place or that, walking beside his mother, talking to her, listening, looking up into her face, holding her hand, hearing her speak the lines of the Bible, the stories, all of it he remembered now, and told Elizabeth. All.

The stories themselves. After the sewing was put away, or when he had gone to bed, or in the pale, sunlit early mornings, lying beside her, she had told or read to him, every story in the world, it seemed. He told them now, the stories of enchantment and transformation and fabulous beasts, of spindles and ginger-bread and black lakes out of which naiads came singing, into which swords plunged, of rainbow's ends and rocks of gold and mice that spun and cats that talked, of dragons slain, tasks set, trials undergone, everlasting sleeps, rewards, banishments, dis-guises, spells, wonders. He told her the stories, and then what his mother had told him of her own story. Every day, sitting beside her, or else standing at the narrow window looking out on to the rain. He told her and, in telling, gave everything to her, as he had never before given, gave of himself.

'Elizabeth.'

Perhaps she heard him.

After a month, when she was still alive, defying them, because there was nothing more to be done for her there he took her home. She could neither move nor speak. She would live, or, suddenly, die, they said. He knew. Meanwhile, he must live, in the spotless, silent house, feed her, clean her, move her, dress her, undress, brush her hair, cut her nails. Talk to her. Talk. And at

245

night lie in the narrow bed on the other side of the room, straining to hear her still breathing, even in his own sleep.

When he had help for a few hours he went out, to walk in the air. 'Have a bit of life,' the woman said.

He walked along the flat, wet sand, or on the path beside the sea when the tide was high, neither happy nor unhappy, but settled as he had never hoped to be, content enough, giving to her what he had never before given. For now he had everything and the past was wholly returned.

Only at night, in his dreams, he wandered the empty hospital corridors, hearing the tap drip and the window left unfastened bang loosely in the wind, seeing the grass and weeds growing up through the cracks in the paving stones, and he longed then for that life and mourned it all and woke in terror, unable to find his way out of the building, which they had locked against him, and back to Elizabeth.

Only at night, in the dreams, he lay beside the dying, the old woman Annie Hare, Ettie Marshall, the old men, re-claiming each one, restoring them, too, briefly to life, and then consigning them to death again, as he watched with them.

'Elizabeth,' he said, waking, anxious. Needing her.

'Elizabeth.'

Perhaps she heard.

Twelve

'Will you be there?'
  'Yes.'
  'Not late?'
  'No.'
  'Will you ever be late?'
  'No.'
  'Will you always be there?'
  'Yes.'
  'Every day?'
  'Yes.'
  'Until I'm dead?'
  She did not laugh at him. She had never laughed. The anxieties, clearly written on his pale-skinned, serious face were too intense, she felt them as he did.
  She met him every day at the gates of the school, always arriving there too early, so that when he looked out of the window at the end of the afternoon, he would see her there. Her own anxiety matched his, her own need. She might have asked him, 'Will you always be there? Until I am dead?'
  During the day, when he was not with her, she worked on the hats and at clothes too; she had taught herself to sew children's gowns, out of silk and lawn, using the smallest of stitches, to smock and tuck and embroider. Word had spread, people sent to her from miles away. Miss Desmond displayed the garments, and

they went for grand christenings and outings from the houses of the county rich. She was not happy when he was away from her but she was perfectly at ease, perfectly occupied, the work she did satisfied her. But when he came home, it was put away and then her whole attention and interest was for him.

He was clever. She read to him, borrowed books for him, taught him, talked to him, answered his questions, kept up with him easily until he was eleven. After that his interests narrowed and focused, he gathered speed and left her behind. What remained were the pictures and her stories. Nothing changed that.

'What will I do? What will happen? How shall I get there?'

'On the bus, from the crossroads.'

'Will you come on the bus with me?'

His face tightened, his eyes darting in panic. (He had won a scholarship to the King's School twenty miles away. She had worked with him, and for him, night after night, though it was never in doubt. His cleverness astonished her. She went in awe of him now.)

'I shan't go.'

She sat beside him at the table.

'Listen ... ' She made him face her. 'I will be here. You will be there, at school. That will make no difference to anything else. Has it ever? It's only miles. What are miles?'

'Away.'

'You will go. *Must* go. There is nothing for you here.'

'I shall be afraid.'

'For a while, and then you will know what it is like and grow used to it and so not be afraid any longer.'

'How do you know that?'

'Because I know.'

'I want you to come.'

'No.'

He turned away.

On the first day, she walked with him to the crossroads and waited, but when she saw the bus approaching, down the straight road, left him. Must. He had been too closely in her company, too tied to her love, bound up with her in his every thought and movement, waking and sleeping, breathed as one with her, as though he had not been separated from her body at birth. She sometimes feared that she had obstructed him, for all their happiness, for all their richness of life, for all their love, and that he was marked by it.

At the end of the day, she had waited some distance from the crossroads, not wanting to shame him in front of others. But he had come out, running and stumbling towards her and fallen anyhow into her arms, crying with relief.

'I thought you might have gone. I thought you wouldn't be here and I would never see you again.'

'Why? Why did you think such a thing?'

He could not say. He was silent, pressing her arm to his body. 'I am here.'

'Will you always be here? Until I'm dead?'

'Until you don't want it.'

He stared at her as if she had spoken in some strange tongue, for how could they imagine such a thing, that either would not want the other, now, ever?

They had walked entwined together down the hill towards the house and beyond the house the silver sea.

Thirteen

He remembered his mother's smell. Not a smell of anything. Her smell, the smell of her flesh and her hair, the smell of her clothes. Like a small animal he had sought it out and nuzzled towards it.

The cottage had smelled of cloth and the steam from the hot iron against felt and straw, of the cold flagstones on the scullery floor, of books, of the salt sea. (Though by the time he had left her it was changed, by the shrivelling and wasting of the flesh, desiccation, ageing, the slide into death. For all he had not known it, or refused to know. Things were the same, he said, when he returned from the hospital, nothing would have happened, things would be as they had been, and the cottage, the sight of her, her smell miraculously restored to him. Nothing could change, he would not allow it, he had power. So he said. She is well. Things will not change. So he believed.)

Sitting beside Elizabeth now, he knew her smell, it was familiar, antiseptic, inhuman, masking the other smell of her illness, the bodily, orifice smell. And this room had its smell, cold and sickly, of perfumed air, linen, pillows, an inanimate smell. But close to her, through it, he smelled Elizabeth.

'We'll go for a walk.' (For he spoke to her, now that she could neither move nor speak, now that he had nowhere else to go, for hour after hour, told her everything, or as much of it as he could bear to remember, dare to speak.)

The room was full of a soft, diffused light coming through the half-drawn curtains. He had fed her, spoon by careful spoon. It was the middle of the afternoon. No voices. No sound.

Elizabeth lay, eyes open, silent, motionless on the high bed.

'We'll walk, up the hill, away from the town. Past the Baptist chapel. The gulls are crying. We'll stop here. There's the smoke from a train. Look back. There's the sea, you know that, over the rooftops. Our rooftop. You know that. There's a woman with a dog. We don't know her. She doesn't look at us.

'Past the church and out on to the straight road. There, you can see the forest. Daft, isn't it, to call it a forest? Only we do call it that. She does.'

They had walked this way before, from the town towards the crossroads and the forest, rather than along the shingle beach to the next bay, and then further, to the cliff and the cave and the rock pools. He would take her there, tell how it felt to have the sea anemone suck his finger into its soft mouth, feel the bright, satin weed, smell the salt fish stench deep inside the cave.

Tomorrow, perhaps, or the next week.

But she had seen inside the cottage in the evening when the lamp was flaring, seen the hats on their stands and the beautiful embroidery, heard the hiss of steam from the iron. Seen him, as he sat at his books. Seen his mother at work. Seen how it was between them. He had shown her everything in the room, the furniture, piece by piece every ornament, every scrap of ribbon and trim. The shining steel scissors lying in the centre of the table.

After so long, she knew.

'We'll go back then, Elizabeth. You'll be tired. It's a good stretch.'

Perhaps she heard.

He reached over and held the beaker to her lips, pressing the corner of her mouth so that the water dribbled in, massaging it down her throat with his finger, wiped what ran away into her neck, which was most of it. He took the ivory-backed brush and brushed the front of her hair where it had flopped forward out of place. Moved one arm, then the other, set her hands in new positions.

251

The room was still. He did not speak again. She had had enough of walking, enough pictures put into her head for this day.

'Elizabeth.' He bent and touched his lips to the paper-dry skin. Smelled her smell.

'Elizabeth.' Drew the curtains.

Left her.

Perhaps she heard.

Fourteen

Behind the medical school, a park led to playing fields but beyond that rose the violet-blue hills. When he had first seen them, even in the midst of his despair his heart had leaped, for they seemed to be a horizon that was utterly private to him, the hills beckoned and promised. The buildings would house him, in them he would learn his skill, they were merely necessary, but the hills reassured him with the promise of an escape.

He was afraid of everything he saw, though he must keep the fear hidden; he seemed to stand outside things even as he was in the midst of them. He was alarmed and intimidated. He would work here. The rest was an alien landscape full of strange faces and voices loud with confidence. He kept back in the shadows that fell from the huge building across the grass.

But he wanted the hills. He was inland here, and glad of that, tired for now of the sea and the everlasting sound of it dragging up, dragging back, the coldness of it and the seagulls' cry. He could not have said so, fearing to betray and afraid of his own disloyalty. Longing to leave meant a rejection of her and of his home and he could not admit that. But the thought of the violet-blue hills filled his mind now, in the dusk, as he leaned out of the window of his room on the evening before his departure. He longed for the space there, now, even for the corridors and high ceilings and echoes of the hospital buildings. He was tall, he felt stifled in the cottage, his arms and legs might at any moment have protruded through a window, a door, as they extended beyond his cuffs and the hems of his trousers, his head might have pushed through the fragile ceiling to the sky. She had to look up to him now.

Everything was ready for him, everything clean, mended, ironed, folded, labelled, packed into the canvas bag. His room was already empty of him.

The sea soughed softly, creaming on to the shingle.

He had worked, driving himself forward, for only this, that she could be proud. He would fulfil her wishes for him.

When he was ten, he had taken up a wounded bird from where it lay broken-backed on the shingle, and tended it, keeping it in a box in the scullery and, when it died, he had dissected it meticulously, studying the way it was made, its wings, frame, skull. It had been a thing of great beauty to him in death just as in soaring raucous life; and coming upon him, she had said, 'You should think of doing that. Tending things.'

'Yes.'

'But not birds. Don't waste yourself.'

And so he had turned his attention to people, looked at them, studied their bodies, their shape, their movements, noting deformities made by age or disease, the tell-tale signs of illness. He read them. It was always clear to him. It was the old he studied the most, and there were many of them in these streets, shuffling, deaf, awkward, hump-backed, thinning, struggling against time and the forward surge of the rest of life. He recognised their fear and their loneliness, answered to them as he watched them, he warmed to their frailty and their simple power of endurance, as he felt alien from the others, vibrant, assured ones thrusting forwards into life full of heedless, casual strength, milling round him. He had no friends, as she had not, longed for none, shunned company. What he needed of human closeness, influence, presence, he took from her, as he had taken everything else, his breath, it seemed. He saw the world through her eyes and what he knew of those other worlds he had learned from her. He was in tune with her ambitions and desires for him, liked their quiet, steady, close way of life together. It was as though the same

254

blood flowed in and through and round them both, as if he fed from her breast and they had never been separated.

Yet in his head now, he saw the line of violet hills and from them he took something quite new, some strength or life or inspiration, some hope and sustenance, and as he took it, concealed it.

He had told her everything. She had been with him as he had first gone into the hospital buildings, saw them as he described them, every ceiling and moulding, every archway and doorway, the interview room, the lecture halls, the laboratories and dissecting rooms, the covered walkway that led to the hospital, the smell, the echoes. As he had looked, listened, spoken, written, judged, she had followed him, as he told it to her afterwards. As he had done so, it had been the same as on the day he had first gone to the infant school, when he had gripped her hand, eyes closed, describing, remembering and struggling to tell of his bewilderment, the sense of strangeness he had felt as he had sat at the low table, with a plate of mashed potato and gravy before him, and, for a few seconds, had stood outside himself, looking on, had thought, 'I am. I am. I am. Here. Here. This is me. I am eating potato. I am. Here.' But he had never been able to convey that. He had carried the particular potato and gravy smell with him forever. As he had looked down at the plate of meat and fried potato in the hospital, he had known it again, in exactly that way, the sense of standing outside his body looking down, saying, 'I am. I am. Here. Now. Eating. I am.' But the person who sat among the others at the refectory table staring at the plate, at the plate of fried potato, the meat, had not looked up, had not been aware of him, had not heard. 'I am. I am. Here. Now. I am here. This is.'

She had asked, 'Did you eat?'

'Yes. Fried potato. Meat. Fruit pie. You queue up.'

'So it was cold?'

'Yes. When I got a place at a table. Yes, it was cold.'

The first of years of cold, snatched, hospital food, the smell of the potato forever in his nostrils.

But then there had been the line of hills. Those he had not

255

spoken of. She did not know of their existence. When he thought of them now, his stomach flared with the excitement of something he did not understand, some secret, clutched to him, for in truth they were simply hills in the distance, and of no possible relevance to him, or to the life he would live now.

The other flare was of fear, and that too he had pushed down and out of reach, out of consciousness. Because he knew, as he had looked at her that morning, every morning for weeks, saw again the infinitesimal changes, in the skin beneath her eyes, in the eyes themselves, and in the slight cautiousness in her movements as if she feared not so much pain as some falling apart and dissolution. There was no acknowledgment between them, of her illness or of his watchfulness, but that she was ill was something quite certain and known to him, inside her some terrible thing, some flaw, long dormant, was beginning to work like yeast, in stealth and darkness. If he had closed his eyes he thought that he might have seen it, like a stain spreading and seeping through her veins.

But nothing was said, nothing could be said, she went about life as before, self-contained, purposeful, working or walking, or sitting quietly in the chair, by the window or beneath the lamp reading, or else staring ahead of her, hands resting on her book.

She was proud, she said, and determined for him, hungry for his future. They had achieved this together and he was to go away. That was all. But would come back, in a few weeks, and then, regularly, time after time, until he came back to her forever. It was only, she thought, a temporary absence.

Fifteen

'I am not old. I am young. Nothing changes.' But her own face looking back at her from the oval mirror was changed. She saw her young face overlaid by this unfamiliar, older one, not lined but curiously fallen, the skin bleached as cotton cloth.

'I was Florence Hennessy who became Flora Molloy.'

And then the tide of memory rose up and drowned her.

When she woke from her drowning it was three o'clock in the morning. She sat at the open window, seeing the moon play upon the shifting surface of the water, bathing the shingle.

What confused her was the inconsistency of time, and its unreliability. She could no longer depend upon it, for this day had lasted a hundred years, moving forward as indetectably as growth, and the previous eighteen years had lasted less than a moment. That much she knew, yet the shock of it was still great to her and terrible. She remembered the falling snow that had surrounded them, could have stretched out of the window and felt it soft as a cold feather in the cup of her hand. She saw the infant's eggshell skull in the pale eerie snowlight.

The sea slipped up over the shingle, lost its footing, slipped back again.

The house was light and empty as a paper house. There was no

257

life in it, nothing stirred in the air around her. She felt transparent and brittle as a chrysalis discarded.

When he had walked away she had thought that he might have drained her life out of her and taken it, trailing behind him like an invisible cord, but she saw that he had not, that he was separate, whole and entire, and that the cord had shrivelled and crumbled away into nothing at last.

She regretted nothing. Her life here with him had been her absolute fulfilment; everything had led to it. Yet now her lack of discontent, the satisfaction she had had for so long from so little, seemed strange to her. She remembered her early passion for her independence and to make her mark upon life, away from her mother and Olga and the dark house, the excitement at what she saw all around her, her fervour of hoping.

Over the next days and weeks alone it was the pictures that came back to her, slowly at first, a recollection now and then, a reminder in the way the light fell and the pattern of clouds, but soon, with urgency, crowding into her mind. Instead of other memories, which seemed to recede, she had these. It delighted her that they were not lost, but imprinted still, clear, fresh, detailed. She needed no other reminders. She had only to sit at these windows and almost unbidden they could come quietly back to her with a clarity and vividness that the faces of people did not have, and she rested in them and was sustained by them day and night.

Sixteen

She slept the day that he left and for hours of every day after, great draughts of sleep, and, when she was not sleeping, floated through time, unthinking, unfeeling, as it grew dark and light and dark again around her, as the tide rose and fell.

And when finally she woke, coming to herself again, for a few minutes it was as if he had never existed and the years with her son had never been, that she was alone, as she had always been alone, in some strange place – the house called Carbery, Miss Pinkney's house, the room in the lodging house of Miss Marchesa, the convalescent home, the Bloomsbury flat. She had moved on from one to the next until she had ended here, and settled at last. Yet now, the purpose of it gone, she felt detached, as if she might simply move on and away yet again, and then again, in an eternity of hopeless change.

But she was ill and for that reason, as well as to await his return, must stay.

She felt intermittently feverish, and drained of all energy. She did not want food, only had a craving for cold water, which she drank from the scullery tap, cupped in her bare hands.

On the second evening, she took the lidded basket and a linen bag, in which the scraps of fabric, the ribbons and braids were stored, and emptied them out carefully, and arranged them on the table, shading the spectrum of colours precisely, until they began to form a picture. The scraps held their life here, his childhood and the years of his growing up and all of her work and purpose with them. Looking at them, Flora looked at every day, every month, every season, in darkness and in light. She began to cut them into even pieces, to piece the picture meticulously together, arranged and re-arranged until her eye was satisfied, then began, little by little, to sew. The stitches were minute and exact. She had time, she thought, to finish.

She walked less now, and never far, and paused for breath, standing on the shingle beneath a steely sky, watching the gulls soar and the boats come sweeping in. No one paid attention to her, no one came.

When she was not sewing, she slept, or sat at the window, getting up now and then to drink the water which alone seemed to sustain her.

He wrote, twice, sometimes three times each week, and his letters were life to her, joy, interest and satisfaction. Yet, reading them over and over again, she felt apart and that already the ending was embarked upon. But he thought of her, he said, in everything.

That he was profoundly unhappy in everything he did not say. Only the work, the excitement of learning, steadied him, so that the moment he woke he turned his mind to it in anticipation, and to hold back the demons of fear and uncertainty.

He went about his daily routine, from lecture room to laboratories to hospital ward, easily for all his unease.

Only the idea of staring into the face of death disturbed him, only the corridors leading to the mortuary held terror during the early days, so that he lay awake, anticipating that journey, steeling his nerve, plunging violently in and out of dreams in which the dead floated like corks on the surface of the water.

He had his studies and his ambition, he had the time in which he wrote the letters, and in which he read his mother's letters to him; he had the picture, which he carried within him, of the cottage, and the view from his room of the wide seashore. He had the line of hills.

He did not go to them, knowing that in reaching them they would lose all interest for him, all power to enchant. When he had free time he walked or cycled out in other directions, alone or with anyone who cared for his company. He told them nothing of himself. That he had learned the habit of closeness and self-containment from her over the whole of his childhood he perfectly understood, and occasionally, looking around him, listening to the others, he was disturbed by it, felt awkward, uncertain where or how he might find his place in their world. They had an ease and a sureness which he lacked and sometimes envied. Then, the hills would hold out hope for him, and he did not mock himself for the power he invested in them.

For the rest, he studied the working and the healing of bodies and minds, and longed and at the same time did not long, to return to her. And the small, hard stone of terrifying knowledge, that his mother was ill and would never be well again, lodged like a bitter kernel within him.

Seventeen

The sea roared in to drown her and the gulls swooped to gorge on her flesh. The pale slabs of sky were dead and staring as fish-eyes, framed in the cottage windows and the walls of the cottage pressed inwards until she could not breathe. The silence boomed in her ears but when she cried out, there was only emptiness to hear.

Her pride was no longer of use to her.

The ghosts slipped in then. Turning her head quickly, standing in the shadows of the stairwell, she might have glimpsed them – but whether they were the ghosts of the dead or of the living she could not have discovered.

(Leila Watson's address, torn up and discarded. Olga's letters left unanswered, and in the end, unopened.)

She dreamed of her mother and saw in the mirror that her own face was become like her, though years too soon. She understood well enough that it was her punishment. Rejection bred rejection from one generation to another and her pride turned in upon her.

She was thin and hollow as a straw.

But now and then a little shard of memory broke off and floated back to her like a feather on the outgoing tide, to nourish her. A glimpse of a picture came into her mind, a fragment of Miss Pinkney's voice, comforting.

'Come to us,' Leila Watson had said. And held out her arms,

and the shelter and consolation she had so despised turned on her to mock her.

Once, Tadeusz was in the room, laughing with Lawrence Molloy, before they turned and left together and a tunnel of forest trees and blackened bushes echoed to their fading voices. They had spoken to her in the language of Tadeusz, which she could not understand.

Her skin burned up. Only when his letters came did she get up and struggle to wash and dress and go about the cottage, tidying pointlessly. (The sewing was finished, the cover she had made folded and wrapped and put away, and her life with it.)

Once or twice, a face peered in through the windows, until, mistaking some real living person, some passer-by, for one of the ghosts, and in any case hating the staring slabs of sky now, she drew the curtains across all of the windows save one.

In the town, here and there, people mentioned her. It was noticed that she no longer walked on the beach, no longer collected work from Desmond's shop.

Once or twice, Miss Desmond herself came and knocked, knocked, knocked on the door of the cottage, out of concern, Miss Desmond, not bent, not frail, not changed in any way save to have become very old.

But Flora had slept and the knocking had sounded only through her dreams, making her afraid but not waking her.

Miss Desmond had gone away (and written a letter to Hugh Molloy, and so, in the end, perhaps, brought about a resolution).

She might have dressed and gone out, walked through the town to the doctor and presented her illness, but she shrank from what would follow, the inevitable, public end to her life, not from pain but from failure and humiliation. She would not relinquish anything now, would not weaken as she had once weakened. She might have written to him. He would have come to her, needed, perhaps, an excuse to do so. She longed for it and in the last days thought of nothing but his voice, his presence, his footstep, his body filling the small room, all of her remaining energy was concentrated upon it. But in her waking dreams and odd bursts of

263

feverish delirium, she saw him not coming to her but running, running away, growing smaller to nothingness in the far distance.

Outside a storm blew, the gale howled for admittance, its breath fouling the window panes. Doors slammed and gates were broken and lay on their sides anyhow. And then, quite suddenly, the sky cleared, the sun shone on to the surface of the calm, exhausted sea, and glanced off it through the thin bedroom curtain and into her face and after a while awakened her.

The room was filled with light and she lay in it and upon the frail, brilliant beam of it, held, caught, suspended. Her skin shone like silk. Her eyes were lit like tiny fires flickering in the sockets. The child lay beside her on the white pillow and the pale curtains were blown about like clouds in the breeze and the silence all around her was dazzling.

*

Coming in exultant from the cold morning, Molloy saw the letter addressed to him in the unfamiliar hand of Miss Desmond, lying, brilliant upon the dark floor.

Eighteen

'I fear for her,' Miss Desmond had written in her strong, clear hand. 'Something is very wrong.'

The paper made a soft sound, shaking in his shaking hand. But for that moment at least he still believed in his own power to save her.

He ran down the hill from the railway station, his canvas bag pounding against his back. Ahead of him, the sea was a painted sea, the waves stiff, varnished things, the sheen on the surface of the water iridescent. A gull hung motionless, white on the white sky.

When he opened the door, the silence roared out to meet him, and in that moment he thought she came to him and touched him and he was caught up and held in her love for him, meshed in its gilded netting as it tightened around him.

He shut the door quietly and then all his powers drained from him, and he knelt, sobbing, his hope lying shattered about him on the floor.

At the end she had felt only relief and gratitude that he had not come to her, had not known of her illness at all; so she had believed.

But finding her in her bed, curled away from him as if in

rejection, he was aware only of his own love and need for her and his desolation.

He would bear guilt, if not for the rest of his life at least for the most part of it.

That night, he lay beside her and sent for no one, told no one, wanting her to himself. He had pushed away the knowledge that when he had left she had had her dying upon her. She had said nothing of it. He had been glad of that, and of the freedom it had allowed him.

Now, he wondered how he might so much as draw his next breath without her. He did not touch her that cold, quiet night, and scarcely slept. He was only conscious of the absoluteness of the silence and the stillness within the room.

He begged to have known her dying, to have felt her last warmth, and because what he begged could never be granted, after his distraught, angry questioning, he spoke to her, promised her, asked her forgiveness endlessly. Her death would continue to draw him; in trying to make up for it, for his absence from her, for her aloneness, he would spend a lifetime watching over the dying of all the rest.

The darkness of that night was moonless and starless and impenetrable. But when the light came, it filled this room of birth and death, and the brightness blinded him.

It was later that he found the cover she had sewn, coming upon it at the back of a cupboard, in looking carelessly, hurriedly for some trivial thing, and at first he pushed it aside. But some flash of familiar colour caught his eye and he took it out, and unfolded it, and traced every detail, saw every piece of fabric and ribbon and braid, and that she had sewn up the pieces of their lives and bound them together.

When he left the cottage, walking away up the hill for the last time, he carried it with him.

Nineteen

For there had been precious little else to take. What she had given him had been everything that was invisible, intangible, life, love, ambition. And the things she had told him of what mattered in her past. She had painted the pictures for him so exactly that he knew these things as she had known them, saw them through her eyes, her memories became his. The gallery. The white corridors and high empty spaces filled with light. The picture of the young woman before the open window. The rain falling on London. A pleasure steamer making its slow way back up river in the soft, starlit dark and the sound of an accordion, the sound of singing. The glowing, dim-red cavern of the Bloomsbury flat, the walls hung with rich patterns, lamplight, pigeons cooing on the ledges above the London streets and squares. Children running with kites in the billowing wind on the hill high above the green slopes and the hollows with their clumps of trees. (But of Henrjyk Tadeusz she had never spoken, to anyone in her life again. And who remembered Tadeusz now?)

The brilliant white light and blown steam and spray and speed bursting from the great canvases of Turner, the roaring skies, the service of clouds everywhere.

His own name, given him after the dead boy Hugh, sitting sloe-eyed, solemn-faced and expectant in the back of the open car, for the last time.

The stone stairs that led to the top of the castle tower and the parapet looking out across the flat lands to where he might just make out in the distance the silver line of sea.

Her smell. The sound of her voice. The sight of her. Her warmth as he reached her, arms outstretched, hurtling down the hilly streets of the town. And in a drawer of the chest, beneath clothes which he bundled up to throw away, hardly bearing to touch them, smelling her smell in every scrap, every crevice of cloth, a book in a language he did not recognise, with her name in a handwriting he had never seen.

For days the sea had been immensely still, the sky clean and pale. But after he left, walking away up the hill, the clouds came streaming in and the tide rose and the rain fell, blackening the water.

Twenty

Flora, dead. But no one else. The rest might live on forever.

Miss Marchesa, grown as old now as the old she had made her
living from, looked after in her turn in one room of the lodging
house. Miss Marchesa, who steeled herself on waking each
morning for the interminable sameness of another day, listening
for the sound of water running in basins above, for footsteps on
the stairs, and the slamming of the front door. (But those noises
did not come now.)

The boy Hugh, dead for so many years, was not dead for so much
as a day in the house called Carbery, but remembered, loved,
spoken of, by the very old, to the children and their children, who
came after. (The photograph of him, in a silver frame, standing on
a table, the pastel portrait hanging on the stairs, a crayoned
drawing of Moses in the bulrushes, and another, of a mythical
beast trampling on flowers, in the old nursery, quite familiar to
them all.)
   Though, gradually, the grand houses like Carbery lost their
grandeur and the gardens were overgrown and neglected by the
old, and, after their deaths, built upon.

Of course Olga did not die. Olga might never die. Olga danced
and sang and went to parties sprightly down the years into old

age and on, brightly into eternity. And wondered very often about her sister and did write, but the letters went unanswered. Flora might come here, she thought once, might make a life of some sort in this country. But of what sort? The piece was turned this way and that beside the jigsaw, time after time, but would never quite fit, was not, after all, in the right place and so in the end was discarded.

Miss Desmond did not die. Miss Desmond reached the age of one hundred quite comfortably, and Miss Lea the same.

And Leila Watson lived forever, among the sheltering, cocooning hills and woods and green roofs and leafy branches, among the old of her family and the children, and thought without fail of Flora, and prayed for her, every day, and at last ceased to question and be troubled and simply commended her to God. (For God and his church took up a great deal of her life now.)

No one else died then. No one else might ever die. All were immortal.
Only Flora.

(But perhaps Tadeusz, now or then, in this country or that? But it was never known.)

Molloy took all the deaths of the world upon himself after, took on death itself, it seemed, embraced it and made it his own to make up for the guilt of his betrayal of her. Though every death he kept vigil over could not atone for hers, nothing in life at all made up for that.

He had shrivelled to a hard, dry pith within himself and his life blood seemed to have stilled and desiccated within him.

And so it had been. Until now, and Elizabeth, lying motionless, eyes wide, month after month in the bed.

He waited, attending her with endless love, perfect care. He took her everywhere as she lay there, told her everything he had to tell.

Perhaps she heard.

His days, which he had feared would be sterile, empty husks, were crammed full of her needs and the fulfilling of them. His need for her.

The year turned. Spring came in very gently, a pricking of vivid, translucent green.

The blackbirds scuttled under the snow-white pear tree.

The year shifted a little.

The blossom fell.

He woke at dawn and the room seethed with a familiar silence.

She had lain still for months but now her stillness was quite other and absolute.

Beyond the window, the sky was pearl grey and cloudless.

He got up, went to the cupboard and took out the quilt, and laid it on the bed, to cover her.

'Elizabeth,' he said.

Perhaps she heard.